Just a
Regular
Boy

Also by Catherine Ryan Hyde

So Long, Chester Wheeler

Dreaming of Flight

Boy Underground

Seven Perfect Things

My Name is Anton

Brave Girl, Quiet Girl

Stay

Have You Seen Luis Velez?

Just After Midnight

Heaven Adjacent

The Wake Up

Allie and Bea

Say Goodbye for Now

Leaving Blythe River

Ask Him Why

Worthy

The Language of Hoofbeats

Pay It Forward: Young Readers Edition

Take Me with You

Paw It Forward

365 Days of Gratitude: Photos from a Beautiful World

Where We Belong

Subway Dancer and Other Stories

Walk Me Home

Always Chloe and Other Stories

The Long, Steep Path: Everyday Inspiration from the Author of Pay It Forward

How to Be a Writer in the E-Age: A Self-Help Guide

When You Were Older

Don't Let Me Go
Jumpstart the World
Second Hand Heart
When I Found You
Diary of a Witness
The Day I Killed James
Chasing Windmills
The Year of My Miraculous Reappearance
Love in the Present Tense
Becoming Chloe
Walter's Purple Heart
Electric God/The Hardest Part of Love
Pay It Forward
Earthquake Weather and Other Stories
Funerals for Horses

Just a Regular Boy

A Novel

Catherine Ryan Hyde

LAKE UNION
PUBLISHING

Text copyright © 2023 by Catherine Ryan Hyde, Trustee, or Successor Trustee, of the Catherine Ryan Hyde Revocable Trust created under that certain declaration dated September 27, 1999.

Published by Lake Union Publishing, Seattle

www.apub.com

Amazon, the Amazon logo, and Lake Union Publishing are trademarks of Amazon.com, Inc., or its affiliates.

ISBN-13: 9781662504372 (hardcover)
ISBN-13: 9781662504358 (paperback)
ISBN-13: 9781662504365 (digital)

Cover design by Shasti O'Leary Soudant
Cover images: ©Milosz Guzowski / ArcAngel

Printed in the United States of America
First edition

Just a Regular Boy

1. REMY

Chapter One

What's Coming

Remy Blake was five years old when his father drove him away from Pocatello for the last time. Remy didn't deep-down believe it really *was* for the last time. That seemed impossible. Still, it made him nervous that his father kept saying so.

"But I can write *a letter* to Lester," he said. Because he had been told there would be no phone. "If I say it out you'll write it down for me. Right?"

"Nope."

"Why not?"

"No mailbox up there."

"Can't we just keep driving until we get to one?"

"That'd take all day. And what do you think we'd be using for gasoline? Except for a little we brought as an emergency ration, and for the chain saw, there'll be no gas."

"We could just go to a gas station like we do at home."

"This *is* our home now, son. And there are no gas stations."

Remy squirmed in his seat, telegraphing the discomfort he'd been trying so hard to hide. He always wanted his father to be proud of him, which meant he had to be tough and brave. But Lester was his best friend—had been since they were both learning to walk—and it was hard.

"Why can't I call him on your cell phone?"

His father laughed.

During the time Remy hoped he would answer the question, his father took a pack of cigarettes out of the pocket of his flannel shirt. He shook one out and lit it from the glowing tube of cigarette lighter he'd popped out of the truck's dashboard.

The windows were both down, which whipped Remy's hair into his eyes, but it was worth it not to have to breathe much of that awful stuff.

"There's no reception up there," Remy's father said at long last. "Because there are no cell towers."

Remy wondered sometimes if the long pauses before answers were his father's attempt to get Remy to figure things out on his own. But he was never right at the edge of understanding, so he hoped that wasn't it.

"What *do* they have up there?" Remy asked.

It was a brave act, because his tone of voice made it clear that the question straddled a line, doubling as a complaint.

"Son," his father said, in that voice he used to make a proud speech, "up there in our new home, we'll have the most important thing a person can have: freedom. And the greatest freedom there is, well, that's got to be the freedom to survive what's coming. If you don't survive, then you got nothing. Nothing's more important but that you survive."

Remy had never asked his father what was coming. He didn't figure it was anything he wanted to know.

———

Remy was fast asleep when they arrived. His father had to shake him awake.

He hoped to be carried to bed in a fireman's carry as his father sometimes had done. Instead he was set on his feet and expected to march. It was an omen of what was to come, though he only knew so as a vague sensation at the very back of his mind.

He didn't know anything about the place yet, because it was dark. Weirdly dark. In fact, it was a dark Remy had never seen before. Never imagined. There was no moon that night, or it was down—Remy didn't know which. There were no streetlights anywhere. No lights from a neighbor's porch because, he would later learn, there were no neighbors.

He would have expected his father to carry a lantern or flashlight. He felt sure he had seen such things being packed. Instead his father only lit wooden matches from a box, one after the other, creating a tiny point of light for them to follow.

It was cold, and completely still.

In time, and in a moment of fumbling in between matches, Remy saw the vague outline of a doorway as they passed through it, and felt his feet touch down on wooden boards, a relief from the sense that his new world was nothing but hard dirt.

"Turn on the lights," he said, standing still and attempting to look around himself.

It was no warmer inside than it had been on the march from the truck.

His father laughed. "There are no lights," he said.

"How can there not be lights?"

"There's no electricity out here."

"But we'll have it later, right?"

"You don't seem to get it," his father said.

Remy felt strong hands at his waist. Felt himself lifted as high as his father's head, and set down on a thin mattress.

"Go back to sleep," his father said.

"Wait. What don't I get?"

"There's no electricity out here. There never will be. There are no electrical wires. There are no power poles. This is the wilderness. Now go to sleep, and I'll show you what's what in the morning."

Remy curled up on his side on the thin mattress, shivering. He found a single scratchy blanket and pulled it over himself. Still his teeth chattered. And his bladder was uncomfortably full.

"Where's the bathroom?" he asked quietly, the words seeming to split the darkness in a vaguely rude manner.

Again his father laughed.

Remy wanted to ask why everything he said was funny all of a sudden. But it felt like challenging his father's authority, so he never did.

"All around you," his father said after a time.

"How can the bathroom be all around me?"

"This is a hundred and seventy-five acres of bathroom. Do the deer ask where the bathroom is? Or the bears? No, they don't. They go where they are."

"There are bears?" Remy asked, his eyes feeling wide in the dark.

"There are bears all over Idaho. You know that."

"They never came onto our street in Pocatello."

"There are no streets here."

Which, by that time, Remy could have figured out on his own.

"So what do I do?"

"I can give you the matches and you can go outside and pick a tree."

"By myself?"

"Yes, by yourself. This is about you learning to toughen up."

"Oh."

Remy fell silent for a long time. He did not ask for the matches, or go outside. He decided to try to hold it.

But soon, overwhelmed by the cold, he chose to risk another thinly veiled complaint.

"Is there heat?"

"There's a woodstove," his father said. "Makes this little tiny place real toasty warm, real fast. But that's for tomorrow night. Can't very well split wood in the dark, now can I?"

Remy did not answer.

His eyes had begun to adjust to the near-total darkness. He could see that the ceiling was not far above his head. But that was all he could see.

"You want my blanket?" his father asked.

It came out of nowhere, startling Remy.

"No," Remy said. "Then *you'll* be cold."

Another long silence.

Remy nursed an uncomfortable knot in his stomach. It was the tightening brought on by fear. He knew the sensation. But in the past it had been with him for only a flash of a moment. Just until an instance of perceived danger had passed. Or at least in one sense that was true. In this dramatic a case of it, anyway. In another, more subtle, way it had been there in his gut since his mother died. And it had been growing. He didn't really know why it had been growing, except that it felt like it had to do with watching his father. What he said and did.

Remy sensed that between that tightening in his gut and the teeth-chattering cold he might never get back to sleep.

"Hey, Dad?" he asked quietly.

"I don't want you to call me 'Dad' anymore."

"Oh," Remy said, more shocked than his simple reply reflected. "What do you want me to call you?"

"Roy."

"Why?"

"Because it's my name."

"But why—"

He never got the chance to finish the question.

"Because a father is an authority. A boss is an authority. The ultimate authority is the government. And authority is enslavement. It's just a way of amassing power. Everybody just wants power over everybody and everything else. I'm not raising you to be a slave. So you don't bow down to anybody anymore, and that includes me. We are free men, both of us. We are equals."

Remy said nothing in reply.

There was really nothing in what his father had said that Remy understood. And yet, inside his head, there did seem to be some wordless sense of understanding.

In that moment, though he could not have defined or explained it, Remy understood that his childhood was over.

———

When Remy woke in the morning, it was light.

He had been sleeping in his clothes. He hadn't even taken off his sneakers.

He was in a tiny, unadorned cabin. It was no bigger than their old one-car garage in Pocatello. It had no kitchen, no separate rooms. No furniture except the two platforms of single beds, his being up near the ceiling like a loft. It had the potbellied woodstove his father had mentioned, and only one small, dirty window.

His father was not inside the cabin.

Remy wasn't sure how to get down from his loft. And the mattress felt wet. At first he instinctively blamed it on the cabin. The roof probably leaked. But it was vaguely warm, and had a familiar smell.

It fell together in his head slowly, and in stages. To his immense shame, he had apparently wet the bed.

He flipped onto his belly and wiggled off the side of the platform, hung from his fingers for a moment, then dropped onto the cabin's wooden floor, hurting the balls of his feet right through the thin rubber soles of his shoes. Only then did he see that there was a rough wood-and-rope ladder at the other end.

His clothes were soaked through with his own urine. The back of his hair was wet with it. He knew the bed above him was still wet. And he was so humiliated by the situation that he resolved to do nothing to acknowledge it.

He would change his clothes if his father brought clothes in from the truck, but nothing more. If his bed was still wet when he climbed up into it that night, as it likely would be, he would do nothing about the situation except to bear up.

His stomach cramped painfully from hunger, and his mouth was uncomfortably dry from sleeping with it open all night. His teeth felt filmy and bad, as if he hadn't brushed them in weeks. And there was nothing he could do about any of it as far as he could tell.

He opened the cabin's only door and blinked into the bright, cold morning. He saw only trees, with beams of sunlight shining through their branches.

His father was nowhere to be found.

———

Remy wandered the woods for what seemed like an hour without finding his dad.

He paid careful attention to the direction of the sun, and tried to keep the cabin in sight. If he let it slip from his sight, he tried to remember well which direction he would need to go to see it again.

His hunger pangs grew alarmingly painful, and his lack of food made him feel weak and a little dizzy.

As he wandered—the sun gleaming into his eyes through tall trees, then disappearing behind their branches, then coming out and blinding him again—he listened to a distant sound.

Thwack. Thwack. Thwack.

He did not walk in the direction of the sound, because he worried it might be a bear, doing . . . well, Remy didn't really know what bears do. That was part of the problem. And he did not want this to be the morning he found out.

But after listening to the thwack for several minutes, he decided it was likely to be his father splitting wood. They'd had a woodstove in Pocatello, too. In fact, it had been their only source of heat. So it was not that Remy was unfamiliar with the sound. More that he had allowed the fear of bears to get into his head and run the show up there.

He cautiously followed the sound.

He paid no attention to the direction he would need to go to find the cabin again, because he was sure he was about to locate his father, and then it wouldn't matter.

In time he came to a clearing with several downed trees, and more standing deadwood, and he did see his father there, splitting a large round of wood with the blunt end of a splitting maul and a cast iron wedge. He saw that the trunk of a downed tree had been cut into stove-size pieces with a chain saw. The chain saw sat silently on a stump by his father's side. Remy wondered why he hadn't heard it. Maybe he had slept through that part.

He watched his father work for a time, apparently unnoticed.

His father had his shirt off, and was dripping sweat in the clear, chilly morning. His huge belly poked out over his belt, looking uncomfortably constrained by the waistband of his jeans. Remy could see the forest of hair under his father's arms every time he raised the maul. His back was surprisingly hairy, and his skin gleamed white, as though it had never seen sun.

Thwack. Thwack. Thwack.

Soon Remy grew bored watching, and set off for the cabin again. Maybe he could find the truck, and the load of belongings his father had packed. Maybe he could get his hands on a change of clothes before his father witnessed the humiliating truth.

He wandered away from the clearing, and immediately got his directions turned around and got lost. The sun seemed much higher overhead, though he couldn't imagine how so much time had gone by, and he felt unsure about using it to guide his travel.

He walked around in what might have been a circle, then panicked and started to run, his stomach cramping wildly with hunger, his mouth painfully dry.

Finally he stumbled across something unexpected.

It was water.

Remy wasn't sure if it was a small river or a large creek or stream, but it looked fresh and inviting. It ran quickly, cutting down through the sloping ground, twisting and turning, with a pleasant gurgling sound.

He walked closer.

The water was bright and clear, and looked about deep enough in a few places to reach his waist. A dead tree had fallen, and created a wide pool by slowing and redirecting the current. Remy got down on his knees and leaned over the pool. At first all he saw was himself. His own reflection. It startled him, not because he didn't understand reflections and know to expect them, but because he already looked different to himself. He looked dirty and disheveled. He looked like a wild thing.

Then he saw a movement that caused him to look beyond his reflection. There were fish gliding through the slow pool, weaving in and out of the branches of the downed tree. They were silvery, with a prism of colors reflected on their sides, and a bright flash of red under their throats. They seemed to float effortlessly in the shallow water.

Remy watched them for a time, fascinated.

Then he leaned in, reaching down with his cupped hands for a drink. The silvery fish skittered for shelter and disappeared.

Remy filled his hands and drank from them.

The water was brilliantly cold, and tasted almost sweet. Better than anything he could ever remember drinking.

At that moment a loud and sudden noise launched him into the air.

"Bang!"

Remy flew forward and landed in the freezing pool on his hands and knees, scraping and bruising himself on the stony bottom. The shock was deep, like being plunged into ice water.

He whipped his head around to see his father standing over him, laughing.

"What'd you do that for?" Remy asked, feeling further bruised by his father's laughter.

He instinctively rolled over so that his back would be wet. Maybe then his father would never have to know he had wet himself. Maybe the flowing water would even wash away the smell. He could already feel his limbs going numb from the shocking cold.

"Because you made a fatal mistake," his father said.

"I don't know what that is," Remy said, standing up in the freezing water.

"It means you did something that could get you killed."

"What did I do?"

He climbed up the shallow bank and stood dripping and shivering in the early morning sun. His sneakers bubbled over with creek water, and made a squishing sound when he moved. He saw that behind his father sat a wheelbarrow piled high with cut and split stovewood.

"You turned your back."

"On what?"

"Well, see, that's just the problem. You never know on what. Could have been anything back there. But you weren't paying any attention. I walked right up behind you, and you didn't even hear me. So if something was stalking you . . . hunting you . . . wanting to take you out . . . well, you're just a sitting duck, my friend."

"I'm not your friend," Remy said. "I'm your son."

It was an angry statement. Remy didn't entirely know where all that anger was coming from. Before his life was over he would know that his father was trying to equalize them, and that—as a young boy—he didn't want an equal. He didn't want to be a free man. He didn't want to be any kind of man. He wanted to be a child, and be cared for as a child.

At the moment, he was five, and only knew it bothered him.

Also he knew he wanted his mother back. But since that was impossible, he wanted his father.

"You're not my anything if you don't survive. I have a lot to teach you."

Remy's teeth had begun to chatter, but he talked through it as best he could.

"Who would hunt me? There's nothing out here. There's nobody here."

"You just never know."

"Like a bear?"

"Like a person. A bear would rather keep to itself. If you don't surprise it, and you don't have any food for it to go after, it'd rather not have anything to do with you at all. But people. People are lethal."

Remy didn't know what that word meant, nor did he really want to know. For that reason, he offered no opinion.

"Now, come on," his father said. "Let's get this stovewood back to the cabin and get you dried out."

—

Remy was sitting in front of a fire in the black potbellied woodstove when he broke down and spoke. He was wearing a change of clothes and warming up fast.

"Dad?"

His father heard him. He must have. There was barely room to fall down in the tiny cabin. His dad was staring out the small, dirty window as though expecting bad news. He must have heard Remy. But he didn't act as though he'd heard. It scared Remy. It felt like an escalation of their troubles.

"Dad?"

At first, nothing.

Then his father turned his head vaguely in Remy's direction.

"Who?"

"You."

"And who am I?"

"Oh," Remy said. He steeled himself to do it. He hated every minute of this, but his father seemed to be giving him no choice. "Roy?"

"Yes, Remy?"

"What do we eat here?"

"Mostly I'll be hunting and fishing for our food."

Remy felt his mouth fall open. He waited for his father to turn his head and see why he wasn't answering.

A moment later, his father did just that.

"What's the problem, Remy? You got a weak stomach for hunting?"

"No, sir."

"No, who?"

"No, Roy. It's just . . . that'll take so long."

"Oh, we can eat before I go hunting."

"How?"

"We have supplies."

"Where?" Remy asked, looking all around himself.

He even looked up at the ceiling, in case there was something hanging up there—some treasure he hadn't noticed—unlikely though it seemed.

"I'll show you," his father said.

He got up and walked out the cabin's door.

Remy followed him down a path worn into the weeds. Away from the truck. Seemingly in the direction of nowhere and nothing.

In time a structure came into view. Not until they were nearly on top of it, though, because it was all done in camouflage, though Remy didn't know the word to call it. Only that it was that mottled look, like the uniforms his father and his friends had worn to go out for their paintball wars on the weekends. Back when his father still had friends.

As they got closer, Remy saw it was not a permanent structure. It was more of a tent. But it was massive. The kind of tent a whole big party of campers might use to come together and eat. In fact, it was two or three times the size of their new living quarters.

"Why can't we live in *this*?" Remy asked. "There'd be a lot more room."

"Because there are no beds and no stove."

"We could *put* beds and a stove."

"And a bear could tear right through the side and get us."

"Oh," Remy said. "I thought you said they wouldn't mess with us."

"If we were eating, though."

"Oh. If we were eating."

Then he said nothing more.

His father unzipped the tent flap, and they stepped inside.

It took Remy's eyes several seconds to adjust to the dim light. When they did, he saw that almost every square inch of the space was stacked with supplies, right up to the tent's ceiling. Most were in cardboard cartons or wood crates, labeled with a black marking pen. But Remy couldn't read.

It was all on wooden pallets or shelving to get it up off the bare dirt. On top of the cartons sat stacks and stacks of what looked like huge plastic jars, all full of jerky, and foil packets of something, and energy bars, and granola bars.

"What if the bears break in and eat all this?"

"That's why it's all in bear canisters," his father said.

It was clear by his tone of voice that his father was proud of himself for having thought of everything.

"Where did we get all this?" Remy asked, trying to keep his jaw from dropping.

"At the store. Where else?"

"But when did you bring it all up here?"

"The last two weekends, when you were at Lester's."

"Oh," Remy said.

He did not feel entirely surprised. He knew his father had been doing something weighty and secret with that time, which was exactly why he hadn't asked any questions.

"It looks like enough for a year," Remy added.

"That's exactly what it is. A year's worth of supplies, beyond what food I can get hunting and fishing. After that . . . if we're lucky and there's an 'after that' . . . I'll have to do another supply run."

"But . . . ," Remy began. He was having trouble framing the question.

"But what, Remy? Say what's on your mind."

"Where did we get the money to buy a year's worth of stuff all at once like that?"

"I sold the house."

"Oh," Remy said.

His father's words had landed in his stomach like something heavy. As though he had swallowed a lead fishing weight. He had thought if they didn't like it here they could always go home. Remy watched as that comforting idea evaporate. It hurt to see it go.

His mother had loved that house. His mother would have been horrified. But Remy had been trying not to think about her.

His father unscrewed the lid on one of the giant jars and handed Remy a granola bar.

"Here. Eat this for breakfast. And stay in the cabin so you don't get lost. I'm going to go out and bag us a deer."

———

Remy's father was gone all day. Remy sat inside, wondering if it was possible to die of boredom.

When his father got back, he had bagged exactly nothing.

16

They ate dehydrated stew that his father reconstituted in a pot on the woodstove.

Then Remy went to the bathroom outside, checking carefully for bears. There was no toilet paper. His father had instructed him to use leaves or grass.

After that he put himself to bed on the still-wet mattress, utterly devoid of hope that his life would ever be better than that dismal first day.

Chapter Two

It's Beginning

It was nearly a year later before anything happened that even hinted at his father's view of the world being correct.

They were low on supplies, and his father had been putting off driving to civilization for more. He said he was only concerned about leaving Remy alone, but Remy wordlessly perceived that his father was afraid and did not want to admit it. Remy did nothing special with that information in his head. His only reaction to the situation was to bring home more fish, to slow down the exhaustion of their food stores.

That morning Remy padded back to the cabin with a rope stringer of four good-sized cutthroat trout.

Remy was a better fisherman than his father. His father was too impatient, and would not stay quiet or hold still. He would stand up to rearrange his underwear or scratch an itch, and then the fish would know to hide.

Remy prided himself on his fishing. But, though his father had begun teaching him the proper use of a rifle, he was not anxious to learn to hunt.

He walked barefoot, as he always did when there was no snow on the ground. Partly because the soles of his feet were calloused and sturdy. Partly because he had long ago outgrown his shoes. His father's pride at having thought of "everything" had not been fully earned.

In the intervening winter, Remy had needed to insulate his feet with two or three pairs of socks and then plastic bags. But it was not winter again yet.

As he neared the cabin, he saw his father outside, on guard.

He was down on his belly behind a low wall of sandbags. Remy hadn't seen his father fill the sandbags, but he figured they must be filled with dirt, because there was no sand within a thousand miles as far as Remy knew. His father had one of the hunting rifles propped on top of the sandbags, aimed at nothing. He was looking at the world through the rifle sight, as if whatever he expected to happen would happen so fast that there would be no time to aim.

Off in the distance Remy noticed a thick, billowy column of smoke.

"It's only me, Roy," he said as he walked up behind his father. He knew better than to surprise the man at a time like that. "I brought trout for breakfast."

"It's beginning," his father said, his voice low and dark.

"What's beginning?" Remy asked.

He knew in his head he should be afraid, but he didn't feel afraid, because the smoke seemed so far away.

"The conflagration."

"I don't know what that is," Remy said.

"It's like a fire, but . . . more. Much more. It's when a whole civilization burns itself to the ground."

At that, Remy began to feel afraid. Not so much for himself and his father, because it still seemed very far away. It was clear that his father had taken them where no conflagration could ever find them. But the hairs at the nape of his neck stood on end because he thought of Lester, and the people he knew from his old neighborhood. He did not express this out loud to his father, because his father had long ago made it clear that he felt no sympathy for those left behind.

"I'm going to go make a fire," Remy said, "and cook these trout."

"No!" his father said. Shouted, really. "No, you can't make a fire. Someone will see the smoke."

Only then did Remy understand that they might have reason to fear for themselves and their own safety. It was a chilling feeling, like plunging naked into the freezing creek for his occasional bath.

"I'll cook them inside in the woodstove," he said.

"You're not using your head, boy. Smoke will still go up the chimney."

"Oh," Remy said.

He stood for a time, the stringer hanging from his hand. His father never turned to look at him.

"So they just go to waste, then?" Remy asked.

"Salt them and dry them in the sun."

His father still never looked at Remy. He still never took his eyes off that column of smoke.

———

Later, in the afternoon, Remy announced to his father that he was going for his daily walk.

Remy walked miles every day. Two or three hours at a time. It was the only thing available for him to do. It was the only part of the day during which Remy did not feel he was dying of boredom. And in the evening, it helped him feel tired enough to ease the sensation that he was about to jump out of his own skin.

After nearly a year, walking had begun to feel like survival.

"Don't go today," his father said. "It's not safe."

But Remy wanted to go. Badly.

Not only could he not bear the idea of missing his daily walk, but he wanted to move closer to the conflagration and see what it really was. Yes, it made his skin tingle and the little hairs on his neck and arms stand on end. But he wanted to cautiously peek in on what was happening to a world that, against his father's advice, he still thought of as his own. Despite his extended absence from it.

He broke out the big guns.

"But you said you're not an authority over me. You said you don't want me to be a slave. You said I'm a free man."

Remy's father turned away from the column of smoke for the first time Remy could remember. He looked at Remy, but not into his eyes. More like at his nose area. His brow furrowed in distress.

"I'm trying to teach you, though. You don't seem to know how to be safe yet."

"You said people only learn when they're free. That you can't force learning on anybody. And that people who try to force you to learn are probably trying to teach you all the wrong things."

Several nervous seconds ticked by. Then Remy heard his father sigh, and he knew he had won.

"Take a rifle," his father said. "And don't go anywhere near the paved road, whatever you do. And if you see anybody, hide. And if anybody sees *you*, don't lead them back here. Hide until they're gone."

"Okay," Remy said.

Still, it seemed like an awful lot of orders to give to someone if you really believed they were free.

———

Remy walked to the paved road, just as he had been told not to do. It felt bold and exciting, and he had missed that feeling. He had missed being able to *do* something.

He had barely stepped out onto the pebbly pavement when a car came around a bend in the road.

He dove for cover behind a stand of brush. But it was too late. They had seen him.

He heard the car pull over to the shoulder and stop, idling close to where he hid.

"Hey, kid?" someone called a moment later.

Remy did not respond.

"Kid? I know you're right behind those bushes. We're not gonna bite you."

Remy stood up.

His stomach buzzed with fear as he did so. His face burned and tingled with it. His head swam. But still he did it, almost without thinking. And while he likely could not have explained why in words, he knew why.

He desperately missed people who were not his father. He missed talking to real people so much that it was worth a considerable risk to try it.

He saw two men standing outside their car. More of a utility vehicle, actually. It had writing on it. And their dark-green khaki uniforms had writing on the sleeves. But Remy couldn't read what the writing said.

"What're you doing out here all by yourself?" one of the men asked.

They were younger than his father, and slimmer. And cleaner. Remy wondered how clean he was in their eyes. Clean enough, he figured. He had bathed in the creek the previous morning. And he had insisted that his father cut his hair every month or so when it started to get tangled and itchy inside his collar.

"Hunting," Remy said.

He raised the rifle so they could see it. Not raised it at them, not as if to shoot, but just lifting it by his side, pointed at the sky. His father had taught him never to aim his rifle at anything unless he was "fixing to shoot it."

The two men exchanged a glance that Remy could not interpret.

"Aren't you a little young to be out hunting by yourself?" the other man asked.

"My dad is not too far back there," he said, despite its being a lie.

"Even so," the first man said. "Handling a gun at your age?"

"I'm good with a gun," Remy said. "I'm nine."

Remy did not know how old he was anymore. But he knew he was not nine.

Meanwhile he felt a buoyancy in his chest because they were actual people, and they were talking to him.

"You sure don't look nine," the man said. "But anyway. Can you get your dad? We need to tell him something."

"No, he won't come. He doesn't like to talk to people. Just me."

Again the two men exchanged a measured glance.

A strange length of time passed in silence. Remy wanted to ask them about the conflagration, but he wasn't sure he should. Also he could no longer remember the word.

"Will you give him a message for us?"

"Yeah," Remy said. "Okay."

"You won't forget? It's important."

"No, I won't forget."

"I'm guessing he knows this road ends six miles up ahead?"

"I don't know if he knows that," Remy said.

He hadn't known it, but his father might have.

"That means there's only one way out of the area. I'm sure you've noticed there's a wildfire burning to the south of here. It's pretty dangerous when there's only one road out. We're not literally telling you to evacuate. Just to be on your guard. It's a good twenty-five miles away, and right now the wind has changed and the fire is being driven farther south. But the weather is a fickle thing."

"What's 'fickle'?" Remy asked.

He was still positively elated to be talking to them, and didn't want the exchange to end.

"Changeable."

"Oh."

"So just tell him to keep a real good eye on conditions and get out fast if it starts coming this way. Okay?"

"Yes, sir. I'll tell him."

"Don't forget."

"I won't forget."

Regrettably, the men climbed back into their car and drove away.

The most exciting thing to happen to Remy in a year was now in the past. It was a letdown he could feel inside his chest, like something had gone missing in there.

He wondered how long it would be before anything real happened to him again.

—

Remy thought about it all the way home. And it was nearly an hour-long walk.

If he didn't tell his father, they might be trapped and burned alive. If he did tell him, his father would know Remy had defied orders and walked out to the paved road.

And beyond that lay something more amorphous and confusing. Something Remy could feel but not directly understand. If he told his father, then his father would know he had been wrong, and there was no conflagration. That it was not society burning itself to the ground. Just a regular old wildfire.

Remy knew his father didn't like to be wrong. But it went even further than that. Remy got the distinct impression that his father *wanted* the conflagration. That he would be disappointed to learn it had not yet arrived.

But for Remy to know and not tell . . . that was another deeply uncomfortable feeling. In this odd moment, his father was wrong about the world, and Remy knew better. Remy knew more. It made him feel as though the earth had tilted on its axis and now everything was weirdly off kilter.

When he arrived back at the cabin, his father was still lying on his belly in the dirt, viewing the world through the rifle sight over his miniature sandbag fortress. A thin curl of cigarette smoke rose above the big man's head.

"It's just me, Roy," Remy said, though he knew his father must have known that already. Otherwise Remy would be dead.

"I was worried," his father said, lifting his head away from the rifle. He spoke with the cigarette bouncing at the corner of his mouth. "You were gone too long."

"I was gone just how long I always am."

"Well, it seemed longer."

They stood considering each other for a moment. Remy caved inside. He couldn't bring himself to do it.

He walked around the fortress and checked the drying fish, then let himself into the cabin. He would watch the wind direction himself. For now.

Maybe later he would feel braver.

—

He sat on his loft bed for the rest of the afternoon, staring out the window, willing the wildfire to turn around and move north, in their direction. Because then they would have to leave this place.

But the wind continued to blow the fire south. Even the smoke moved away, until in time there was no evidence of fire that Remy could see.

It was as though the best day of his new life had never happened at all.

—

Remy couldn't sleep that night. He had been lying awake for maybe an hour when he decided he was a big enough man to do what needed to be done.

"Roy?" he asked quietly.

"What is it, Remy?"

"Are you asleep?"

"I was almost asleep. What do you want?"

"It was only a wildfire."

For a long moment, he heard no movement, and no sound.

Then his father turned on the flashlight, lighting up the room. Remy thought that was too bad. The reason he had been brave enough to speak was because of all that darkness.

"The smoke, you mean?"

"Yeah, that. It was just a wildfire. It wasn't what you thought it was."

He couldn't see his father, because his bed was directly under Remy's. So that was good, at least.

"And how do you happen to know that?"

"I saw some people."

"You saw people?" His father's voice came out hard, and half the way to shouting. "You weren't supposed to get near anybody! You were supposed to hide."

"Well, I did. But it turned out they'd already seen me."

"You could have been killed."

"I wasn't, though. They were okay."

"Nobody is okay. Where did you see people?"

"Just . . . you know. On my walk."

"How close to here?"

"Not close at all."

"You didn't go down to the paved road, did you?"

"No, sir. I mean . . . no, Roy."

A long silence fell, and Remy thought maybe the talk was done. He hoped it was, anyway. Through the filthy window he saw the tiniest sliver of a moon, nearly new. He liked the moon, so he sat up in bed to see it better. His mother had liked the moon. When the thought of her smashed through, as it sometimes did, it always felt devastating to Remy, like something that could split him wide open. He tried his best not to go there, but now and then it smashed through.

"What kind of people were they?" his father asked, bumping him out of the past.

"Just regular people. Men."

"Hunters?"

"No. Not hunters. They were . . . you know. Official. What's that word you use?"

"Authorities?"

"Right. That."

"How do you know?"

"They had clothes with writing on them. And writing on their car."

As soon as the second sentence was out of his mouth, Remy realized his mistake. He toyed with the idea of saying the car had been driving on the dirt road between the real road and the cabin. But that would only make things worse. In his father's view, the only thing worse than Remy too far away was a stranger too close.

"So you're lying to me now."

"I just don't want to get in trouble. I'm always getting in trouble with you."

"Then why don't you just do what I—"

But he cut himself off and never finished, as sometimes happened when he realized he was talking like a father, and not like a free man to another free man.

"So you met two people from the government," his father said. "And they told you there was no cause for alarm. Nothing out of the ordinary. Just a wildfire. That's not surprising. That's exactly what they would want you to believe."

Remy made a mental note not to share any more knowledge he might have with Roy. If he ever happened to stumble on any again, that is. Because he didn't know who was right and who was wrong now, but he did know there was no point in giving something to a person if you happened to know it was something they really didn't want.

Chapter Three

Canada

Remy crouched barefoot near the creek's widest pool. He purposely stayed as far back from the bank as he could manage, so the fish would not see his movements.

It was late autumn, with a strong bite of winter in the air. First snow could be any day, and his father had not yet gone out to resupply. It was beginning to scare Remy.

He drew his fishing pole back, cast high and far over his head . . . and the baited hook never came down again. He had made the humiliating beginner's mistake of letting it hang up in a tree branch over his head.

That had been his last hook. And if he didn't catch a fish that morning, he wasn't going to eat.

Remy tugged gently to see if he could free the hook without breaking the line. When it didn't budge, he sighed deeply and began to climb the tree.

It wasn't a particularly easy tree to climb. It had lost its leaves, so at least he could see where he was going. But there were no branches on which to brace his feet until he'd shimmied up the scratchy bark of the trunk a good seven or eight feet. And then the little branches were so dense that they poked and gouged him all over as he tried to move around. He was able to identify his hook easily, because it had a shiny silver lure to attract the trout's attention. He moved gingerly along a limb toward it, breaking away as many small branches as he could, but getting scratched up anyway.

When he reached out for the hook and lure, the branch broke, and he felt himself hurtling helplessly toward the ground. He landed hard, feeling the wind rush out of him, accompanied by an explosion of sharp pain. He had landed on part of the branch, and felt something give on that side of his torso. He knew he had probably broken a rib, or multiple ribs, but there was nothing to be done about that. You didn't do anything about injuries out here. You just moved forward in spite of them if you possibly could.

Remy sat up gently and felt around the injured area, but it hurt to touch it. And it hurt to draw a full breath. So he resolved to avoid doing both of those things, at least as much as was humanly possible.

He pulled slowly to his feet, uttering a litany of "ow ow ow ow" sounds under his breath.

In his only bit of luck in as long as he could remember, the branch with his hook was lying near his left foot.

He bent down to retrieve it, this time keeping the expressions of pain to himself. He might as well practice, he figured, before he got back to the cabin. His father would not want to hear it.

He broke the tangled line near the branch, bit off the excess as close to the hook as possible, and retied the tackle onto the line coming off his reel.

Then he did a careful underhand cast into the deep pool.

He tried to keep his baited hook as far away from the downed tree as possible, because he lost a lot of tackle there. The trout were wily. They would wrap the line around a branch and then break it, or simply swim into a wooded abyss where Remy could never reel them in, and where forcing the issue would only result in a bare, broken line flying back through the air toward his face.

But that's where all the fish were. In the dangerous area. Well. Dangerous for Remy. Safe for them. It was that kind of game. It was almost a form of war.

Remy sat for nearly an hour, gently experimenting with how deeply he could breathe without bringing on that jolt of pain. When he overdid it, and the jolt hit, it felt like someone trying to crack open his torso with a splitting maul and a cast iron wedge. It made him feel sorry for deadwood.

He did not get so much as a nibble.

Breathing shallow breaths, he slithered along the cold ground, tugging his bait closer to the downed tree. He sat for several minutes, but still got no interest from the trout, so he tugged it a little closer.

Suddenly his ears filled with the familiar zipping sound of line being pulled off the reel. He tried to react quickly, but it hurt to move his left arm. By the time he had stopped the reel and tried to reclaim line, there was only that sickening solid feeling that told him the line was hung up on something.

Figuring he had nothing to lose, he rose painfully and walked right to the edge of the water. Not seeing his hook, or a fish, he waded in.

He found the end of the broken line wrapped around a branch. But the fish and the hook were gone.

Remy stood in the cold water for several minutes, feeling the disastrous nature of the morning settle fully into his gut. He almost cursed out loud, the way his father did when any little thing went wrong, but Remy was learning not to express anything he felt. Other than the little "ow" sounds he'd made when first exploring his injury, he kept things to himself now. And the better he learned that lesson, the better everything seemed to go.

His feet were growing numb, so he stepped out of the water and walked home empty-handed.

When he got back, his father was lying in the hammock out in front of the cabin.

Remy walked right up to him, feeling resentment seethe in his belly. They were out of food, and his father wasn't hunting. He was hunting less and less and taking life easy more and more. It was maddening to Remy, and impossible to understand.

His father opened his eyes and looked Remy up and down.

"Not like you to come home empty-handed," he said.

"We're out of hooks."

"You're supposed to preserve the hooks at all costs."

"I know what I'm supposed to do. *You* try it sometime. It's not that easy."

Remy waited in silence, assuming his father would know what came next. But Roy only squinted into the sun and then closed his eyes, as if napping.

"You need to go get supplies," Remy said.

His father sat up, and in doing so, unbalanced himself and almost fell off the hammock. He ended up with his feet braced on the ground, holding tightly to the ripstop nylon on either side of him. He looked Remy dead in the eyes.

"That's a pretty naïve thing to say to me."

"I don't know what that means. But I had to say it. How could I not say it? We're out of food. We're out of fishhooks. We're out of propane. We're down to three matches. We really only have enough gasoline for one trip in the truck."

"And you think the stores are just open in the next town, like nothing ever happened?"

"I don't know what I think," Remy said. "I just know I'm hungry and there's nothing to eat. We can't just sit here and starve. And freeze to death. There's no more gas for the chain saw. And you're not cutting stovewood anyway. It could snow any day now, and without stovewood we'll freeze."

"I can siphon gas out of the truck's tank."

"But you need that gas to go get supplies."

"There may not be any supplies anywhere. I don't think you get that."

"Well, we have to try something!" Remy shouted.

It hurt his broken rib. Or ribs.

He had never shouted at his father before. But their situation was growing desperate.

A moment's silence fell.

"I guess I could drive out and see what's what," his father said. It was clear by Roy's voice that he was terrified. It put the fear into Remy, too. "If no stores are open, and no one's around to care anyway, maybe I could break into one. Or if there are abandoned cars I could siphon gas out of one's tank."

"Anything," Remy said. "Just do something."

"I doubt the truck'll start after all this time."

"It's on the trickle charger."

"But that's probably run down, too."

"I start up the generator and charge it up when it runs down," Remy said.

He had never told his father that he'd been doing that, and now he stood quietly as the news sank in. Remy had invested a lot of energy in making sure they could leave this place if his father ever agreed to such a thing. And he saw the end of their supplies coming, even if it seemed his father did not.

"Well, aren't you just the little genius?" his father said after a time. It did not sound like a compliment.

"I just know we need supplies. We're almost out of stovewood and we're almost out of matches. How can we make a fire with no matches?"

"People make fires by rubbing two sticks together."

"Roy. We need supplies."

His father sighed, and Remy knew a good thing when he heard it. It was the shift he'd been pushing for.

"You stay here," Roy said, his voice quavering.

"I can come."

"No way. Not a chance in hell. It's too dangerous. You stay here." His father took him by both shoulders, his fingertips digging in. It hurt, but Remy didn't let on—didn't say so, and was careful not to let it show on his face. "This is very dangerous, what I'm about to do. I might not make it back. If I don't come back, you'll have nothing. You'll have to head out of here on foot. Bring a rifle. Don't go out the way we came. Go north. Take the compass I gave you and head north."

Remy's brain swam with fear, and his side ached.

"Why north?" he asked, knowing it would only get colder the farther he moved in that direction.

"We're only a couple or three dozen miles south of the Canadian border. I don't know what the border looks like up there, but if you're on foot in the wilderness, you can probably step right over. Border crossing stops are pretty much only on roads, so far as I know. See if you can't walk right over the border into Canada."

"Why Canada? What's wrong with this country?"

"Use your head, boy. The fact that our society has fallen apart doesn't mean theirs has. I mean, in the great scheme of things it's probably the whole world order. But some countries'll fare better than others, and I wouldn't trust this one any farther than I could pick it up and throw it." He shot a wistful glance over his shoulder in the direction of the truck. "Wish me luck, boy."

Remy said nothing. Not because he didn't want his father to be lucky, but because he'd been struck mute by his fear of the moment.

"Oh, wait," his father said. "Before I go."

He walked into the cabin and came out holding a full can of something. When he got closer, Remy saw it was beef ravioli. His favorite.

"Yeah, yeah, okay," his father said. "I've been holding out on you. This was purely for emergencies."

He extended the can and Remy took it from him.

"But the can opener is broken," Remy said.

"You can open it with the hunting knife and a mallet. But save me half, in case I come back empty-handed. If I don't come back at all, you can eat the other half."

And with that, he turned away and walked to the truck.

"Get a new can opener," Remy called after him.

"Remains to be seen what I can get," his father called back.

Remy waited, his teeth clenched, to see if the truck would start. The engine turned over several times, a bit weakly from the sound of it, and Remy's heart fell down into his gut. But a second later it caught and fired up, and he inhaled deeply because he had forgotten it would hurt.

"Ow," he said, grateful that his father was too far away to hear.

—

Remy started a fire in the woodstove with one of the three remaining matches. The wood that lay piled in the cabin beside the potbellied stove was all they had left. But it would be enough until his father came back.

If his father came back.

It was a ridiculous luxury to have a fire going during the day, but Remy was cold and miserable and in pain, and he wanted to eat his ravioli hot. He could always pay for his excesses later by taking the wheelbarrow out into the surrounding forest and picking up downed deadwood.

He opened the can with the hunting knife and a mallet, carefully puncturing the edge of its lid one cut at a time. It took ages. The knife would slip and pierce the lid too far from the last cut, leaving a bit of connective metal that would not budge. Then Remy would have to try to keep the knife right on that troublesome bit of metal as he brought the mallet down again.

It was frustrating, and slow. And it hurt.

When he finally got the can open, he warmed it on top of the woodstove, salivating at the smell of it.

When it was properly hot, Remy ate it.

He did not save half of it for his father. He ate it all.

He ate it all because it hadn't been his idea to hide a can of his favorite food from a hungry boy. And because it hadn't been his idea to wait until they were starving before venturing out for supplies. And it hadn't been Remy who'd been lying in the hammock when he could have been out hunting. It hadn't been Remy's idea to leave Pocatello and come to this miserable wilderness in the first place.

Roy could be angry, but he couldn't squeeze the ravioli back out of Remy. It would be too late. His father could feel however he wanted about it when he came back.

If he came back.

—

Night fell, and his father still had not come back. And Remy was getting scared.

He was tired, and sleepy, and wanted to go to bed, but he felt he should probably stand guard. If his father had been captured, someone might know Remy was here. They might be coming for him.

He put on three pairs of socks, wrapped himself in his scratchy blanket, and took up one of the rifles. He lay on his belly behind the low wall of the sandbag fortress, and tried to stay awake.

In the morning, he decided, if the sun came up and nothing had changed, he would head out on foot for Canada.

He did not succeed in staying awake.

The slamming of a vehicle door launched him up out of a sound sleep. His breath ragged, his heart pounding in his throat, Remy aimed down the walking path in the dark, his finger on the trigger.

The moon had reached its first quarter that night, and, as his eyes adjusted to the light, Remy felt grateful that the moon was there to help him. It felt almost as though his mother were looking down on him and wanting him to survive.

In time the dark shape of a man emerged from the trees. Remy could see the bright glow of his cigarette in the dim moonlight.

"Don't come any closer!" he shouted, his voice wavering with panic and cold. "I'll shoot you. I will!"

He watched, frozen, as the lighted tip of the cigarette rose to the level of a big man's mouth, glowed more brightly, then dropped to the end of a long arm.

"I mean it! I've got a gun!"

"Remy," the dark shape said. "It's me. Roy."

Remy lowered the rifle and collapsed into shaking. He wanted to say something angry to his father, but he couldn't speak yet. He was too overcome by the bulk of his fear draining away and leaving him.

"That was good, though," his father said. "Good to know you have the right instincts." He came closer and stood over Remy, his cigarette glowing in the dark. The fiery tip brightened and lengthened as his father took a long draw. "Come help me get all this stuff out of the truck."

"Tonight?" Remy tested his voice and found it still shaky. "Right now?"

"We at least have to bring in what the bears would eat."

Remy sighed and pulled to his feet. It hurt his ribs, but he kept that to himself. He followed his father out to the truck in the moonlight.

"Why were you gone so long?" Remy asked, his voice stronger.

"I had to make a few trips. I couldn't fit everything into the truck in one trip. And I had to go to a bunch of different stores."

Remy stopped dead on the trail.

"Wait," he said.

His father stopped, too.

"What?"

"So you just went to a bunch of stores? And everything was just . . . regular? You just bought stuff like in the old days?"

"Well, *up here*," his father said. "It's very remote up here. The cities might be a different story."

He turned away and began to walk again in the dark.

Remy trotted after him.

"Wait," he called, but his father kept walking. "Wait. Did you ask them what it was like in the cities?"

"Of course not," his father called over his shoulder. "Nobody wants to talk about a thing like that."

They reached the clearing where the truck was parked, and Remy couldn't believe his eyes. There sat what he guessed to be three truck-loads of stovewood, stacked on either side of it.

"Wait," Remy said. "You *bought* wood?"

"And food, and all the other supplies we need."

"But why did you *buy* wood?"

"You said yourself it's almost winter."

"But . . ."

"Just help me bring this stuff in, Remy. I'm tired. I want to go to bed. Go get the wheelbarrow and put all the empty bear canisters in it, and bring them out here. It might take you a few trips. If we can put all this in the bear canisters now, we can leave it out here till morning."

Remy sighed as silently as possible.

His father was right. The food that was not canned had to be in canisters, and it had to be now. He was sleepy, and his ribs hurt misera-bly, and the thought of reaching and stacking sounded almost impossi-bly painful. But they had a rapidly approaching winter to survive. And it had to be done.

As he walked off toward the supply tent in the moonlight, he heard his father call after him.

"And even if it's not bad in the cities . . . yet . . . that doesn't mean it won't be. You know. Any time now."

Remy did not reply.

—

They lay in their bunks, Remy trying to sleep. But it was almost morning. He could see a slight glow between the trees when he opened his eyes and looked out the window.

"If you're awake," his father said quietly from below him, "I'm going to tell you something. But I don't want you to freak out."

Remy felt the fear seize his insides again. His insides were so tired from the fear. He was so tired.

"I'm awake," he said.

"I've been having chest pains."

"Like . . . like what kind of pains?"

"Like angina, or maybe some kind of blockage."

"I don't really know what that means," Remy said.

But his gut told him that it meant his father was sick. His mother had been sick, and look how that had turned out. The frozen spot in his insides grew wider, and colder.

"It means my heart is not so great. Not so strong right now. But if I take it a little easier, everything should be fine."

"You should see a doctor if you're sick."

"Right, like I can just go all the way into the city and go to a doctor, and be safe. Use your head, boy. I'm safer here. And I'm okay. You saw with your own eyes what I was able to do today. I just think it might be better if I didn't split wood until I take some time to rest up and heal."

"Is that why you haven't been hunting?"

A long silence. Remy wasn't sure what to make of it. But it only stoked the fear. It felt as though the cold fear in his poor, tired gut had been with him forever and was never going away. It was exhausting. It was wearing him down. Tearing him apart.

"I can fire a gun all right," his father said, startling him. "I wasn't so sure about dragging a deer home."

"Maybe I could help with that," Remy said.

But the truth of the matter was that, with freshly broken ribs, he probably could not. But maybe he would just have to do it anyway.

One way or another it was going to be a very long winter.

He lay awake for a long time, one odd little part of his mind wishing he could have left this place on foot and headed for Canada. Yes, it would have been rough, and terrifying. Yes, he very well might have died.

And yet, somehow, in that moment, life simply dragging on like this felt like the worst possible outcome.

—

When he finally rose again, Remy helped his father put away their new store of supplies, and tarp the stovewood against incoming weather.

In addition to a great deal of other canned and dried food, his father had bought two dozen more cans of beef ravioli.

If Roy ever noticed that Remy hadn't saved any for his return, it was never mentioned.

Chapter Four

What Kind of Man

Remy was ten days short of his eighth birthday when his father died. But he didn't know it. He didn't know how old he was, or remember the date of his birthday. He had no idea how long they had been living in that desolate place.

He awoke that morning to see that his father was gone.

The rifles lived in a corner of the cabin by the door, and one was missing, so Remy rolled over and fell back asleep, confident that his father had only gone hunting.

When he finally woke up for good, he climbed down from his bunk and tended to a few basic chores, such as splitting and hauling stovewood.

Winter was coming on again. Remy didn't know how his father had been feeling lately, because after the night they discussed his heart, almost a year earlier, it hadn't been mentioned again. But his father knew they needed to stock up on meat for the winter. They both knew it. Roy had taken charge of the hunting, while Remy had taken over the stovewood detail. Nothing was more important than that they survive the winter, so they focused only on that. At least, as far as Remy knew.

His ribs had healed, but they had healed badly. They ached in cold weather, and limited his ability to twist his torso as far as he otherwise might. It still hurt to slam down a splitting maul, but Remy had learned to do it anyway.

Pain had simply become a condition he had no expectation of living without.

His father didn't come home for breakfast, so Remy ate a cold can of spaghetti and went back to splitting wood. He didn't have a watch, but he had learned to follow the angle of the sun.

The sun moved all the way down to the western horizon, and still his father had not come home.

Remy wanted to go out looking for him, but he knew better than to leave the cabin at nightfall. If he got lost in the dark, he would freeze to death. So he ate plain tuna straight out of the can and put himself to bed.

When he woke in the morning, his father still had not come back.

That was when Remy fully came to understand fear. He thought he had felt it all along. But in that fulcrum of a moment, he realized he had only understood a sort of miniature fear, like fear's little brother. From that moment forward, it would be the genuine adult article setting up living quarters in his poor beleaguered gut.

It would be the full-size monster of fear.

He jumped down off his loft bed and went out searching.

He had no way of knowing which direction his father had taken, so there was a great deal of time and a little bit of luck involved in his search.

The sun was almost directly overhead when he found his father.

Roy was lying facedown on the hard dirt, his rifle splayed out near his side. Behind him lay a young buck, his hooves hog-tied together. Remy touched them both, one after the other. They were both in a fairly advanced state of rigor mortis. Remy didn't know the words, or what caused the process, but it was different from any living body he'd touched, and he wordlessly knew they were dead. And he'd more or less expected that. When his father had not come home the night before, he had already known.

Remy was not surprised.

As to what he *was*, feelings-wise, in that moment he felt very little. Mostly a stony kind of shock that made him feel as though he were walking in a dream.

He picked up the rifle and walked back to the cabin, where he got the shovel out of the supply tent. He carried it back to where his father lay, and attempted to dig a shallow grave. Actually, he attempted to dig a suitably deep one, so the animals could not get to his father's body. But the ground was so hard. He worked on it all afternoon, and only managed to get it about knee deep.

Then he tried to move his father's body into it, and failed utterly.

He tried for close to an hour, and literally was not able to budge Roy's huge frame even an inch or two.

That was the moment when he started to cry, and he didn't stop for the balance of the day. It felt as though he was crying tears of frustration. Looking back, he realized there were other reasons to cry, but on that day it was hard to feel his way around in the blank, hazy shock.

He had no choice but to carefully memorize the clearing and never, never come back to it again.

He dragged the deer back to the cabin.

The deer was young, and therefore fairly small as deer go. And the way was downhill. Still, it wasn't easy.

But Remy had to do it. The deer had given his life so Remy and his father could eat. Not voluntarily, but that only made its fate more tragic in Remy's eyes. And Remy's father had given his life so that Remy could eat the venison the deer provided.

Remy was going to eat the deer no matter what that required of him.

By the time he got it back to the supply tent he was exhausted, and it was almost dark. It was cold, cold enough to go to a hard frost overnight. So Remy left the dressing of the deer until morning, stringing it up over the branch of a tree to keep the wild animals from getting it.

Still crying, his nose stuffed and running and his eyes swollen, he let himself into the cabin and ate a can of sardines. Remy hated sardines. His father had liked them. Remy ate them because they were the only food inside the cabin, and he was too utterly exhausted to walk back to the supply tent for something better.

He put himself to bed in his father's bunk, because it didn't matter where he slept anymore. The lower bunk could just as easily be his bed now.

And that was the moment it hit him. Really, fully hit him. Both of his parents were dead, and he was completely and utterly alone.

Remy cried himself to sleep for lack of a better option. For lack of *any* other option.

———

In the morning, he decided he needed a plan.

His father had told him to head for Canada on foot if he didn't come back. But that was because, at the time Roy had said it, Remy would be without supplies. Now he could stay here most of a year, until he ran out of everything, and then head for Canada. But why stay in this awful place a year? Why stay a moment longer than necessary?

Actually, there was one reason Remy could think of to stay. Maybe his father had been right all along about the state of the world. Maybe this was the only safe place in the whole country. Maybe it was his one and only shot at survival.

Still, he would run out of supplies. Sooner or later he would have to try to make it to someplace else.

Remy's mind ran so fast, and in so many directions, that he tired himself out and needed to lie down again.

No matter how hard he tried to rest and think of nothing, his mind kept returning to Pocatello. Lester still lived there with his parents, right on the block where Remy had grown up. At least, he hoped they still did. Maybe they would take him in. And even if they wouldn't, probably they would know what to do. It was such a relief even to think about showing up on their familiar doorstep.

But Pocatello was hours away by car. If there even still *was* a Pocatello.

Yet Remy felt he had to try.

He decided he would load the truck with as many supplies as he could, and attempt to drive it to some kind of civilization. He didn't figure he'd make it all the way home. Someone would stop him, clearly able to see he was too young to drive, and to be out in the world on his own. If his father was wrong, he didn't know what they would do. Put him in some kind of orphanage, maybe? If his father was right, they would kill him.

But he would die here, too. Given enough time.

The fear blazed so strongly in his belly that he could not have stood up if he'd tried, but Remy decided he would do it. He would have to. He would attempt to save himself by driving someplace. Anyplace, really.

But first he had to stay long enough to eat that deer. Too much had been sacrificed so that he could. There was no way he could bring himself to let it go to waste.

It relieved him to know he had to stay longer. He would do the unimaginably brave thing because he had to do it. He really had no choice. But it was an immense relief to be able to push it a few weeks down the road.

It was only twenty days later when Remy finished the last of the venison.

He loaded the bed of the truck with canned goods, jerky, and creek water in every bear canister he'd managed to empty out.

He had clothes that fit, one change of clothes, and a pair of decent sneakers, because his father had gotten them for him on his second and last resupply run. He loaded the change of clothes and both rifles into the cab up front, his skin and muscles buzzing with fear.

Then, on what was supposed to be the last trip from the cabin, he decided he hadn't eaten the bones of the deer clean enough. He stayed, and chewed on them until there was nothing left to strip away, then broke them and sucked out what marrow he could. There were a lot of bones, and it was not a quick or easy job.

He threw the bones out for the wild animals, not bothering to carry them far from the cabin, because he wouldn't be there when they came scavenging.

He walked halfway to the truck with his blood pounding in his ears, then remembered that his father sometimes made venison soup from the bones.

He carried them in a pot to the creek, washed the bones, and filled the pot with water. Then he carried it back to the cabin. He built a fire in the outside firepit and set the water on to boil. He sat for what felt like forever, waiting for it to heat. He boiled the bones for a couple of hours to get the most out of them, then fished them out with two sticks and scattered them in the dirt again.

As he did, he watched the sun cross the sky and decided it would be too late in the afternoon to set off, even if he took the hot soup with him. That was a relief. He could feel the bulk of the fear drain out of his spine, his cells. He breathed as deeply as his badly healed ribs would allow.

He would have to stay another night.

He sat for a time, rising and stirring the broth occasionally with a long branch to help it cool.

46

When he sat back down in the dirt after the last stir, he saw and felt something touch his eyelashes.

He looked up.

Framed against the angry gray afternoon sky he saw snowflakes drifting down toward his face. The fear jolted him again, because he knew he would have to leave. Right away. He could not stay another night, because if it snowed hard, the truck would be blocked in by the drifts. The dirt road would be impassable—possibly until the spring thaw.

Remy sat that way for what might have been a long time, watching the flakes fall, feeling their shocking coldness touch his face, one flake at a time. Under and maybe beyond his paralysis of fear, he felt as though someone was telling him to go. Pushing him to go. For the second time in his life, it skittered through his mind that his mother might be looking down on him. Looking out for him.

He fetched the truck keys from inside the cabin and climbed inside.

He turned the key the way he had seen his father do so many times. The engine groaned as the starter weakly cranked it a few times. Remy didn't know if it would start, and he couldn't tell if he wanted it to start or not. Maybe he wanted both, in equal measure, if such a thing were possible.

A moment later it roared to life, startling him.

Remy had never driven before. But fortunately the truck had an automatic transmission, so he didn't imagine it could be all that hard. Take the brake off. Put it in drive. Steer it carefully so he didn't hit anything. He could always go very slowly until he got the hang of the thing.

He turned it around in the wide clearing his father had used as a parking spot. Roy would have done it in one sweep of the wheel. But it took Remy a while.

Then he drove off down the dirt road, absorbing an awkward truth: he could fairly comfortably reach his feet down to the pedals, or he could see well over the dashboard, but not both at the same time. He had to sit up straight and high to see where he was going, and the truck inched along even without Remy's foot on the gas. But if he needed to slow down going around a curve, he had to slide down until he was more or less looking at the dashboard instruments to apply the brake.

He made it a couple of miles this way, and then the road made a sharp turn.

Remy slid down and stomped his foot on what turned out to be the accelerator.

The truck flew off the road in a spot where the ground dropped away. If it had done so nose-on, things might almost have been okay. But Remy steered wildly to try to make the curve, and the truck ended up going off sideways.

It landed on its passenger-side wheels, then flipped over and came to rest on its side. Remy, who had not been able to wear a seat belt and still reach the pedals, came down hard on the passenger-side door, breaking the window with his head.

He lay still a moment, dazed. He tried to rouse himself to some kind of action, but something wasn't working right. His brain sent no signals, or his muscles failed to receive them. There was some kind of vibration buzzing like a swarm of bees in his chest.

In time, when he was able, he touched his temple. His hand came away bloody.

Still numb from the adrenaline of the moment, he shinnied out the truck's sliding back window. He tried to jump to the ground from there, but slipped and fell before he could.

In the dusky light, he saw bear canisters and cans of food scattered everywhere.

He took a step, cried out in pain, and fell to the ground, scraping the heels of his hands. He rose again, but he could not put weight on his right leg.

He crawled up to the road, and for a moment he didn't move. He only looked down over the wreckage of what had been his very best plan.

Then he stood and hopped a few steps toward the cabin. Then a few more. He found a fallen branch on the edge of the road, stripped away its leaves and twigs with his pocketknife, and used it as a makeshift crutch.

He knew at his current rate of travel it would take him hours to hobble back to the cabin.

The snow fell harder, and swirled all around him. It would cover his scattered supplies and make them nearly impossible to find until the spring thaw. But he could carry nothing. Moving himself along the road was the best he could manage.

The adrenaline began to wear off, and the pain was right there to feel. He had knocked his head hard. He had probably broken his leg. And there was something very wrong with his right shoulder, which made walking with a crutch challenging.

But there was nothing he could do about any of it except to get himself indoors for the night.

The only option remaining to him was to set off on foot for Canada. But even that required two good legs.

Maybe he could manage it in the spring.

———

When he arrived back at the cabin, he had nothing to eat but venison broth.

He drank almost all of it, then gingerly put himself to bed, his teeth gritted against the pain. He had not so much as an aspirin, and sleep seemed out of the question.

In the morning he would have to make his way back to the truck and poke around in the snow for a wheelbarrow full of supplies. He could melt snow just outside the cabin for drinking water, but without the food from the truck, he would starve in just a matter of weeks.

As he lay shivering under his father's blanket and three tanned deerskins, he heard the wild animals coming for the bones, which he had left close outside the cabin. At first he didn't know what kind of animals they were, but as they began to fight each other over the find, their growling and snarling identified them as coyotes.

Maybe they would come again the following night because of Remy's mistake. Maybe every night. Certainly they would come for his father's body. And then, maybe they would get bold and come for *him*.

Many times from that day forward Remy would miss his father. But, that night, he hated the man with a passionate heat. If Roy had been in front of him in that moment, Remy would have tried to tear the man apart with his bare hands.

What kind of a man takes a young boy to a place like this and then leaves him completely and utterly alone?

2. ANNE

Chapter Five

Need

Anne jogged in place while she waited at a busy intersection with her friend Miri. She was a little out of breath, and in no hurry for the light to change.

It turned green immediately, and they ran across the street together.

Anne had grown up with Miri. They had been friends since grade school. But now Miri lived in Texas, they saw each other only once a year, and Anne might have given her friend the impression that she was keeping in better shape than she actually had been.

A few blocks later, Miri spoke up. It seemed astonishing to Anne that her friend could speak so effortlessly as she exercised.

"Boise has changed a lot," she said as they ducked around a man feeding quarters into his parking meter.

"How so?" Anne managed, albeit breathlessly.

"It used to have more of that small-town feel."

Anne stopped, though she knew it wasn't supposed to be the end of the run. She just gave up and admitted she was winded. She stood on the sidewalk, feet splayed, hands braced on her thighs, trying to catch her breath.

It took Miri half a block to notice.

When she did, she walked back to Anne with a slightly twisted smile on her face.

"What happened?" Miri asked.

"I might have exaggerated my fitness level."

"I *knew* it."

"Don't gloat."

"I'm not gloating. It's just that we're not as young as we used to be, hon, and we have to beat the years. Stand up for ourselves. Come on. Don't just collapse there. We'll finish with a brisk walk instead."

Anne sighed, and fell into a fast stride beside her friend—who, she hated to admit, was right. It's better to do what you can, fitness-wise, than to do nothing at all. Well. Everything-wise, really.

"How can you say Boise used to be a small town? It's the biggest city in the state."

"I didn't say it used to be a small town. I said it used to *feel* like one."

"I'm surprised it doesn't feel tiny because you're comparing everything to Dallas–Fort Worth now."

"I remember my hometown."

They drew level with Anne's favorite coffee place. Anne slowed one step and looked wistfully in its direction.

"Sure," Miri said. "Why not?"

Anne dug around in her belly pack and realized she had not brought a mask. Miri noticed.

"I have one," Miri said. "I'll go in."

"Thanks. I'll have a macchiato. A *skinny* macchiato," she added quickly. In case her friend was inclined to judge how much of a drink she had just earned.

Miri masked up and walked into the coffeehouse, and Anne chose them a table on the outside patio.

She fell immediately into unpleasant thoughts about Louisa, and her marriage, and when Miri got back outside with the drinks, her friend seemed to read her mind.

"So," Miri said, sitting across from her. "The elephant in the room. What's with you and Chris?"

"Oh, you noticed."

It iced a portion of Anne's gut to hear her friend say it out loud. Because that meant it was real.

Anne stirred her macchiato for a moment, trying to decide how much to say. But Miri was her best and oldest friend, and if she couldn't talk to Miri, then she was genuinely alone in the world.

She purposely looked away from her friend as she spoke.

"I think he might be seeing someone else."

"Nooooo!" Miri said, drawing the word out long. "No way. He's not that kind of guy."

"Are we sure there's really a 'kind of guy'?"

"Positive. I've tried every one of them, and this I know. This is my one true area of expertise—the kind of guys who cheat. Benefit from my research. I don't think Chris would do that to you."

"Well, he's pulled away."

"Since when?"

"Since we had to send Louisa back."

"Oh. Louisa. You haven't talked about that much."

"I know I haven't. I'm sorry."

Anne sipped her hot drink for a moment, knowing it was time to talk about it, but not feeling quite ready.

"The thing about it is," she said after a time, "it's that perfect heartbreak of a situation, because there's really not much assurance that she'll be okay with her mother. But there's not a damn thing we can do about that. And Chris, well . . . he's just not a person who handles heartbreak well. Take the dogs. We lost Scout and Dixon a year ago, not even two months apart. I don't remember how much I told you about this at the time. Chris said, 'That's it. No more dogs. It just hurts too much to lose them.' And you know me. I don't live my life without dogs. So I said, 'Look. I'm getting two more dogs. If you don't want to get attached to them, don't.' And I went out and got these two at the shelter. He was mad that they were three years old, because he just figures that's three fewer years before we lose them. He wouldn't even look at them for pretty much the first six months."

"And now he adores them, of course."

"Right. But I think he resents me for it."

"And a child is not a dog," Miri said.

"Right, I know that. And you know I know that. I'm not comparing the two. I'm just talking about the willingness to make emotional attachments."

"How are the kids doing with it?"

"With which?"

"I meant Louisa."

"Oh. Well. Not all that well, as far as I can tell. They were fosters themselves. It's not like they don't know how it feels."

They sat in silence for an extended time. Anne had grown addicted to staring into her coffee cup. She could feel herself doing it, but she didn't quite know how to stop.

"And there's a big showdown coming up," Anne said suddenly, surprising herself. "Because I want another foster. And it's going to be a real battle. But I can't stop wanting it, Miri. It's just how I feel, and I can't change it. And I know exactly what he'll say. Well, not exactly. I know two ways it could go. He'll either say no, absolutely not. Or he'll say straight adoption, and nothing so heartbreaking as fostering this time. Something more predictable. The situation, I mean. I'm not calling a child a 'something.' And I feel exactly the opposite, Miri. Exactly the opposite. Everybody wants the easy ones. Everybody wants to avoid the heartbreak, and all these poor kids just languish, waiting for somebody to take a chance on them, because they're not neat and safe. They have damage and nobody wants to deal with that damage. Well, I do. I want to take a child who desperately needs to be taken. I want the one who *needs* me." She fell silent. Sat stony still. Then she shifted slightly in her seat, and braved a look up at her friend's face. "Do you think that's a bad sign?" she asked.

"About what?"

"About me. Wanting to help a really damaged child because they need me? Is that, like, some kind of psychological issue?"

"Don't know," Miri said. "I'm not a psychologist."

"Right."

"But a psychologist might not be a bad idea."

"For me? Or for me and Chris as a couple?"

"Yes. All of the above. Now let's talk about something a little less stressful, and then we're going to finish this run."

It was the last thing Anne wanted to hear. Dead last. In that moment it even ranked behind difficult adoptions, and her husband's possible affair.

———

It was four nights later before she brought it up with Chris.

They were propped up in bed together, but not asleep. Anne was moisturizing her hands and face, and Chris was doing something on his tablet. She couldn't see what. He wasn't hiding the screen from her. It was just not at a good angle in relation to where she sat. She didn't want to lean over to see, because it struck her as a suspicious gesture.

She looked at *him* instead. He didn't seem to notice.

He was shirtless, his longish dark-blond hair tousled. Even after all these years, seeing him without his shirt filled her with a pleasant mix of familiarity and a touch of excitement. He was a handsome man.

Surely she was not the only woman who had noticed.

"Can you take the kids to school tomorrow while I take Miri to the airport?" she asked.

"Sure," he said. "Why not?"

He didn't take his eyes off the screen of his tablet as he spoke.

"I'm thinking about counseling."

He shifted his eyes away from the screen. They landed on her face, but not quite at the level of her eyes.

"Okay," he said.

"Just that easy?"

"If you feel like you need it, I'm not going to tell you not to go."

"I meant for both of us."

"Oh. For both of us."

"Are you against the idea?"

Chris sighed. Then he pulled back the covers and rose. He walked away in just his plaid pajama bottoms, and, for a brief moment, Anne thought he was literally walking away from the conversation. But he only walked into the bathroom and left the door open.

"Not dead set against it, no," he called back through the open door. Anne could hear the sound of him urinating. "But not entirely sure what you think our problems are."

Because he was in the next room, where he could hear her but they could not make eye contact, Anne got brave.

"Are you seeing another woman?"

For about the count of three, only silence came back to her. She died a number of little deaths in that silence.

"No," Chris said.

Then he flushed, and walked back to rejoin her.

"The silence was weird," she said.

"The silence was because I was shocked. It stunned me that you would ask."

"You've been so distant."

"Big jump from distant to actually, physically having sex with someone else."

It would stick with Anne, that sentence. What he said and how he said it. Because it sounded as though he was parsing what it meant to be seeing someone else. As though anything short of the complete sexual act didn't count at all. But in that moment it was only a vague feeling at the back of her mind.

He climbed into bed and turned off the light on the nightstand, pitching the room into darkness.

"Where did we land on the counseling?" she asked.

"Tell you what. Find a counselor. Go see him. Or her. Figure out what feels wrong in your life. And then if you tell me I need to be there, too, I'll go. Is that a reasonable response?"

"Yeah," she said, a little surprised. "It actually is."

He rolled over. Fluffed his pillow. Settled into a comfortable position. Anne assumed they were done talking for the night.

It surprised her again when he spoke.

"You want another foster," he said. "Don't you?"

"Yes. Or a straight adoption. Or foster to adopt. Yes, I do want that."

No reply from him.

"Is that going to be a fight?"

"Here's the thing about that," Chris said. "I really don't think it pays to have that fight tonight. Because it's not like the perfect kid is just sitting on the shelf waiting for us. It's probably going to take time before the right kid presents himself. Or herself. It took a year to get matched up with Louisa. So let's get a good night's sleep and push that fight down the road. Maybe by the time it comes up again we'll have a therapist as a referee."

It all sounded quite reasonable to Anne. Once again she found herself surprised.

—

In the morning, the kids came spilling down the stairs at exactly the same time, jockeying and elbowing each other for first place on each step.

They stopped dead when they saw Anne.

"What are you doing here?" Peter asked.

"Nice greeting."

Janie cut around him and wordlessly planted herself at the breakfast table, bracing her elbows on either side of her place mat.

"I didn't mean it like that," Peter said, looking embarrassed. "I just meant . . . I thought you'd be driving Miri to the airport."

"We're running a little late."

"Oh."

He walked over to Anne with his awkward teenage gait and offered her a kiss on the forehead. He was taller than she was. And she couldn't remember when that had happened. It seemed to have been during the previous night. She opened her mouth to ask him when and how he had gotten so tall, but she knew that was the kind of question kids found corny and humiliating, so she closed her mouth again.

She took the conversation in a different direction.

"I made eggs. I figured you guys eat enough cereal."

"What kind of eggs?" Janie asked, sounding mildly suspicious.

"Poached. On toast."

"Oh, good. I like that."

"Where *is* Miri?" Peter asked, settling at the table and looking around himself as though she might magically appear anywhere.

"She's upstairs packing."

"Oh."

Anne turned back to the stove and began the task of fishing the eggs out of the simmering water and draining them on paper towels. With her back still facing her children, she said something that she'd been wanting to say for a very long time. Something that felt as though it lived in her throat but never quite came up into the light.

"I'm not sure we've talked enough about Louisa going back to her mother."

The sentence was met with stony silence.

Anne popped up the four slices of toast, placed two on each plate and an egg on each slice, and turned back to the kids. They were staring at the table in front of them. Peter was rolling the edge of the cloth napkin in his fingertips. His fingernails were bitten down to the quick again, and his cuticles had been bitten as well. They looked angry and red, the way they had when he'd first come there to live.

She set their breakfasts in front of them and sat across from them at the table. She looked directly at them. They did not look back.

The dogs came bounding through the doggy door from outside, wagged their way to the table, and sat, each a few inches too close to one of the children. It was the closest to begging they were allowed to get. They were both enormous, seventy pounds for Plato and eighty for Jasmine. Jasmine looked like a golden Lab maybe mixed with some mastiff, or something else big, and Plato was black and long haired, with a white chest freckled with black spots.

"If you don't want to talk about it right now," she said, "that's okay. But I want to be sure you know you can if you want to. Anytime you want to. One way or another, don't let your breakfast get cold."

They both picked up their forks immediately. They still did not look up.

Oh dear God, please don't let me raise emotionally stunted children, she thought.

It was bad enough she'd been raised that way herself.

And why was it that wanting to do better than your own parents never seemed to translate into actually doing better? Something about knowing how, obviously, but it seemed to Anne that a person should be able to learn these things as an adult.

Janie pulled a piece of crust off her toast. Anne stopped the transgression before it could happen.

"Do *not* give Jasmine any of your toast."

Janie popped the crust into her own mouth, as though that had been the intention all along.

Then, surprisingly, the girl spoke up, her voice thin and tentative, her mouth still full.

"I just don't really know if she's okay."

"Louisa?"

Janie nodded weakly. Her head was tilted forward, causing her long, straight hair to fall over her face. She seemed to be hiding behind it. And she had always insisted that her clothes be oversize, probably for the same reason. Anne knew exactly how she felt, so she didn't try to push or advise the girl. She just let her pick out baggy clothes.

"Well, that's the thing," Anne said. "That's just the problem. We really *don't* know if she's okay. That's why it felt like maybe something we could talk about."

Her children only ate in silence.

"Okay. Well. One of the reasons I brought it up today is because I'm thinking about finding a therapist. And that's something that's available to you kids, too. If you feel like you want it."

"You and Dad?" Peter asked. His voice sounded hopeful and almost excited.

Anne's heart sagged, and her face felt hot. The kids had noticed, too.

"First me. Then probably your dad and me. And you if you want. Maybe as a family. I'm not sure yet. Just . . . you'll let me know if you want to talk, right?"

Before they could answer, Miri came down the stairs dragging her comically huge suitcase. So in that moment Anne's private conversation with her kids was over.

——

"I talked to Chris last night," Anne said in the car.

"About . . . ?"

"Kind of everything, I guess."

"Define 'everything,'" Miri said.

"I brought up counseling. He's open to the idea. He says he's not having an affair. It didn't really feel like he was denying that he's been distant. He just said there's a lot of real estate between being distant and actually, physically having sex with somebody else. Or words to that effect."

"Whoa," Miri said.

For a minute or so, Anne only navigated through traffic. She kept her eyes on the road and asked no questions.

"Which part of that was paraphrased?" Miri asked after a time.

"The part about the distance between the two things. I forget exactly how he put it."

"So he said 'actually, physically having sex.'"

It made Anne's stomach tingle to know that Miri's mind had seized on that. Because her mind had seized on it, too. She might not have known it consciously at the time he said it, but in that moment it felt clear.

"Yeah," she said. Her voice sounded hesitant to her own ears. "He did. Why? What do you make of that?"

"What do *you* make of it?"

"I'm not sure. That's why I asked. Just kind of . . . that maybe he's parsing what classifies as cheating."

"That was my thought. Deep flirtation. Worst case, maybe affair of the heart. But I could be wrong."

"But you're the expert," Anne said.

They got to smile again over that, if a little ruefully. It was a relief.

"Well, I'll say this for you," Miri said. "You dove in headfirst and got a lot done."

"That's because you pushed me. You're a very pushy person, you know that, Miri? That's why I like it when you come visit. I *need* a push now and then."

"Everybody needs a push now and then," Miri said, just as the sign for the airport exit came into view.

"*You* don't seem to."

"O.P.P.," Miri said. "Other people's problems. O.P.P. are always easy. It requires a damned impressive set of chops to take on your own."

———

Anne sat in the therapist's office, watching him scribble something on a pad. It was three weeks later, and halfway through their first session, and she still wasn't sure how she felt about him.

He was in his sixties, with salt-and-pepper hair and a neatly trimmed beard. Though she hadn't told him so, Anne had chosen him because he was just the sort of father figure Chris might accept.

"You keep coming back to that," he said.

"Which part?"

"The part about need. About wanting to help a child in need."

"Sorry," Anne said.

It was a ridiculous thing to say, and she knew it the moment it came out of her mouth. She was paying this guy—or at least their insurance company was paying him—big money to say whatever was on her mind.

"It wasn't a criticism," he said.

"Oh. Okay. What was it?"

"Just a mild flag. When something pops up multiple times like that, it indicates to me that it's important to you."

"It just concerns me," she said, squirming a bit in her chair. No matter how much she shifted her weight, she couldn't seem to get comfortable.

"So I gather. It seems almost as though you're asking me if it's a pathology."

"Okay. Well. I'll ask straight-out, then. Is it?"

"Unless I'm misunderstanding your relationship to the issue, it sounds like a virtue. Like you're wondering if you should weed it out of your life, but meanwhile everybody else is ready to give you an award. Maybe it comes from something in your past. Maybe it's an issue that has a psychological explanation. I don't know. It's only our first session. But I do want to say this about it. My job is to help people heal from the past so they can move on from it. But that's working on the assumption that the issues are causing damage. If a patient grew up in a household full of alcoholics, that person might decide to be a lifelong nondrinker. But abstaining from drink is not a problem that needs to be solved. It's a habit the person is safe and fairly well served to keep. Maybe a person grew up with bad parenting. Neglect, let's say. Then they grow up and decide their own children will have everything a child needs. It's an issue from their past, but why would they want to fix it? Wanting to help a young person in need is not exactly a failing. The only time we might tackle a positive behavior like that is if it's gone out of balance and is starting to negatively impact your life."

They both sat a moment, saying nothing. He might have been looking at Anne, but she was looking away from him, so she wasn't sure.

"I guess," she began, "then . . . I'm hoping you'll tell me if it's gone out of balance and is starting to negatively impact my life."

"I can't tell you that."

"You can't?"

"Not really, no."

"Why not?"

"Because it's not what I do. I don't look at your life and make pronouncements about it. I talk to you about your life and help you see it in a better perspective on your own. And even if it *were* my job to judge a thing like that . . . it's only our first session. I'll ask *you* to tell *me*. Is it causing problems?"

"My husband would say so."

"So it's causing problems in your marriage."

"Yes."

She expected him to answer. He didn't. He seemed oddly at peace with silence. Anne had never gotten the hang of that.

"Then I guess I have to stop doing it," she said.

Still no response.

"Right?"

"Not necessarily."

"But it's causing problems in my marriage."

"That's pretty much the definition of a marriage, wouldn't you say? Two people are what they are, and they want what they want. Some of that works well for the other person, and some of it causes problems. The two people try to find some compromise or common ground. If they can't, and it can't be lived with, then the marriage is over."

It seemed to her a strangely blunt way to end the speech. As if he had just pronounced that her marriage was over. It struck her for the first time that such a thing might prove true.

"You're saying I might have to leave my husband."

He made a light huffing noise. Anne couldn't tell if it was a stifled laugh or an expression of exasperation.

She almost said she was sorry. But this time she caught herself.

"I will never tell you to leave your marriage or stay in it. That's not how this works. I just try to help you to see your own situation more clearly so you can choose what you think is best for you."

"And also it's only our first session," she said.

He cracked the first smile she'd seen on his face, and that was the moment she felt they might both be on the same page.

"Indeed," he said. "Is your husband coming to the next session?"

"I don't know. I'd have to ask him."

"You don't have to push. He can take time to warm up to the idea if he'd like."

"He won't come next time," she said. Her voice sounded firm to her for the first time. "I'm not going to ask him yet. Before I try to understand my marriage I'm going to try to understand *me*."

Her statement felt final to her, and she was surprised when he had more to say.

"If you want your marriage," he said, "you can probably have it. If you want to help another needy child, you can probably have that. Maybe you can have both. But if you can't, then you'll have to decide what's most important to you."

But there was no real decision-making to be done in this case. Even as he said it, Anne already knew where that decision, if needed, would land.

3. REMY

Chapter Six

Dying, Then Waking

Remy put himself to bed for the last time on what he had accepted would be his final night on earth.

It was the third of April, but he didn't know that. He had no idea of the date, or his own age, or how long he had lived alone in the cabin after the loss of his father.

If anyone had been there to ask him, he likely would have concluded he'd lingered on in that horrible wilderness for two or three years after his father's disappearance. In fact, it had been less than six months. The fact that his answer would have fallen so far from the facts reflected that Remy was no longer able to judge time—not even segments of time as obvious and distinct as a number of winters. It was all just a haze in his mind.

He hadn't spoken to anyone in months. In fact, he hadn't spoken at all, not even to himself. Speech seemed like a distant concept to him, as though he had lived without it longer than he had initially lived with it, though that assessment was also warped.

As to his father's disappearance, he really had no idea where the man had gone, or when. And of course the why was an unfathomable mystery. If he tried to think about it—and the truth of the matter was that he tried *not* to think about it—he could find nothing in his mind but confusion. Yes, at one time his father had been there with Remy. Later, at some indeterminate point in time, he was no longer there. Remy did not know anything more. The memory of finding his father's body, and of unsuccessfully attempting to bury his father's body, had been completely repressed.

Remy hadn't eaten in more than six days. There was food in the supply tent, though it was dwindling. The problem was that Remy could not get to the supply tent to retrieve it. He had been snowed in. A drift of snow from a week-old storm had piled up against the cabin door, and Remy wasn't strong enough to move it. The window opened several inches, so he had been able to reach out with a cup and bring in snow, which he had melted on the woodstove. It did not open enough to allow him to wiggle out.

He had thought of shattering the window and breaking out the wooden frame with the butt of one of the rifles. That would have allowed him to get out to bring in more food. But then the window never would have closed again, so Remy would have frozen to death in his bed in the night.

He had been urinating and defecating—at least, back when his bowels had had something to evacuate—in a cooking pot in the corner, and the window would not open enough to allow him to dump the pot. The smell was constantly sickening to him.

But the existential crisis he faced that night was not about elimination, nor even about his lack of food.

Remy was out of stovewood, both inside the snowed-in cabin and outside it. There was simply no more available to him. All the deadwood and downed wood he could find had been dragged inside and burned. There were trees everywhere, including a few downed trees, and he had broken up the smaller branches as best he could. But there was no way to make the trunks and larger branches stove-size. He had siphoned all the gas from the ruined truck, and now the gas was gone. The chain saw would no longer start.

He tucked himself into the lower bunk, humming in his throat the way he did when the terror needed taming, and wondered what it would feel like to freeze to death. It was a scary thought, dying. And yet, on another, entirely different level of himself, the idea felt strangely welcome.

Maybe death would feel like nothing at all. Maybe it would literally be a portal into nothing. It was a comfort to think about knowing nothing, and feeling nothing. Everything he had been feeling for years, everything he could imagine feeling ever again, was deeply unwelcome.

He covered himself with both blankets and all three tanned deerskins.

There was a chance it might be enough, and he might wake up. But he didn't think it was a very good chance, and he wasn't even sure which outcome he hoped for.

In fact, the most telling clue to his mental state was this: he could no longer find it in himself to care.

Remy lay awake for several hours, wondering if he was dead yet, and, if so, how he would know.

———

When Remy woke, it was late the following morning.

He lay perfectly still with his eyes closed, afraid to open them. He assumed he was dead. He thought when he opened his eyes, he would see where one goes after death. And that was a terrifying thought.

Finally, unable to bear the suspense a moment longer, he shot his eyes open.

He was in the cabin.

He touched his own arms and face. Pinched himself. Poked at himself. He could see his breath billow out as steam, but a much fainter steam than he'd been used to seeing since the winter had set in.

He could hear a wet dripping sound, like rain. Somewhere outside, water was tapping on the ground and running off to . . . wherever. Downhill, he supposed.

He sat up, the blankets and skins falling away, and looked out the window. The snow, which had come up higher than the bottom of the glass pane for days, had disappeared.

Remy got up and walked to the window and looked out, noticing as he did that it was strangely warm inside the cabin. He threw off the coat in which he had slept. It was not particularly uncomfortable to walk around in just his T-shirt and underpants. At least, not by his new standards of discomfort.

The midmorning sun was beating down on the cabin and every-thing around it. The snow was melting fast.

Remy opened the window as far as it would go. He turned his head sideways and stuck his face out. It was warm. Springtime warm. The temperature had warmed by about forty degrees in just one day.

And he was alive.

For the third time, Remy looked up at the sky and wondered if his mother was intervening on his behalf.

His stomach painfully cramping, his every muscle and cell weak with hunger, he walked to the door and put his left shoulder to it. He gave it all the strength he had, which admittedly was not much. It opened about three inches.

The snowdrift was still there, but it had half melted, and sunk down. Rivulets of water ran downhill away from the door. The problem was that, though the drift was smaller, it was also quite dense and heavy with moisture.

Remy backed all the way across the cabin.

He took a running charge at the door, hitting it hard with his left shoulder. The uninjured one.

It hurt, but he didn't cry out. He never did anymore. Why express pain? And, more importantly, express it to whom?

The door gave another few inches.

Remy tried to squeeze out, but only managed to get himself stuck there, the door painfully compressing his chest. For a moment it filled him with a claustrophobic panic. The panic motivated him to push harder, but for that moment nothing moved. Remy was giving it everything—every ounce of energy and strength he could muster and then some. Nothing was budging.

And then, just like that, the snow shifted. Slid on its half-melted base.

The door flew open another foot, and Remy tumbled out onto the wet ground.

Without even going inside to put on clothes or shoes, he stumbled to his feet and ran to the supply tent.

Remy's leg had healed, and he could move fast if he needed to. But he was not the same as he had been before that injury. His right leg was now shorter than his left, and less than perfectly straight. It didn't hurt much to put weight on it, though it ached in the cold no matter what he was doing. He was able to run, but it was an ugly, uneven thing. A sort of fast hobble.

He unzipped and threw back the tent door, and grabbed three cans of ravioli, two beef and one cheese. Holding them tightly to his chest, he ran back to the cabin, where he opened them one after the other and ate them cold.

Then, because it was the first food he had eaten in six days, and because he had not been wise enough to eat slowly, he had to run outside, fall to his cold and wet knees, and throw it all up into the melting snow.

It was a terrible waste. About twenty-five percent of his remaining food supply, gone without nourishing him.

He ran back into the cabin, dressed, and hobbled back to the supply tent for more. This time he took three granola bars and ate them two bites at a time, allowing long breaks to see if the food was inclined to stay down before taking another two bites.

When he had managed to hold and digest the food, he hiked out to the site of the crashed truck. He was hoping the thaw had exposed a few more supplies that he might have missed on his slow and painful trips out to dig and poke around in the snow.

By the time he got there the snow was almost completely melted, save a few places still in shadow. On the ground near the ruined and useless vehicle he found a bear canister full of jerky, three cans of soup, and a big foil ziplock bag of dehydrated stew.

On the wet dirt near the stew, he found the compass his father had given him. It was shattered and rusted, its case bent, its needle lying in the dirt a few inches away.

Remy carried the food back to the cabin, hobbling fast and feeling stronger.

There were three army-green duffel bags in the supply tent. He packed one of them full of the remaining food, his change of clothes, and a rifle. He loaded the rest of the ammunition—which wasn't much—into his pockets.

He ate one of the cans of soup, then did what he had been yearning to do for years: he left that place.

He headed out on foot—barefoot—with the blankets and skins draped over him like a massive cape, and the heavy duffel on his shoulder.

He knew the weather could turn again at a moment's notice, and that without shelter he might die. But the snow was melting. The world was thawing. And, in a thaw, the chances of consistent warming were better than the alternative.

Besides, it was a chance he was willing to take. Nothing was worse than staying one more day in that horrible place, utterly and abjectly alone.

He headed north, toward Canada. In case his father had been right. Maybe he could call Lester's house from there. He certainly couldn't walk to Pocatello.

No, north to Canada was his best shot.

At least, he thought he was heading north to Canada. The sun was directly overhead, and without a compass it was hard to know for sure.

—

Remy walked all day.

He was used to walking for hours, but not with anything weighing him down. The skins and blankets were heavy. The weight of the duffel felt nearly unbearable.

Three times during the day he stopped, dropped his belongings, and ate the contents of one of the cans of food, just to lighten his load. He left the cans discarded on the forest floor behind him. It was all soup, and all a kind he didn't like. Because that was all that was left over after eating his favorites first.

Still, the farther he walked, the more weighed down he felt. Removing three cans of soup had not provided much relief.

It wasn't until the sun had nearly set that Remy realized it was setting to his right. Which meant he was going south.

Remy knew how to navigate by the sun, so he couldn't imagine why he had made such a basic mistake. He briefly toyed with the idea that Pocatello was acting as a magnet, drawing him closer.

He sank down onto the pine needles and leaves and cried.

In the morning he would have to retrace his steps and start all over again. That meant two hard days of walking without really getting any-where except back to where he'd started. He wondered if he even had enough food to get him to Canada. He wondered if his father would turn out to be right about the border. What if there was a wall or a fence? Would somebody shoot him or arrest him for trying to cross the border? He had never crossed a border, and had no idea what the rules might be.

Still crying, he found a flat area with several downed trees. He draped the skins over two of them to form a makeshift shelter underneath, wrapped himself in the blankets, and cried himself to sleep.

He woke in the middle of the night, and needed to step out of his little cave to urinate.

The stars were brilliant—more stars and brighter stars than he had ever seen. In Pocatello they were washed out by the lights of the city, and at the cabin he had tried not to go out after dark because of bears.

The thought hit him like a hardball to his stomach. He had no protection from the bears.

Was all his food in bear canisters? Had he left anything half-eaten, or out?

He zipped up quickly, then turned and ran back toward his belongings . . . and stopped cold.

Down the hill he saw lights on in windows. Not a lot of them. Maybe six that he could make out. But there were people living down there.

He stared for a long time, then crawled back into his little shelter.

He checked all the food as best he could in the dark. He had two slabs of venison jerky and two granola bars that had not been secured in bear canisters. He put them in the canister with the dehydrated stew.

Then he peered out and looked down the hill, just to be sure he had not imagined what he thought he'd seen.

The lights were still there.

———

When he woke in the morning, it was not yet dawn. He pushed the skins away from over his head.

He checked his food stash, laying out and counting what he had. It was enough to eat well for two or three days, but he could make it last longer if he rationed it.

He sat staring at it for a long time, his mouth dry.

He had found no water on the long hike, and there was no more snow to melt.

It was dawning on him that he had no way to get water.

Remy had always had access to water—good water—at every moment he'd lived in the wilderness. The idea that he might walk to some spot that had no creek running through it had never occurred to him.

He stood and looked down the hill.

He could make out about twenty houses in the morning twilight, and one little business with gas pumps. And there was a paved road running through it. The town was almost nothing. Remy wasn't even sure if it qualified as a town. And yet it looked intimidating to him. It was more civilization than he had seen in years.

He opened both bear canisters and consolidated all the food into one, eating a granola bar and some jerky that wouldn't fit.

He carried the empty plastic jar down the hill.

He hid behind trees as he neared the closest house. Its backyard was facing him. It had a board fence, but the fence was only about four feet high. He waited and watched, but saw no one. Maybe the owner of the house was still asleep.

It was still very early. Barely light.

He slithered closer.

Then, all in one big effort, he ran to the fence and scaled it with one hand, still holding the empty bear canister in the other. It wasn't easy, but Remy was light and fit, and the adrenaline made him feel as though he could do anything.

He dropped onto the dirt inside the fence.

He saw pots of soil with no live plants inside them, and a couple of kids' bikes lying on their sides. And a hose.

He ran to it, and stuck the end of the hose into his bear jar. It had no nozzle on the end. He turned on the water and watched it fill.

Before he could get a full jar of water, he heard a dog barking in the house.

He picked up his half-full jar and ran for the fence, not even bothering to turn off the hose. He was just swinging himself over the top as the back door opened and the dog came charging out.

Remy dropped down hard on the other side, but did not manage to stay on his feet.

When he got up and ran back uphill, he noticed that almost all the water he'd managed to get had spilled.

He could still hear the dog barking. When he looked over his shoulder, he saw an older woman standing by an open gate in the fence, holding the huge dog by the collar.

"Kid?" she called to him. "What're you doing, kid? Where'd you come from?"

Remy looked where he was going again, and just kept running.

When he was out of her sight, he sat down in the dirt and drank the water. There were maybe three good swallows left.

Then he got up and started searching for his belongings. He hadn't properly noted where he'd set up his camp. It took him over two hours to find it.

He sat there all day, and did not hike out, because he knew for a fact that when he retraced his steps north, there would be no water.

No, he would have to wait here until after dark. Then he would have to go back down into that terrifying civilization and find a hose that was not inside a yard. He would have to drink a whole bear canister of water, about a gallon, then refill the jar for the trip.

It would be heavy.

But there was nothing else he could do. He had to have water. Everybody has to have water.

Chapter Seven

Trap

It was after sundown but before complete darkness when Remy made his way down the hill to the scattering of houses.

As he got closer, he stopped behind each tree he passed, and waited. To see if anyone was watching. To see if anything moved.

Everything seemed quiet and still.

Remy watched for a long time, a chill mixed with tingling sensations running up and down his spine.

Maybe his father had been right.

Remy had seen only one living person in this little gathering of houses. Nothing and no one seemed to move. Granted, he only came when it was dark. And there were lights on in the majority of houses. But maybe their occupants were long dead and the lights were on all the time. Maybe the lights would be on until their bulbs burned out and the houses fell forever into darkness.

Maybe Remy was one of only a very few people alive in the country. Or even in the world.

Remy was now utterly lost inside his own head. Lost in the conundrum of what to accept as reality. With no one else around, no one to talk to, and no one to talk to him, his brain seemed to obsessively flip an idea upside down and then flip it back again. Over and over this seemed to happen, until he had no perceivable sense of which reality might hold more weight.

He had lost perspective, the way a person might if looking at a photo of a common object, like a rock, but with nothing else in the photo for size comparison. Could be something you could wrap up in your fist, or it could be a continent.

Remy no longer knew which world was real.

Better get ready to head for Canada, he decided.

Maybe things would be better there. And if not . . . well, Remy tried not to think about that.

He looked back at the house. The one whose yard he had breached. That older woman he'd seen, holding on to her dog's collar. Was she a lucky survivor? Or was she one of the ones doing the killing? It was impossible to know.

Flip. Flip back. Remy was effectively lost. It was impossible to decide.

He moved a few trees closer.

There was a large object sitting in the dirt behind the fence—the four-foot board fence that marked the house where the scary dog lived. Remy couldn't make out what it was, so he crept a little closer.

It looked like a huge bottle of water.

As he approached it, he saw it was one of those multiple-gallon plastic bottles with a small neck and mouth. The kind you turn upside down and drop onto your water cooler. Remy had seen them at his mom's office, back when his mom was alive.

He crept a little closer.

It wasn't a sealed bottle. The plastic cap had been removed, the neck of it peeled away. Then the cap had been loosely replaced. The bottle was a little more than half full of water.

Remy pulled in a deep breath, and could hear and feel it shudder with his fear.

He came out from behind the tree, hobbled very fast downhill, and grabbed the bottle. It was heavy.

As he turned to run away with it, his eyes were drawn to the light in the upstairs of the house. The older woman was standing in the window, looking down on him.

Remy froze a moment, looking at her in return.

She raised a hand in a gesture that might have been waving to him. Or it might have been a threat. It might have been a salute to some authoritarian power that had taken over the country, just as his father had said it would.

The world flipped. Flipped back.

Remy ran all the way back to his camp, despite the way being uphill and the bottle being heavy.

He poured half the water into the empty bear canister and drank the rest. As he tipped the big bottle back, too much water came out all at once, and he wasted a lot. It rushed out, wetting his face and his shirt, and the ground where he crouched.

When he had finished the water, he tucked in, wrapping himself in blankets under his roof of tanned skins. He tried to sleep, to prepare himself for the big day ahead. He would have to spend a whole day walking back to where he started, though it was unlikely he could even find the cabin again. Then he would have to head north and walk for two days or so to reach the border.

His water stash wasn't much for three days of walking.

Or maybe he should trust that the people who lived down the hill from him were innocents who had survived the conflagration, just like him. After all, one of them had left water out for him. Maybe she wanted to help. Maybe she would even call Lester's parents in Pocatello for him.

Then he thought of his father. And he knew what his father would have said.

"That's exactly what they would want you to believe, Remy."

Flip. Flip back.

It's a trap, Remy, his father whispered in his ear. Or it seemed that way, anyway. It might well have only been Remy's frightened mind playing tricks on him.

He lay awake for hours, too cold and frightened to sleep.

Maybe the water she'd left him had been poisoned.

The possibility hit him hard, like something physically slamming into his torso. He had drunk almost half of it, with no thought that it might be dangerous.

He lay terrified and still, waiting to see if it would kill him. But halfway through that terrible night he still felt fine. And he was thirsty again, so he drank the rest of the water, which he figured he had proven was safe.

Now he was out, with nothing to drink on the trip.

The only solution he could think of was to stay right where he was for another day.

The moon hung almost full, and very bright. As though his mother were lighting the way. Remy picked his way carefully through the forest with the empty water bottle. The one the lady had left for him.

All the lights were out in all the houses. Which meant someone had turned them off. Which meant someone was alive in every house. One of the bulbs might have burned out since he was last here watching the houses. But not all of them.

That proved there were survivors. It did not prove that they were innocent, nondangerous survivors.

He left the empty water bottle right where he had found it.

Now all he had to do was come around the following night to see if she had filled it again.

He carefully picked his way back to camp in the moonlit night.

It's a trap, Remy, he heard in his ear again. But this time it felt more clearly like his own brain saying the words. *They might kill you if they catch you.*

Remy would have to be very, very careful. And he would have to get out of this place as soon as he could.

As he sat with these problems, he saw a movement. He looked up and jumped at the same time, ducking for the cover of the downed trees.

But it was only a deer.

The deer startled when Remy startled. Then they both froze and just considered each other for a time.

The rifle was no more than five feet from his right hand. He could very slowly and carefully reach for it. It would be a lot of food, if he could shoot it. Weeks' worth, if he dressed and dried or salted it properly. It would be hard without the supply tent and the firepit he'd had at the cabin. And he hadn't brought any of the salt. But maybe he could figure out a way to do it.

He started to reach out with his right hand. But as he looked into the dark pools of its wide-open eyes, he realized the deer was very young. Barely a teenager. And yet he saw no adult deer around. Somehow this baby was out in the world alone.

Remy dropped his hand to his side again, knowing he could not shoot it.

It was hard enough to be out in the world alone without people taking shots at you. Without everybody trying to kill you.

As if reading his thoughts, the deer flashed its white tail and bounded away, disappearing into the thickly forested slope.

Remy slept all day to make up for the sleep he had lost in the night. And that was just as well, he decided. He *should* sleep during the day. It was the only thing he dared do when the world was light.

———

When Remy woke again, it was dark. But the moon was high and bright, and, once his eyes had adjusted, it was all the light he needed.

He took stock of his food, and was alarmed to see how much it had dwindled.

It was barely enough for two days. And it would likely take him at least three days to walk to Canada. And then what? It's not like Canada had a set table waiting for him as he stepped over the border.

No, if he was going to walk out of this place, he would need more food. *A lot* more food.

He picked his way downhill again.

All was dark and still below him. No lights on in any houses. He crept cautiously to a spot near the fence of the older woman's house.

The huge water bottle was half-full again.

He picked it up and struggled back to his camp with it, wondering if the fact that the first water hadn't been poisoned made this water safe. Not necessarily, he decided. She might be waiting to gain his confidence.

He filled both empty bear canisters with water and then sipped carefully at what was left in the bottle. It tasted normal, so he drank the rest.

Then he went back downhill in search of food.

Food was harder, of course. Because, unlike water, nobody left food outside. But he had to at least try. There was that little store. The one with the gas pumps out front. Maybe there was food there. Maybe he could break in and take enough for his trip.

It wouldn't really be fair to the store's owner to break in. Remy already felt bad about that, even though he hadn't done anything wrong yet. He felt bad simply because he had put it on his mental table for consideration. But he figured the owner of the store wouldn't die if Remy took some of his food. Remy would die if he didn't.

He crept up to the back doors of the little convenience store. They were glass double doors, in aluminum frames.

Remy pushed quietly on them, but of course they were locked.

He peered inside with his face close to the glass, and saw things he had only vaguely imagined for years. Things he remembered as though they'd been a pleasant dream about paradise, not as though they were common items he'd once taken for granted.

He saw row after row of potato chips, and corn chips, and tortilla chips, and pork rinds. Peanuts and mixed nuts. Those snack cakes with the sugary coconut on top. A whole floor-to-ceiling cold case filled with juices and sodas and milk and beer.

The only way to get to any of it would be to break the glass doors, but Remy had nothing with which to break them. And even if he had gone back out into the forest and found a stout branch, he would wake the whole town by doing so.

He turned to walk back to his camp, defeated in a way he could never remember feeling before.

And then, as if his life was not dismal enough in that moment, he soon realized he had lost his camp in the dark woods.

He wandered around in what might have been circles, for what might have been hours, knowing that if he could not find his belongings, he would have no warmth, no water, no protection, no food.

The frustration began to build into a storm inside him, and then something . . . just . . . happened.

Remy would not have been able to name or describe the something that happened, even if there had been anyone around wanting him to. Maybe if called upon to say, he might have claimed that he unexpectedly broke into thousands of pieces.

His heart took to pounding, and adrenaline poured into his blood. He began to run wildly, with no attention paid to his direction. But then a minute later the feeling changed, and he couldn't move, so he fell and huddled and melted into a pile of panic and distress in the cold dirt.

He couldn't go to Canada, because he didn't know Canada. And he didn't have enough food or water to get there. He couldn't call Lester, because he had neither Lester's number nor coins for a pay phone, and he couldn't ask a grown-up to do it for him, because they might kill him if he tried. Everybody had food and a safe, warm house. Everybody but Remy. Remy had nothing. And it wasn't supposed to be that way, and it wasn't fair, and he didn't know what to do about any of it because he was only a kid. And a kid is supposed to have somebody looking after these things. Every kid in the world had somebody looking after them. Unless they were all dead. But even if they were dead, right up to the moment of their deaths they'd had someone to look after things for them.

Only Remy was expected to do for himself.

It wasn't the slightest bit fair.

The list of all the things he didn't have or couldn't do rolled through his head, seemingly without end, and he vaguely heard himself making strange noises that might have been sobs but sounded like hiccups. And then, just at the bottom of that well, when there seemed to be no more room to go downward, the feeling changed. Everything changed.

Now Remy was angry.

He raised his head to see that it was barely light.

He stood, and looked around, and saw that he was standing no more than a hundred feet away from his makeshift camp.

He walked to it, the rage roiling in his gut, and all through his blood. It felt good. No, it felt great. Because it felt strong and able instead of scared and helpless.

He picked up the rifle and marched back down to the convenience store.

It was morning twilight, but still very early, and Remy saw no one.

He marched up to the back doors and shattered their glass with the butt of the rifle. He ducked under the aluminum divider that separated the top and bottom panes of the door, and stepped through the broken glass, and gathered as many bags of chips as he could possibly hold in his arms. Then he ducked out again.

Two big- and scary-sounding dogs were barking from somewhere. Maybe above the store? Remy heard a door open, and an older man's voice called out to him.

"Hey, you! Hey, what the hell? What the hell, boy?"

And then the dogs were after him.

They would have caught up with him eventually, but they didn't seem to want to go too far from home. They nearly caught him. He could hear and feel them, nipping the air near his heels. But then they pulled up and circled back to their owner.

Remy disappeared into the woods.

He had dropped several of the bags of chips, but he still had about six bags clutched to his chest. And he still had the rifle. He could feel it digging into his ribs.

He carried them back to his camp and crawled under the deerskin roof, where he began tearing the bags open and stuffing handful after handful of chips into his mouth with filthy hands.

While he ate he thought nothing, and felt nothing.

In time the chips ran out and so did the adrenaline. And Remy knew two things.

First, that he hated dogs. They were terrifying.

And second, he had shards of glass embedded in the soles of his bare feet.

He sat out in the early morning sun for a few minutes, picking them out as best he could with his long fingernails.

Then he realized a third, very important, thing: he would have to move to a new camp.

In the brightening sunlight, Remy saw that he had left a trail of blood all the way from the convenience store to the spot where he sat.

4. ANNE

Chapter Eight

Wild

Anne was driving through downtown to her therapy appointment, and she was in her brand-new car. She hadn't had a new car for a decade, and she was not the least bit prepared for the level of technology she now possessed.

So she was surprised—no, more than surprised, shocked and startled—when the car began to ring like a telephone.

She pulled over to the curb and stared at the car's information screen, which seemed to be indicating an incoming call. It took her at least two rings to realize that the car had synced itself to the cell phone in her purse.

She touched the screen as indicated, to pick up the call.

"Hello?"

"Oh," a woman's voice said. "Anne?"

It was Edwina. Anne would know Edwina's voice anywhere. It filled her chest with a nervous elation. If Edwina was calling, it probably meant she had a new foster child she wanted Anne to meet. Her voice seemed to be projected through the car's speakers, as if Edwina were a song Anne could listen to on the radio.

"Yes. It's me, Edwina. It's Anne. Is this good news?"

"Oh, honey, I'm sorry," Edwina said.

"What are you sorry about?"

"You think I'm calling with good news."

"But you're not?"

"Sorry, no."

"Well, why *are* you calling, then? It's not *bad* news, right? Did something happen to Louisa?"

"No! I mean, not that we know of. There are home visits, of course. Welfare checks. But there's been no news. And no news is good news in this line of work."

"So you're calling because . . ."

Anne briefly connected to the world again, and looked out through her windshield. There was a car waiting for her to leave—apparently hoping she was about to vacate the parking place. She waved him on, and the driver frowned and hit the gas again.

"I'm so embarrassed," Edwina said, her voice filling the interior of Anne's new car. "This was the most classic, perfect example of a buttdial I've ever been involved with. I mean, I didn't literally use my . . . posterior. But I think you know what I mean."

"Oh," Anne said. It came out quietly, like a light breath. She knew they could both hear her disappointment.

Edwina talked through the awkward moment with a flurry of words.

"Somehow I have you and one other foster parent in 'favorites' on my phone. I don't even know what a favorites list is, and I swear I never added anybody to it. I mean, not on purpose. I don't even know how. But yours is the first name on the list. So if I'm accidentally on favorites, then the slightest little touch or bump on my phone and it calls you. I heard it ringing, but by the time I'd figured out how to stop it, you'd already picked up. New phone. I feel like I'll never figure the darned thing out."

"I hear you," Anne said. "I have this brand-new car, and I was driving downtown in it, and all of a sudden it started ringing."

"The car?"

"Yes. The car."

"How can a car start ringing?"

"That's what I was trying to figure out. Apparently it syncs itself to my cell phone."

"Wow. Strange. Well. Ain't technology grand? Supposed to make our lives easier. And it does, I suppose, until it turns on us and makes them harder."

A short, awkward silence fell.

"I thought you were calling to offer me a foster child," Anne said.

"Sadly, no."

"You know I applied for one. Right?"

"I did know that. But right now there's nobody."

"Oh. Okay. I guess the right child will come along at the right time. It's just weird. It feels weird, you know? Because you can't help noticing that there are kids all over the country. Needing help. Falling through the cracks."

"True," Edwina said. "But this is not all over the country. This is Ada County. Not so eventful here, relative to some places. I think that's the good news, don't you? Always best to live where not much happens. But you could always move to New York or LA and have your hands full."

Anne sat in silence for one beat. Maybe two. Through the windshield she was able to see the stoplight at the intersection in front of her. It changed from green to yellow, then to red. An SUV ran the light rather badly.

She was sure Edwina was about to end the call, so she opened her mouth to speak. To prevent it. But before she could, Edwina said something. A cryptic something, but intriguing.

She said, "There's just that one situation . . ."

Anne sat up straighter. She focused intently on the screen in her car's console. As if she could squeeze more information out of it by staring.

"What situation?"

"No. Nothing. Never mind, Anne. I never should have brought it up."

"But it *is* a child?"

"Yeah. More or less."

"How can it be more or less a child?"

"It can't. I'm sorry. I didn't mean it that way. At all. I just meant . . . it's not really a situation of a *foster* child . . . yet."

"I don't know what that means," Anne said.

"I never should have mentioned it."

"But just as a friend," Anne said. Her voice sounded a little too close to pleading. At least, to her own ears. "I mean . . . we're friends. Right?"

"Of course we are."

A long silence. Or, anyway, it felt long.

"Is this a child that hasn't been removed from the home yet?" Anne asked. Because Edwina wasn't saying more.

"No."

Another silence. A bit more brief this time.

Then Edwina restarted on her own.

"We haven't . . . caught this child yet. Wait, strike that. 'Caught' is a terrible word. It sounded terrible. I didn't mean it to. I'm making him sound like an animal. But anyway, his situation is almost that way. Almost the way you'd need to catch an animal to help him. But clearly it's just this bad situation he's been put in. I'm not trying to make him seem any less than human."

"So we're talking about a child living on his own?"

"Seems to be. It's always possible that an adult is living homeless in those same woods with him. But nobody's seen one."

"So a teenager."

"No. The people who've been calling it in, they make him to be somewhere in the seven-to-ten range."

Anne only sat for a moment, absorbing what she'd been told.

Then she said, "That young? How is that even possible? And wouldn't you call the police and have them search for a kid that young?"

"Oh yeah. We did. We do. But right at the moment, nobody can find him. They even brought search dogs up there. They followed his scent for a while and then lost it. It's like he's all over those woods and his scent is everywhere. He seems to be evading everyone, and we're not sure how. And we're especially not sure why, because he really needs the help."

"If you bring him in, can I foster him?"

"Probably not," Edwina said.

It burned, and stung.

"I thought I was your number one foster home."

"Oh, you are. But I'm not sure this is a child who can be fostered."

"What kind of child can't be fostered?"

"This one. At least, from what I've been told. He doesn't seem to be . . ."

But then Edwina did not finish the sentence.

"Doesn't seem to be what, Edwina?"

"I'm trying to decide on the word."

"Okay."

"I guess the word I'm searching for is . . . domestic."

"He doesn't seem to be *domestic*?"

"Right."

"Aren't all human beings domestic?"

"One would think. But the calls we're getting on this kid . . . well, they make him out to be a wild thing. A wild child. Like the proverbial boy raised by wolves."

"In *Boise*?"

"No. No, not here. And not all that close to here. Not even in our county, but it's so remote up there. If they bring him in, they'll probably turn him over to us. Coeur d'Alene is having staffing issues because of Covid."

"And this is where?"

"Oh, totally up in the middle of nowhere. Along the road that goes north through all that national forest land. I forget the route number. They call the little town Blaire, but it isn't much of a town. Unincorporated. I think they told me the population of the place was in the forties. Two people have been calling this child in. One is an older woman who's concerned for his welfare. The other is the guy who owns the only convenience store in town, and he seems more concerned about his store. The kid's been stealing from him. Multiple times. It seems to be how he's feeding himself. The first night he broke in. Broke the glass doors on the back of the shop, which made the owner very unhappy. Now he comes down out of the woods when the store is open, waits till no one is paying good attention, and just runs through and takes as much as he can. The guy sics his dogs on the kid, but they don't really bite. They just chase him away. Which is not much of a theft deterrent, because by that time he's got what he came for and he's running away anyway. So it just keeps happening. I'm telling you all this off the record, Anne. This is not any kind of official transfer of information. It's just that I know your ears perked up when I said there might be a child. I'm just telling you all these details so you know you don't want *this* one."

A pause. About two beats of silence.

"Uh-oh," Edwina said.

"Uh-oh what?"

"I forgot how much you like a challenge. I just realized that what I said probably backfired on us. Now you'll want him more than ever, won't you? Just forget the whole thing for now, okay? Please. For me.

When we find this little guy, we'll evaluate his situation, and then we'll know more. Look, I should go. I didn't even really mean to call."

"Right," Anne said. "Got it."

But as they ended the call, it struck her as a rather fateful thing. Edwina's phone had dialed Anne, seemingly of its own accord, just at the exact right time for Anne to learn this bit of news in the making.

———

"I'm sorry I'm late," she said to the therapist.

He wasn't looking at her. He seemed to be reading his own notes. But they couldn't be notes regarding her session, because they hadn't begun it yet.

Maybe he was refreshing himself on the last three sessions. Or maybe it had nothing to do with her at all.

Anne sat, rearranging her skirt for too long, and in a way that tipped her hand to the fact that she was feeling off balance and uneasy.

"It doesn't really matter," he said.

"Doesn't it?"

"Not really, no."

"Why doesn't it?"

"Because you're paying me for the time between 10:00 and 10:50, and you can use it however you want, including not being here if that's your choice."

He looked up from his notes for the first time.

"I got an odd phone call," she said.

"Okay."

"It was my friend at Child and Family Services."

"You have a friend there?"

"I do."

"Did you know this person before you began fostering children?"

"No. No, we started out strangers. But there have been quite a few children, and when you work with someone for a while, you get to know them."

"Hmm," he said. "That sounds potentially challenging."

She glanced out the window, waiting for him to say why.

"In what way?" she asked when she grew tired of waiting.

"It just seems to me that it might be tricky figuring out where public service leaves off and friendship begins. Take this phone call. The one that made you late today. Was she calling you in an official capacity? Or as a friend?"

"Neither. It was more of a butt-dial."

"But then you did go on to talk."

"Yes."

"As friends?"

For a moment, Anne didn't answer. She was nursing a little glowing ember of irritation with the therapist. But as she opened her mouth to speak, it struck her that the conversation with Edwina had indeed crossed back and forth over those lines. And that it actually *had* been a bit cumbersome and awkward.

"A little bit of both, I guess."

"Tell me what you felt was odd about it."

"Okay. Fine. I will. It's kind of on my mind anyway. She ended up telling me about this boy. This eight- or nine-year-old boy who's living on his own in the woods up by one of the national forests. He's not in the foster system yet, because no one can find him to help him. He's been evading everybody. She said he almost wasn't . . . domestic. Like he was a wild animal, except a human one. Is that even possible?"

The therapist, whose name Anne was too ashamed to admit she had forgotten, set down his notepad and leaned forward in his chair.

"I'm not sure there *is* such a thing as impossible when it comes to the vagaries of human beings. I'm guessing he must have had a home or guardianship at some point in his life, because a human baby is not equipped to survive alone. But if he's been surviving alone for some time, I suppose a child could revert to a state that might seem wild to outsiders."

"But you're saying he wouldn't really be?"

He sat back again with a little thump. Sighed.

"I guess, if called upon to say, I'd be saying all aspects of that situation would be real. The fact that a child did experience domestic life at one time is a factor, but then so is his more recent state. But this is all hypothetical, of course, because I haven't met the child in question, and I don't know anything about him except what you just told me. Why do you ask? Are you thinking of fostering him?"

"I'd like to. I'm not sure if I'd be allowed to."

"But you would take him if you could."

"Yes."

"But you haven't even met him yet."

Anne sat in silence for a time, feeling her face flush. It did seem increasingly like a character flaw, her goal to take on the toughest children she could find. And he seemed to be pointing that out.

Before she could fight her way through the issue in her head, he spoke again.

"You haven't told me about your own upbringing," he said.

"Oh. Okay." She felt herself let out a deep sigh. It felt as though she had just skated through something difficult, and that what lay ahead would be easy. "My dad left when I was six. And you know how when couples with kids divorce, the kids always think it's their fault? And the parents always knock themselves out trying to keep the kids from blaming themselves?" She paused, but he seemed to take her questions as rhetorical. Which they more or less had been. "Anyway, my mother wasn't like that. At all. She told us straight-out it was our fault. There were three of us kids. And she said three was just too many. And that we weren't easy enough. She said we were just too much. Too many and too much. We ruined her relationship with him, which used to be romantic and fun before we came along, and then finally we drove him away. By being too much."

She watched him take notes in silence for a few seconds.

"I certainly can understand the connection, then," he said.

"Wait. What connection? Connection to what?"

His eyes came up to meet hers, which, in four sessions, they almost never had.

"Oh. You *don't*. Sorry. I thought you were telling me this on purpose to explain what's happening in your life now."

Anne only sat a minute, feeling her head grow slightly swimmy. She didn't tell him directly that she didn't know what he was talking about. But her silence must have said it all.

"You have two foster children," he said.

"They're adopted now."

"Okay. Two children. What are their ages?"

"Thirteen and fifteen."

"And you're determined to add a third, because you want to prove that three isn't too many. And you want to help children with deep issues, because you want to prove that no child is ever too much. And your husband is hesitant, so you're pushing him to make the commitment—to assure you that three tough kids isn't enough to make him bail out the way your father did."

They sat in silence for a long time. A full minute or two.

"I'm not trying to sum you up too simply," he said. "I'm not even positive I'm right. I'm just explaining what I thought I heard you telling me."

"I guess that's why I'm paying you the big bucks," she said.

He let the remark go by.

"I just want to reiterate what I said in our first session," he said. "The fact that you do something as a result of an old, deeply internalized experience doesn't necessarily make it a bad thing to do."

She didn't speak, because she still felt a little stunned.

"Tell me more about what it was like growing up," he said. "This time tell me how it all made you feel."

She told him more about it. But she was never quite able to dig down to how it all made her feel.

—

She called Chris as soon as she stepped out of the elevator and into the lobby.

He picked up on the third ring.

"What's up?" he asked.

"How busy are you?"

"Mild to moderate."

"Can you pick Janie up from school?"

"What about Peter? Is he supposed to fly home?"

She stepped out into the blazing late-spring sun. It was a simply dazzling day. In spite of everything going on in her head, the weather hit her, and bent the trajectory of her mood in the direction of good. The world came through. And it didn't always go that way. Anne could go weeks in her head, never clicking into the present, never letting it click into her. That day felt different.

"Peter is going over to Matty's for dinner and staying the night. I told you."

"On a school night?"

"It's not a school night. This is Friday."

"I thought it was Thursday."

"Nope. Friday."

"Are you sure?"

"Chris. You're holding a cell phone in your hand. Look at it."

A pause.

Then he said, "Oh. Friday. Okay. You sure you told me this?"

"I couldn't be more sure. You were brushing your teeth last night and I was leaning in the bathroom doorway. Is any of this ringing a bell to you?"

"Hmm. Maybe," he said. "I remember your telling me *something* . . ."

It was such a perfect example of the way he tuned her out. But she didn't point it out, because it didn't seem to need any more emphasis.

"So . . . Janie?"

"Yeah. I guess I could. And where will you be?"

"I wanted to take a long drive in my new car."

She stepped off the curb and crossed the parking lot to said car, waiting for him to react.

"I've heard more compelling excuses," he said.

"Okay. I'll dig down a little deeper for you. I just got out of therapy, and it was weird, and kind of upsetting. Certainly unexpected. And I need to get my head clear."

She dug out her smart key, and hit the "Unlock" button, and the car lit up. As though it knew her. It almost reminded her of your dog's reaction to your coming home. That flash of recognition.

"Okay," he said. "You'll be home for dinner, though. Right?"

"No. Not sure I'll even be home tonight. If I'm not, there's a casserole in the fridge. Thirty minutes at 350. No preheating required."

"Okay. I guess."

"And if I'm not home by bedtime, feed the dogs, please."

"That's a lot of head clearing."

Anne hit the end of something inside of herself. Some kind of thread that wove through her sense of cool, her patience with her own life. She had been running her life along it, as though coping were a string. And it ran out in that moment.

"I'll see you when I see you," she said.

She ended the call before he could answer, and slid the phone into her purse.

She climbed into her new car, and stared at the map app on its information screen. But no matter how long she stared, she still didn't know how to use it. And it wasn't about to explain itself to her.

She dug around in her purse and found her phone again. She opened its familiar map app and typed in one simple word.

"Blaire."

It was many hours of driving away. Not that she cared.

———

She bought coffee and a bottle of orange juice in the convenience store, hoping for some opening into the topic she wanted to discuss.

The owner was a man in his sixties with a mostly bald head, a grizzled beard, and what seemed to be a naturally perturbed demeanor. He was not masked, which made her briefly question whether she should be. But she quickly put the thought away again.

As he rang up her purchases he glanced almost obsessively at the doors—first front, then back, then front again. She found herself following his gaze almost without meaning to. It took her a couple of sweeps to realize this might be the figurative door into her query, and he might be opening it for her.

"Expecting somebody?" she asked.

He frowned expansively. More dramatically than necessary, as if playing to the balcony.

"Just looking out for thieves," he grumbled.

"You get a lot of them in these parts?"

"I get the same one over and over," he said, handing over her change.

He dropped it into her palm so their hands did not touch.

"That seems odd," she said.

"It's a big old pain in my butt is what it is. That kid's gonna steal me out of the profits that're all I've got to live on."

"Whose kid?" she asked.

But she was leading him. Trying to get him to say more. She knew the thief in question was nobody's kid.

"He'll be a ward of the state if anybody can ever catch him. Do you want a bag?"

"Yeah, sure," she said. "Thanks."

But really she just wanted to prolong the conversation.

"So he has no parents? Nobody looking after him?"

"Not so far as we can tell. If he's got parents, they're doing a piss-poor job of looking after him, that's all I can tell you. And before you say it, that's no excuse."

"It's not?"

"No."

"I was thinking it was."

"You were thinking wrong."

"But if he has no other way to feed himself . . ."

"All he has to do is walk up to one of us and say he's hungry. Any damned person in this town. We'd get him some kind of social worker and something to fill his belly while she's driving up here. There's no excuse for taking without asking. Nobody'll ever catch him at the rate we're going. My neighbor keeps putting water out for him, and no matter what I say, she won't stop, and I think she's a fool. And I told her so, but she won't listen. She doesn't seem to care."

He pushed the bag across the counter. It seemed like a signal that he wanted her to take them and go away. She took hold of the bag. But she did not go away.

"You think she's a fool for giving water to a thirsty child?"

"Yes I do!" he bellowed. Apparently she had struck a nerve. "Yes, it's foolish. It's just plain stupid. I don't want that kid or any other kid to starve, or die of thirst. I'm not a monster. But I think we're all agreed that he needs to come down out of those woods so we can get him some real help. Some long-term help. And when is he going to do that? I ask you. He's going to do it when he's desperate. When he has no choice. So all she's doing is postponing his misery, giving him what he needs to stay out there longer. Now if you'll excuse me, I was in the middle of an inventory. I have to take inventory nearly every day now, just to get some sense of what he got each time. You know. For insurance purposes."

She did not move away as he clearly had intended her to do. It struck her that if he could claim the losses on his insurance, then he wasn't as hard done by as he wanted her to believe. She was sure it was a nuisance in his life, but she felt sorrier for the boy living a wild existence in the forest on his own.

"How often does he come in here and steal?"

"No rhyme or reason to it. Sometimes two days in a row. Other times he'll skip one or two days. I suppose it depends on how much he took me for on his last trip through. Now if you'll excuse me . . ."

"Has he been in today?"

"No, and not yesterday, either. That's why I'm watching the doors as close as I am. He'll be around by and by."

"Well, I'll let you get back to it," Anne said.

She walked out of the little store and back to her car.

She pulled out of his gas pump area and parking lot, but did not pull out of the miniature town. Instead she stopped by the side of the road and shifted into park. The engine hummed quietly as she sipped her coffee. It was scalding hot, and bitter with age. It had clearly been sitting on a hot burner all day.

She glanced at her phone, which she had set on silent, and saw three texts from Chris. She scanned them just enough to be sure there were no emergencies, then powered off the phone and dropped it into the depths of her purse.

When the terrible coffee was gone, she drank the juice. It was getting late, and she was hungry, but not enough to make the effort to do anything about it.

The sun dipped to a long slant and set behind the hills to the west of her, and still she sat, not ready to drive home. There was something wrong with home in her mind. With the feel of it. There was a hole in "home." It felt as though this odd little adventure was her best shot at filling that hole, though she knew in her conscious brain that the hole was in her, and not in the house or the family.

And now it was almost dark. And obviously nothing was going to happen.

She sighed deeply and shifted into drive.

She swung a U-turn in the two-lane paved road, and that was when something happened after all. That was when she saw him.

He was hovering on a hill above the convenience store, his body half-obscured behind a tree. Her headlights, which had been set to auto, had switched themselves on in the heavy dusk. As she turned, they swept across him.

When she saw him, she reflexively stomped on the brake. The lights froze there. Illuminating him. And he froze, too.

The sensation was that they were looking into each other's eyes, albeit at some fair distance. Later she would realize that, with the glare of her headlights in his eyes, he likely didn't see her at all.

His hair was either dark, or filthy, or both. It came down past his shoulders, and stuck out wildly from his head because it was so tangled. It might have been more than tangled, she realized. It might have been matted. His clothes were too tight, his pants too short. She could see his ankles glowing white in her headlights. He was barefoot.

And his eyes. Well. Those eyes. She only saw them for a flash of a moment. It might only have been a second or less. But, in that flash, she saw fear at a level she had never seen fear before. It was something she would see for days, whenever her mind wandered, or when she closed her eyes to try to go to sleep.

Then he bolted. She almost didn't see him go. It was such a sudden movement that it left her with the eerie sensation that he had just vanished.

She watched the woods for a minute or two. But it went without saying that he was not coming back.

The only time she had ever seen a living being that spooked was in an encounter with a wild prey animal. A deer, hit and lying helplessly on the shoulder of the road, instinctively fearing the next person to approach would likely end its life. This had been a human child. But she had to *remind* herself that this had been a human child. It was an odd sensation, to say the least.

It sent a shiver along the nape of her neck as she drove away from that place.

The plan was to stop and find a motel, but she never did. She just stopped for coffee several times, and drove.

———

When she arrived home, it was well after 3:00 a.m. She expected everyone to be asleep.

Peter came bounding down the stairs, taking them two at a time. He stopped cold when he saw her.

"I thought you were at Matty's tonight," she said, looking up to the spot where he stood frozen on the stairs. "What are you doing up so late?"

"I came home."

"Why?"

"I was worried about you."

"Me? Why?"

"Dad said you went somewhere, but he didn't even know where. Or why. And he had no idea when you were coming back."

"How did you even talk to him?"

"I called home to make sure you both remembered I was going to be away. So what's going on?"

"Nothing," Anne said. "Everything's fine."

Peter didn't move. He only stood there on the stairs, his face revealing everything. Anne had always maintained that her son had no future as a poker player. Everything was on display. All right there to see.

It filled her with guilt, what she saw on his face this time. Because you shouldn't do that to a child. What she had just done to Peter, that was terrible parenting in her view. Her mother had used to do that to her all the time. Her parents, or her mother and stepfather, would be having this vicious, almost violent fight. But if Anne asked about it, her mother would say everything was fine. Everything was normal. Bad thing to do to a child. Makes them feel crazy. Makes them doubt their own eyes and ears.

"You know what?" Anne said, and the change in her tone made his face soften. Just that fast. "Come on down in the kitchen with me. I'll make us both a cup of tea."

———

Chris had left her a plate of casserole in the warm oven, and she was nibbling on it, and waiting for the two mugs of water to heat in the microwave.

Before she could open her mouth to explain herself to her son, Janie stuck her head into the kitchen.

"You're home," Janie said.

"You were worried, too?"

"A little."

"Want a cup of tea?"

"Sure," Janie said. "Yeah."

"Put another mug of water in the microwave, okay?"

Janie set about doing that, and Anne addressed them both at once, not waiting for her daughter to finish and sit down. Apparently she had kept them waiting long enough.

"I heard about this child," she began. "This boy."

"Foster?" Peter asked.

"Not really. Not yet. Maybe not ever. It's hard to know at this point. It's a confusing situation. It's unlike anything we're used to. Unlike anything Edwina is used to. He's living . . . wild."

Janie sat down at the table and stared at Anne from behind her long bangs.

"What do you mean, 'wild'?"

"He . . . doesn't seem to have anybody. He's living on his own in the woods."

A silence. Maybe they needed time to take that in. To adjust to that unusual idea. Anne had certainly needed time to grasp it when first she'd heard about it.

The boy's eyes came into her head again, uninvited. Those terrified, wildly spooked eyes. It was disturbing even to remember them. Even just to see them again in her mind.

"Why doesn't somebody from Family Services go get him?" Peter asked.

"Right at the moment nobody can find him."

"Why would he hide?" Janie asked. "Doesn't he want help?"

"My take on the situation is that he's too afraid of people to let anybody help him."

The timer went off on the microwave. Anne was just about to get up to make the tea, but Peter beat her to it.

"Thanks, hon," she said.

"He's going to end up living here," Janie said. "Isn't he?"

"I . . . really don't know."

"But you already went out there," Peter said. "And we all know how you are. You know. Once you get an idea stuck in your head. No offense."

"None taken," she said.

Honestly, she was a little bit put off by his assessment. But she figured she shouldn't be, so she kept those thoughts to herself.

It wasn't as though he was wrong.

"Honestly, I have no idea if he'll be found. And if he's found, I have no idea if he'll be considered a candidate for a foster home. I really don't know much at this point."

Janie spoke up again.

"Did you *see* him while you were there?"

"Briefly," she said.

As soon as she said it, those eyes came into her head again. She could see them so clearly. She could experience his terror all over again, as if she were right there with him.

"Oh yeah," Peter said, glancing at her face. "No doubt. He's coming here to live."

———

Chris was upstairs. In bed, but not asleep. He was lying on top of the covers in his blue bathrobe, working on his notebook computer. Apparently no one was willing to get any sleep until she got home.

He looked up when she walked into the bedroom. She kept moving, though. Kept going until she got into the bathroom, where she began brushing her teeth.

"Got your head clear?" he called in.

She stopped brushing. Spit.

"I'd like to say yes. But I think it's muddier than ever in there."

He never answered, so she went back to brushing. When she'd finished, she removed her makeup, washed her face. Brushed her hair. Moisturized.

Then she rejoined him in the bedroom.

She felt his eyes on her as she changed into her nightgown.

"Here's a question," he said. "And don't be surprised if it sounds a little bit familiar."

"Okay. Go."

"Seeing somebody else?"

She let out a puff of air, and it came out with a sound she hadn't intended. It was a dismissive sound. She definitely felt dismissive, but she hadn't meant to indicate it out loud.

"I'm not going to dignify that with an answer," she said.

"Any special reason?"

"Because it's not a question asked in good faith. You know I'm not. You know if you had to guess what I was doing, that wouldn't be your serious guess."

"Right," he said. "I catch your drift. I always knew it wouldn't be another man. It would be another boy. Or girl."

"You can't possibly be conflating the two."

She pulled back the covers and climbed in. It was a king bed, with plenty of room to leave space between them. And she did.

"Not entirely," he said. "They do have one thing in common, though. They both take a toll on a marriage."

"Can I turn off the light?"

"Sure. If you don't mind the light from my computer screen."

She reached for the lamp and plunged the room into darkness. Rolled away, so her back was facing him. She closed her eyes, but all she could see were the terrified eyes of that boy, and so they flew open again. Almost as a form of self-protection.

"It's really more of an *idea* at this point," she said. "It's a thing that might never come to pass. So maybe we can take our predictions of how much damage it'll do to the marriage and push them down the road a few miles."

For a minute, no answer. Possibly a full, literal minute.

Then she heard him sigh.

"We've been doing that a lot lately," he said. "But . . . sure. Why not?"

5. REMY

Chapter Nine

Finally

Remy lay on his side under the makeshift tent he'd created by slinging the tanned skins over a couple of downed trees. But it was not the original camp. In fact, he changed his location every day, sometimes multiple times a day, in case anyone came looking for him. The store owner, perhaps. Or whoever's job it was to kill people.

He knew he had to get up and move camp soon, but it was hard. It was getting harder every day.

Remy had been out of food for six days. He'd been nursing his water supply, but it had still run out two days previous. He figured there might be some waiting for him behind the older lady's yard, but he couldn't go down there because of the lights.

Last time he had tried to go down into town, he'd had to run back empty-handed because of the lights.

He didn't know exactly what the lights were. He had no idea what created all that light, or what would happen to a boy if they landed on him and he didn't get away fast enough. But one thing was crystal clear: when somebody turned a spotlight on you, that meant you got caught. He assumed the next thing that happened would be someone shooting you, but it also danced through his mind that they might take you alive, and then maybe what happened to you would be even worse.

For the second time in his young life, Remy was putting himself to sleep for what he assumed would be the last time. And it was a relief, too. Because the life he'd been living felt like utter misery, stretching on forever.

In addition to hunger and thirst, he had an infection in his left leg. Down at the bottom of his calf, where his Achilles tendon ran through. Remy didn't know the name of that tendon, but he did know it was infected. It had become swollen and discolored. And it hurt. A lot.

One of the terrible dogs had punctured it with his teeth before circling back for home.

Like their owner, the dogs were losing patience with him.

So he couldn't walk out of this place. Not now and not ever. Because he was starving and thirsting to death, and because his right leg had a break that had healed poorly, and his left one had a painfully infected dog bite. And the hunger would not become less of a problem over time. It would only grow worse. And his lack of water would not heal itself. It would intensify. And the infection in his tendon would not cure itself. It would get more and more infected, and take over more and more of his leg.

And then Remy had the worst thought of all.

He might survive the night.

That's what had happened last time he'd thought he was going to die before sunrise. He had wakened alive, to suffer more.

And it wasn't only his body suffering. Remy was losing his mind. He could feel it going. It was getting away from him more and more every time, and its retreat was picking up speed. It felt like this constant state of utter panic, because he no longer had a solid mind to tell him the truth. Trying to live with his current mind felt like drowning. Like thrashing in water to try to keep it from closing over his head.

He was exhausted from the panic of the thing.

Remy sat up suddenly, and made a decision. But the word "decision" might not be a proper description of the experience. Making a decision suggests a properly functioning mind, and a suggestion that it can weigh one thing against another and reach a conclusion.

That's not what happened to Remy.

Instead the moment just overtook him, and mostly at a level of emotion.

He could not take another minute of this. He would go down into town and let them kill him. Hopefully it would be quick and painless. Hopefully the lights would shine on him one last time, and he would hear the crack of a rifle, and that would be it.

He rose—bravely, he felt—and hobbled painfully down the hill.

It was only dusk. Not dark yet. The little store was still open.

There was a bottle of water behind the older lady's yard. He limped to it, and crouched in the dirt, and drank. And drank. And drank.

He drank the water right out in the open. Not even trying for cover. He drank it not to sustain his body, because he knew he would be dead soon. He drank it because it felt so good to drink water after two days of thirst. And there was precious little good feeling in Remy's life. And, before he left, he was going to take what was there to be taken.

Remy set down the bottle. He pulled a long, deep breath, knowing it might be one of his last.

In short, mincing steps, he hobbled through the back doors of the store, blinking into its bright fluorescent lights.

The owner saw him immediately. The old man. They looked into each other's eyes.

Remy wasn't sure how long they stared at each other that way. Might have been a second or two. It felt like an eternity. Like a whole era in his life.

He didn't move to take anything. He didn't run from being seen. Because, if he ran away, that would only put him back in his camp in the woods, alive. And he was done with that. He was done with alive.

He had reached a spot a long way past the breaking point with surviving alone on cold, hard dirt.

The store owner put two fingers to his lips, and whistled sharply. It made Remy jump.

The dogs came running down from the flat above the store, and burst in the open back doors after Remy.

He wanted not to run. He wanted never to run from anything again. Better to just let the dogs maul him and be done with it.

But his body would not obey.

His body wanted nothing to do with dogs. No matter what he told it, it only ran. Well . . . ran as much as Remy was capable of running. When you can't really put proper weight on either leg, running is going to be a slow, pathetic-looking thing. So they would catch him anyway.

He hobbled out the front door, through the gas pump area, and out into the road, the dogs baying at his heels.

And that was when the lights caught him again.

He turned to look at them, but could see only that overwhelming white. That white that filled his eyes and became his whole world in that moment. They blinded him. He froze in the massive brightness of their beams, knowing it was over.

Then came the impact. It threw him up into the air.

There was a second impact, which Remy vaguely identified as a windshield. He didn't have time to pause and identify it consciously. It all happened too fast. But a windshield feels like a windshield. It doesn't feel like anything else.

He felt himself rolling upward, and then again he was flying.

He came down hard in the road, smacking his head.

The world went black.

Finally, finally. The world went black.

—

Unfortunately—tragically unfortunately from Remy's point of view—he opened his eyes again. He had chosen exactly wrong. He should have died slowly in his camp in the forest. They had not killed him quickly and painlessly. Somehow they had taken him alive, and what they were doing to him was worse than anything he could possibly have imagined.

He woke up strapped down to a bed, surrounded by people who looked like aliens. They all wore more or less matching uniforms of solid white or green or blue shapeless pants and shirts. They had masks on to keep him from seeing their faces. Some of them wore clear shields over their eyes.

They had apparently been experimenting on him while he lay unconscious, cutting into his skin and stitching up the places they had invaded, and immobilizing his limbs with plaster and metal.

And, possibly most disturbing, they were giving him something that made him sleepy and muddy, so he would be unable to resist.

There was only one very tiny silver lining in that hell of a place: whatever they were giving him dulled the pain, which was considerable. Surely that was accidental, and they did not mean to help him in any way. They didn't seem to be there to help.

And there was nothing Remy could do about any of it. He was utterly at the mercy of these demons.

It was an even worse dystopia than the one his father had warned him about. But, in Remy's head, it was a far simpler idea.

Remy simply thought, *He was right.*

6. ANNE

Chapter Ten

Yes

The next time she got a call from Edwina, Anne was quick to assume it had only been a butt-dial.

She was driving again, as luck would have it. She was on the way to her therapist's office, same as last time.

She touched the button on the car's display screen to pick up the call.

"Still haven't figured out how to clear that favorites list," she said. "Have you?" She purposely kept her voice light, so Edwina wouldn't feel bad about bothering her again.

Edwina's voice was not light. It was filled with a gravity of some variety Anne had never heard from her before. And they had been involved in some serious projects together.

"I need to talk to you," Edwina said. "Can you come in?"

"Right now?"

"When you can."

"You can't tell me what it's about on the phone?"

"It's about a child. But it's complicated. I'd rather you come in."

"Give me five minutes," she said.

She did not ask if it was the boy they had discussed once before. The wild boy. Because she knew it was. She didn't know how she could be so sure. She just . . . simply . . . knew.

She clicked off the call and verbally asked her car, working in league with her phone, to call Dr. Klausner.

She got his voice mail.

"I can't make it in today," she said. "But I guess it doesn't really matter. Right? Because I'm paying you for the fifty minutes between 10:00 and 10:50. No matter what I choose to do with it."

———

"I want to take you over to the hospital," Edwina said. "Because I don't want you making this decision about a child you haven't met."

Edwina wore her dark hair up that day, and a gray pantsuit that made her look wildly official, like a candidate in a governor's race. Her lipstick had an orangey tone that struck Anne as unpleasant.

"I already know I'm going to take him," Anne said.

"Please, Anne. Please. Go with me on this. Please stop being Anne for just a minute so we can do this the right way."

That stopped the conversation in its tracks. For a moment Anne just kept looking at a spot on Edwina's desk. When she did look up, her friend's face looked sheepish and ashamed.

"That was a terrible thing to say," Edwina said. "I'm sorry. It just slipped out. I genuinely apologize."

"Whatever," Anne said. But it *had* stung. "Why is he in the hospital?"

"He was hit by a car. He's been three or four days in the hospital in Coeur d'Alene, but he's been transferred here into our care, and for the balance of his surgeries."

It hit her belly like a physical blow. And maybe it shouldn't have. Maybe it should have felt unrelated to her life. Just bad news about a stranger. But he did not feel like a stranger.

"Oh no. Is he okay?"

"Well. No. Of course he's not. He's in the hospital. He's in serious condition. It's probably not life threatening, although the concussion could be the weak link in that diagnosis. But he made it through the first few nights, which is key. It's not likely to be an issue at this late date."

"What does he say about what happened to him?"

"See?" Edwina said. "See, this is why I need to take you to the hospital. You have some false ideas about him."

"Like what?"

"Like you think he talks."

"Oh," Anne said.

A silence fell. Because, honestly, that did bring her up short. And it did help her understand how quick she was being to plunge into water over her head.

Murky water, at that.

"Is it possible that he never learned?" Anne asked after a time.

"We don't know. There's a lot we don't know. Like . . . everything. It's possible that he never learned to talk. It's also possible that it's selective mutism. I've seen this before in traumatized children. But let me tell you what we do know. Even through very heavy sedation, he's absolutely terrified. He lets out this weird, high-pitched shriek whenever a nurse or doctor comes near him. His injuries are extensive, and not all of them are fresh."

She paused, possibly to give Anne time to digest the last sentence. Which was helpful. It required some digestion.

"I'm grappling with what that means."

"It probably means he was abused before he was abandoned. But we may never know for sure. He broke his left leg in the car accident. But his right femur had also been broken. And it clearly hadn't had any medical attention at all. It had just healed the way it healed. The surgeon had to rebreak it and set it properly with some limited hardware, and an external fixator."

"Is that one of those contraptions . . ." But she wasn't sure how to describe what she was picturing.

"Yeah. Big structure outside the limb with pins going through the skin and into the bone. Lots of care required with those, so the patient doesn't end up with a bone infection. When he gets out of the hospital, he's going to need a lot of care. We can provide home nursing. But he has to have a home for that."

"I already told you I'd take him."

"And I already told you I want you to know more about his situation first. Especially with two other children in the home."

"You think he would hurt my other children?"

Oddly enough, it was the first it had occurred to Anne, and it sent a shock wave of fear through her belly.

"I think . . ." Edwina paused. She squeezed the bridge of her nose as if all this was giving her a headache. "I think under normal circumstances we'd want to do a lot more evaluation with him before placing him in a home with other children. But we have two factors throwing us off here. One is that his hospitalization is costing the state a fortune. And we'll pay it, of course. But only for as long as his doctors recommend he be hospitalized. We can't use the hospital like a babysitter. Not at these prices."

"Do we know how long he'll have to stay?"

"Not yet we don't, no. He's in bad shape. Malnourished. Beaten up. He has eleven stitches in his head where he came down on the tarmac after being hit by the car. He cracked some ribs. And get this. He already had five broken ribs from a long time ago, also apparently left alone to heal badly on their own. He has a torn rotator cuff that the doctor thinks is old, but we won't know for sure until they do the surgery on it. His left elbow is shattered. That's fresh. That's another surgery coming up. He has a nasty infection near his ankle. The kind that could be serious if they don't get a handle on it soon. They had to do a ton of dental care on him while he was unconscious. He's a mess, frankly. It could be a while."

"What's the other thing?" Anne asked.

"That's not enough?"

"No, I don't mean injury-wise. You said . . . normally you'd do a lot of evaluation, but there are two things throwing you off."

"Oh. Right. Well. At the heart of an evaluation in a case like this would be whether he's a danger to others. Whether he's capable of aggression."

"I guess that would be good to know," Anne said, sinking underwater in the gravity of her decision again.

"Except right at the moment we know that won't be a problem."

"Because . . ."

"He has two broken legs. He'll be in a wheelchair for months. He'll have a cast or a fixator on his left elbow, and his right arm will be in a sling from the shoulder surgery. He won't walk for months, assuming he ever does. He won't even be able to feed himself for a long time. He'll be on a boatload of painkillers in the foreseeable future. He'll be lucky if he can even stay awake."

Anne's mind was swimming fast, hoping to catch up. She paused before speaking, really allowing the mental picture of his condition to sink in.

"So what you're saying is that he couldn't hurt anybody even if he wanted to."

"What I'm asking," Edwina said, "is if you're willing to foster him during his long and very complicated recovery, knowing you can send him back to us if his behavior is dangerous or aggressive or otherwise problematic as he gets more mobile. And please, Anne. Please, please don't say yes now. Let's go to the hospital, so you can see with your own eyes what you'd be getting yourself into."

"Okay," Anne said. "Fair enough. Let's go see him. And I'll meet him. And *then* I'll say yes."

———

They walked across the hospital parking lot together, Edwina's heels clicking smartly on the tarmac. Anne had worn sensible shoes, cross-trainers, and her steps were silent. And so were the two women, until Edwina stopped walking and spoke up suddenly.

"Oh. I should have told you to bring your vaccination card."

"I've got it. It's in my wallet."

"Okay. Good."

They walked again, headed for the main entrance.

Edwina was nervous and upset. Anne knew her well enough to know it. It was pouring off her in waves. Somehow this case, with this boy, was more than she had encountered before. It made Anne nervous, too, because she thought Edwina had seen everything there was to be seen in her twenty-plus years with the department.

They masked before stepping inside, and were screened just inside the lobby by two masked individuals in scrubs. A man and a woman.

The man took her vaccination card and made notes on a clipboard before handing it back. The woman aimed a thermometer at her forehead and asked her about various symptoms.

She said she had none, which was true.

She and Edwina stepped onto the elevator together.

They rode up to the second floor without saying a word. The silence was beginning to spook Anne, because she and Edwina had always small-talked with perfect ease.

When the elevator doors opened, a bizarre and frightening sound pierced Anne's ears. It was a sound like the screech of metal on metal. It was instantly unbearable.

"What is that?" Anne asked, holding her ears as they stepped out into the corridor.

"That's him," she just barely heard Edwina say.

It set up a lump in her stomach that felt like a rock, accidentally swallowed.

"He does that all the time?"

"No, just when anybody gets near him."

They stopped at a closed door to a patient room, and paused a moment. The sound wound down and disappeared.

A nurse popped out, acknowledging them with an exhausted eye-rolling expression.

"We'll go in," Edwina said. "But it might help if we don't get too close."

They stepped inside, and Anne's eyes fell on the boy.

He bore little resemblance to the boy she'd seen half-hidden behind a tree. He was wearing only a white hospital gown, and he looked clean. In fact, he appeared freshly scrubbed all over. His head had been shaved close to the scalp. The left side of his head was dressed with a gauze pad taped in place. His left leg had been placed in a cast, elevated on pillows. She could see that the cast had been cut away above the back of his ankle, and a drain placed through the skin there to help treat the infection. His right leg was bandaged over the bulk of what she knew was an external fixator, his left elbow in a bulky splint. He had an IV bottle hanging next to his bed, its tube attached to a needle taped into the back of his hand. His arms, legs, and torso were secured to the bed with straps.

But his eyes. She recognized those eyes. She would know them anywhere. Nowhere else in her world had she ever seen that brand of terror in a pair of eyes. It was utterly unique.

She stared into his eyes, and he stared back. He made no sound.

"Hi," she said quietly.

Of course, he said nothing in return. But she thought his eyes might have relaxed just the tiniest bit. They had been stretched open as wide as a pair of eyes can go, and she thought they might have edged just a little bit closer to normal size. Then again, it might have been her imagination. It might only have been wishful thinking.

"We should stand farther away," Edwina said.

Edwina backed up until the far wall of the room stopped her. A curtain separated off the room from what Anne assumed was at least one other occupied patient bed.

Anne did not move.

"Why is he strapped down? Who is he going to hurt?"

"Himself. He thrashes. When anybody gets near him, he thrashes around. He doesn't have one single uninjured limb. He can't afford to thrash."

Throughout that brief conversation, Anne's eyes remained fixed on his, and vice versa.

There was a white plastic chair placed about five feet from the side of his bed. Anne walked to it, and sat. His eyes widened briefly. But when he saw her settle a reasonable distance away, those eyes returned to their slightly-less-than-utterly-panicked state.

"You don't have to be afraid of me," she told him.

Their eyes remained locked on each other.

A strange voice spoke, startling her. A man's voice. It came from behind her. From the direction of the door.

"Well, I'll be damned."

She turned to see two men in blue scrubs standing in the room behind her. Maybe nurses, or maybe orderlies. Anne wasn't sure how to tell. They were wheeling a gurney covered with fresh white sheets.

"What?" she asked.

"I was wondering how he let you get that close."

"Oh. I don't know. I just said hi to him."

"Well, say bye now," the other man said. "Because he's going into surgery."

Anne looked back at the boy, whose eyes had stretched to the maximum possible width. He opened his mouth and began to keen. That horrible earsplitting sound. One of the men moved quickly to his IV as the child began to thrash. Or to try to, anyway. The straps didn't give him much room to move.

One nurse—she had come to assume the men were nurses—quickly turned off the IV drip, unclipped the line, and injected the contents of a syringe into the little plastic vessel attached to the needle in the boy's hand.

In just a matter of seconds, the keening dulled and faded, growing quieter. For a moment his eyes remained wide, but lost their focus and grew dreamy. Then they closed, and the room fell into silence.

But it left Anne shaken. Was this child really someone she was thinking of taking home? Was she up to the task of caring for him? Would anybody be?

"Rotator cuff?" Edwina asked the nurses. "Or his elbow?"

"Elbow," one of the men said. "Surgeon figures the rotator cuff's waited this long and can wait another day or two."

The two men stood on either side of the unconscious boy's bed, undid the straps, and used the sheet underneath him to lift him and transfer him to the gurney.

They wheeled him out of the room, the door swinging closed behind them. And that was that. Anne's first meeting with the boy was over.

To say it had left her full of deeply conflicted emotions would be understating the truth.

She looked at Edwina, and Edwina looked back.

"Still sure your answer is yes?"

"Tell you what," Anne said. "Let me go home and talk it over with my family. Since it affects them, too."

"Now that," Edwina said, "is possibly the most balanced and reasonable thing I've ever heard you say."

Anne rose from her chair, and they walked back toward the elevator again.

"I just wish I'd had more time with him," Anne said.

"You'll get plenty of time with him if you say yes. Did you notice he wasn't afraid of you?"

"Wasn't *as* afraid of me," Anne corrected.

Neither woman said more until they parted ways in the parking lot.

Anne silently noted that her friend Edwina seemed to have crossed an invisible line. Where before Edwina had seemed to warn and discourage Anne, she now seemed to be ever so gently leaning on her to say yes. It made the whole thing feel very real to Anne. And the more it felt real, the more it felt terrifying.

—

She sat down to dinner with her family. She looked around the table at Chris and the two kids, none of whom looked back.

"Family meeting after dinner," she said. "Okay?"

Three pairs of eyes found her face immediately.

Chris spoke with his mouth still half-full of chicken and rice.

"Well, don't just leave us hanging."

Before she could speak—actually, before she could even decide what to say—her cell phone rang in her sweater pocket. It was a thing out of place. Everybody turned off their cell phones for dinner, including Anne on every night besides this one. It was the law of the family, and she had never broken it before.

She opened her mouth to say she needed to take the call. To claim extenuating circumstances. But the phone spoke before she could.

"Edwina Thurgood," it said in that odd female robot voice. Then another ring. Then, "Edwina Thurgood."

"That might be a clue right there," Chris said.

Anne raised one finger in a "Please wait" signal and slunk away from the table to take the call privately in the kitchen.

"Edwina," she said. "Is he still okay?"

"Yeah. The surgery went fine. That's not what I called to say."

"Oh. Okay."

"I just wanted to tell you a little bit more that we found out about him. Just in case it helps you make your decision."

"You know who he is?"

"I said we found out *a little* more. Prepare yourself for the fact that we may never know who he is or how he got put in this situation. I just called to tell you that they found his camp today. Where he was living in the woods. Two days sooner would have been awfully nice, for the state's budget and for the poor child, but I guess they can only do what they can do. Apparently he was moving around constantly, and it threw off the dogs, because his scent was everywhere. Started them going around in circles. So, now, with his camp holding still and all . . ."

"But no ID or anything?"

"No."

"What did they find?"

"I have a complete inventory of his belongings right here in my hands. I'm about to read you everything this kid had in the world."

"Wait," Anne said.

"Wait what?"

"They went through all that just to give me a list of his belongings?"

"No. They went through all that to see if he was really living alone, or if there was an adult out there who they needed to arrest for child endangerment."

"Oh. That makes more sense."

"You ready?"

"As I'll ever be, I suppose."

Something in Edwina's voice made her feel there was a nasty surprise coming. But she shook the thought away again, and decided she was imagining things.

"Two scratchy blankets. Two tanned deer hides. One large olive-green army surplus duffel bag. Two bear canisters. One can opener. More empty junk food wrappers than you could shake a stick at . . ." Edwina paused, and that feeling came around again. ". . . and a rifle, with a small handful of bullets."

For a moment, Anne said nothing at all. She only stood very still and felt the inside of her gut tingle.

"You think he hunted with it?" she asked after a time.

"No indication he had been cleaning or eating any game. Just snack cakes and potato chips."

"Maybe he wasn't very good at it."

"Could have been for hunting. Could have been a terrified attempt at self-protection. There were some scratches on the stock that the sheriff said made him think he'd used it to break the glass out of the doors the first time he broke into the convenience store. No reports to suggest he ever pointed it at anybody."

Anne heard a light sound, and turned to see that all three members of her family were huddled in the kitchen doorway, watching her. Listening to her end of the conversation.

"I thought you'd want to know," Edwina said. "In all fairness. You know. Full disclosure and all that."

"Well, I appreciate it, Edwina. But I need to go now. Apparently my family meeting has already started."

———

"What if he's mean?" Janie asked, her gaze trained down to the tablecloth. "What if we're scared of him?"

"Here's the thing about that, though, honey. He's so badly hurt. He'll be in a wheelchair for months, and he won't even be able to push himself around in it. Neither one of his arms will be working until they heal. So in the short run, if he scares you, you can just . . . not get close to him. Because he sure as heck can't get close to you. In the long run, if he gets better, and we think he's scary or mean, we can ask Edwina to take him back."

"What's his name?" Peter asked, also avoiding her eyes.

"We don't know."

"How old is he?"

"We don't really know that, either. Younger than both of you. Somewhere between seven and ten."

A long, long silence fell around the table. Maybe it seemed longer to Anne than it actually was, because it was the silence before the proclamation. There were apparently no more questions the family wanted to ask. It was something like the moment in a court trial when the prosecution and defense rest, and the jury goes off to deliberate. And there's nothing more you can do except pace and bite your nails.

Janie spoke first.

"I feel bad for him," she said.

"I do, too, honey. But having him here wouldn't be easy. I won't lie to you about that."

The moment froze. No one spoke for a time. Anne found herself watching Chris in her peripheral vision. There was something tense in the watching, as though he might explode in anger. Stomp away. Say something cold. She turned her head to look at him more directly. He looked back. His eyes looked soft, but distant. He seemed to be weighing something, but Anne had no idea what, and it was a hard expression to read.

"I say yes," Chris said.

Anne could not have been more surprised.

"You do?"

"Well. Yeah. A limited yes. Yes to what you just proposed. That we try having him here while he's recovering. And if the kids are scared of him, or he turns the whole house upside down, then we ask Edwina to take him back after that."

"Janie?" Anne asked.

"Yes," Janie said.

"Yes," Peter said, without having to be asked.

Anne slipped her phone out of her pocket and dialed Edwina back. She got her voice mail.

"Yes," she said.

That was the complete message.

———

"You surprised me tonight," she said as she joined Chris in bed.

"It's only a conditional yes. Yes to the situation on a temporary basis. After that we'll know more about what we'd be getting ourselves into."

"Still a little surprised," she said. "Pleasantly, of course."

"I know how important it is to you," he said.

In that moment it came into Anne's head, for the first time in a very long time, that her marriage might just be strong enough to hold up after all.

Chapter Eleven

Mom

Late the following morning she tried to visit him in the hospital again . . .
and almost didn't get in.

"You have to be blood family," she was told at the reception desk.

"He has no blood family," Anne said.

The woman was wearing her mask over her mouth only, and breathing through her nose. Which Anne might not even have noticed had this not been a hospital.

"Then I guess he gets no visitors."

"I visited him yesterday, and so did his social worker. They let us right in."

"Well, they shouldn't have. Maybe her. But not you."

"Listen," Anne said. And she could feel a ball of rage coming up into her chest from down below. "I am his foster mother. And I'm all he's got. And you are *not* going to stand here and tell me that foster parents have no parental rights."

Anne's voice had come up. She was just at the edge of yelling. Several people in the lobby turned to look.

And she wasn't even done.

"I am *not* going to let this stand. He'll be in the hospital for days. Maybe weeks. And he *will* have me as a visitor. He is not going to go through this alone. I have rights, and so does he. I'll get a representative from Child and Family Services to intervene if I have to."

"Keep your voice down, ma'am," the woman said.

"I will not," Anne said in reply. Her voice was firm on this last sentence, but slightly short of yelling.

"Problem here?" an unfamiliar voice said.

Anne turned to see a woman she initially thought was a nurse standing behind her. She was wearing an N95 mask, and also wearing a tag identifying her as Dr. Margaret Gifford. That was good, Anne figured. A doctor would have more authority than a woman staffing the reception desk.

"Yes," Anne said, directing her words to the doctor. "This woman is telling me I have no rights as a foster mom. I want to visit my foster child, and she says I can't because I'm not blood family. He has no blood family."

"Ah," the doctor said. "I think I know exactly which child you mean." Then she shifted her gaze and spoke to a spot over Anne's shoulder. "Let her go up. That poor kid needs any kind of family he can get." She turned to go, then spun back to the receptionist. "And pull your mask up," she added before walking away.

—

When she arrived at his room, Anne found the curtain divider pulled back, and the two beds full, but both with patients who were strangers to her.

She backtracked to the nurses' desk.

"I seem to have lost track of my foster child," she said.

There were three nurses at the desk, but a tall, steely woman took charge immediately.

"Patient name?"

"I'm guessing he's listed as John Doe."

The other two nurses had been chatting with each other, but fell silent. For a few beats, no one moved.

"You're fostering him?" the steely nurse asked.

"That's right."

"Well, you're a braver woman than I am, I'll tell you that much right now."

"I'll show you where he is," one of the other nurses said, jumping up out of her rolling typist's chair.

Anne walked with her down the hall, but distinctly heard someone at the nurses' desk behind her say, "You couldn't pay me enough."

"There's a prejudice," the nurse said quietly. The one walking right beside her. "There tends to be a prejudice among certain nurses here for unruly children who make our jobs so much harder. But I don't think it's fair in this case. There's some resentment because a lot of parents don't raise a kid to accept treatment when it's necessary but unpleasant for them. But that's not fair to this poor little guy, because he apparently has no parents to teach him anything. That's a different situation altogether."

They stopped at a door that did not appear to be attached to a patient room. It struck Anne as more of a utility room door.

"I feel very sorry for him," the nurse said.

Then she opened the door to what looked like a large supply closet. It was empty except for the boy's bed, monitoring equipment, and IV equipment. And, of course, the boy, who stared at them with wide eyes and opened his mouth to shriek.

Anne put a finger to her masked lips. Amazingly, he closed his mouth and did not scream.

"I brought your foster mom," the nurse said brightly.

It changed something in the boy's eyes in a noticeable way. Anne could not have explained or described the change, but she knew it when she saw it.

"You put him in a supply closet?"

"We're out of rooms. We have so much Covid in here right now."

"Is it even properly ventilated in here?"

The nurse pointed to a grate in the ceiling that seemed to cover an air shaft.

"I'm sorry," the nurse said. "I know it's not ideal. But he ends up getting scraps, because the state is picking up his tab. We get some money from them, but not as much."

"So you take it out on him?"

"We still give him the best medical care," she said. "We care for his injuries as well as we would any patient. But we may prioritize him out of rooms, and he has to have his surgeries when we can fit him in, rather than on a fixed schedule. I'm afraid that's just the way it is."

While they spoke, the boy never took his eyes off Anne's face.

"So we don't know when he's having the rotator cuff surgery?"

"No, we have no idea. It'll happen on very short notice."

"I'd like to talk to his surgeon before I go."

"He has more than one. More than two so far. And I don't know if I can get you a consultation with one right now. Or even today. But I could have one of them call you. I'll have to get you on his records as the foster parent."

"In the meantime," Anne said, "can I please get a chair?"

The nurse disappeared down the hall, and Anne turned her full attention onto her new foster son.

"Hi," she said quietly.

At first he held her gaze, but did not try to move or speak. Then his eyes began shifting away from her eyes, landing on a slightly lower part of her face. As though he wanted to look at the rest of her face—her nose, mouth, chin—but they were covered.

It occurred to her that, if a kid is really scared, being surrounded by people who weren't showing their faces might not help.

"I'm not supposed to do this," she said. "But just for a second."

She took hold of her mask and pulled it down to her chin, stretching its elastic ear straps uncomfortably. He drank in her whole face with his eyes. It might have been reading too much in, but Anne thought his eyes looked . . . grateful? Relieved? Something in that neighborhood.

She allowed the mask to snap back into place.

"Here's the thing," she said. "I'm going to be your foster mom. And that means I'm going to be taking care of you. And *that* means no harm will come to you if I have any say in the matter. You don't have to be afraid of me, and you don't have to be afraid of other people when I'm around."

She paused, watching his eyes. They had softened since the door was first thrown open. They had softened more when she'd pulled down her mask. But they hadn't seemed to change as she spoke.

"The first problem," she said, "is that I don't know if you speak. I don't know if you speak the language and I don't know if you understand it. I don't know if anything I say makes sense to you. But here goes. When you're well enough to leave the hospital, you're going to come to my house. And you'll be safe there. I have a husband and two older children, but you're safe with them, too. Now, tell me. Did you understand any of what I just said to you?"

She fell silent, and waited. At first nothing happened at all. It made Anne's heart fall. Would she really have to start by teaching him to speak from scratch, the way she might do with an eighteen-month-old baby?

Then, just as she had begun to accept that hard truth, she saw him nod ever so slightly. It was a subtle movement, but unmistakable. Anne would never doubt that she had seen it.

"Good!" she said. Possibly too loudly.

The boy flinched.

"Sorry. Didn't mean to startle you. That's good, though. I'm really encouraged, because I can tell you things and you understand me. That's going to make so many things so much easier."

A hand touched her shoulder, and she jumped. And the boy jumped because she did. Anne spun around to see the nurse standing behind her again. Empty-handed.

"You couldn't find me a chair?"

"I got you something better than a chair. I got you one of his surgeons."

———

Anne sat in the hospital waiting room for a few minutes. Then she looked up to see a familiar doctor standing over her. It was Dr. Margaret Gifford. She was wearing a clear face shield now, in addition to the N95 mask she had worn before.

"You want to step outside a minute?" she asked Anne. "It would feel good to air out my facial dents."

They walked down the hall together without speaking. Into a stairwell, where they trotted down railed concrete steps side by side. At the bottom of the stairs the doctor pushed open a door, and they stepped out into the brilliant sunlight.

Dr. Gifford lifted her face shield and gently pulled her mask away. Her face not only bore indentations from wearing the mask for so long, but the skin was red and chafed from it.

Anne lowered her own mask to her chin and breathed deeply of the cool, clean-feeling air.

"So you'll be fostering him," the doctor said, squinting into the light. She held one arm up to shield her eyes. "Sorry. I'm pretty much a vampire at this point."

"Please don't warn me not to. Because I'm going to do it."

"I was going to do no such thing. I was going to thank you."

"Oh. Sorry. I've gotten a little defensive, I guess."

"I was relieved to hear that somebody stepped up. This kid needs help. He needs care. But the shape he's in now is scaring people off."

"I don't scare so easily," Anne said.

"Good. So . . . look. Here's what I can tell you, medically. He's in very bad condition, but nothing life threatening. He's going to come through all this. He'll pretty much need to learn to walk all over again. But he's young. He'll bounce back. You may be surprised to hear that the two broken legs don't concern me all that much. I mean, hell of a thing for him to have to deal with, but I trust bones to heal. I'm actually more concerned about the infectious tenosynovitis."

"Wait. The what?"

"The infection in his Achilles tendon. Some kind of animal bite from the look of it. Pretty well advanced, because he was obviously living in unsanitary conditions, and he had no way of getting treatment for it. He got in here just in time. At least, I hope he did. I'm pretty sure we can turn it around. Another handful of days in the woods on his own and it likely would have become gangrenous, and then we'd be looking at an amputation of his foot and half his lower leg. Could still happen, but I like his chances. You'll have to take very good care of that. That and a lot of other things. The pins in his bones. Lots of problems he could get into from here, but we hope to avoid them with good care. I talked to his social worker already, and she said they'll be setting you up with a home nurse. That'll help a lot. But knowing government work, we're not talking live-in. Probably three days a week. There'll still be a lot for you to do. And then of course there's the . . . nonphysical aspects of his situation. I probably don't have to tell you this. I probably don't have to explain this to any sentient human being, but children his age are not intended to live in the wilderness alone. It's as hard on the mind and the nervous system as it is on the body."

Anne was looking past the doctor as she spoke. Staring at the mountains, which still bore a little snow. She didn't look back at Dr. Gifford, who seemed to be waiting for some comment from her. She might have offered a rueful smile, or it might have been too subtle, existing mostly in her head.

"You don't have to convince *me*," Anne said after a time.

"Hopefully you're experienced with foster children?"

"Very."

"Good. But, look. Don't get too overwhelmed about that. He's terrified. He's had plenty of reason to be, I'm sure. But terrified people calm down when they know they're no longer in danger. If you can win his trust, things could take a turn for the better in less time than you might think."

"I can. I know I can. I've already made a little headway."

"Good. That's encouraging to hear. With luck I'll be able to fit the rotator cuff surgery in today. I wanted to hold off. Give the poor guy one marginally functional limb while everything else heals. But the state's having none of that. He has to stay here for observation for a few days, and they want everything done while he has to be here anyway. No additional hospitalization. So, barring emergencies, that'll be today. And you can think in terms of three to five days before you take him home, assuming no setbacks. I can ask the state to cover an ambulance ride so he can be moved by medical pros, but I doubt they'll approve it."

"I'd appreciate the try. And any chance we can get him something better than a supply closet?"

"That gets trickier. We're way over capacity with Covid. We've got patients in corridors. We've got patients in tents in one of the parking lots. We've got a refrigerator truck doubling as a morgue annex. It's just a very bad situation. They wanted to put him in a corridor with about twenty other patients, but I thought with his extreme paranoia and anxiety he'd do better with a door that closes. And, in our defense, it's a very large supply closet."

"That's true. I guess I should just thank you for doing your best for him."

"No problem. We've got his back for now, but after that it's going to be a very challenging few months for both of you. He won't be able to do anything on his own. You'll have to feed him, give him sponge baths. Bring him a bedpan. You're going to be his everything, and believe me, it's a twenty-four-hour-a-day job. It'll be like having a baby in the house. Except hopefully he'll sleep through the night. He'll be on a lot of pain meds, actually, and he'll be quite sedated, so that'll give you some breaks. Well. Good luck."

And with that, she replaced her mask and disappeared back into the building before Anne could say so much as goodbye.

———

She stuck her head into Edwina's office. Edwina was just getting off a phone call.

"Did you bring a sack lunch?" Anne asked.

"I did. But it's painfully boring. If you're offering to take me out to a restaurant lunch, I'd ditch what I packed in a heartbeat."

"Let's go."

As they walked down the hall together, Anne said, "I have some good news about the boy."

"Getting out of the hospital sooner than we thought?"

"No, *real* good news. Actually about . . . him."

"Wait, you went to see him? I didn't know you were going to see him. I was going to tell you I have to get you on his records as his foster mom. So they'll approve you for visits."

"I worked that out," Anne said.

———

Edwina said nothing when Anne ordered the baked brie with little toasts, but she raised her eyebrows slightly when it arrived at their outdoor table.

"Very rich," Anne said. "I know. Yes, that salad you ordered is extremely noble. I'm sorry. No, I'm actually not. It happens to be how I deal with stress."

"You said you had good news about him. And then the subject got changed."

"He understands language."

"You sure about that? You sure you're not watching his eyes and misinterpreting what you see in there?"

"Positive. I explained some things to him. About how he was safe with me, and with my family, and that he'd be coming to my house in a few days. And then I asked him if he understood what I'd just said to him. And he nodded."

Edwina set down her fork, her eyes wide.

"That's a lot of progress."

"I was thrilled about it. Of course, whether or not he speaks is another matter."

"He probably does. If he was around people enough to have language, it's really not that likely that he's permanently nonverbal for some reason. Far more likely that he's scared. But then there is one other tough possibility that I at least have to mention."

Anne felt her stomach cramp slightly at the suggestion that there was something more there to fear.

"What?"

"He could be autistic, or on the spectrum. The keening shriek when anyone touches him. The nonverbal thing . . ."

"I don't think so. When we first opened the door and looked in on him, he opened his mouth to shriek, but I put my finger to my lips to shush him, and he stayed quiet. Did you know they have him in a supply closet?"

"Covid," Edwina said, picking up her fork again. "So much Covid. They're over capacity. It's at least well ventilated, right? Maybe it's comforting for him to be in a small space with no roommates."

"Maybe."

They ate in silence for several minutes. Then Anne looked up to see her friend watching. Staring at her.

"You scared?" Edwina asked. "You look scared."

"I'm always scared when I take on a new foster. This one more than most."

"You know what that means about you, don't you?"

"No. What does it mean?"

"Well, I hesitate to make absolute proclamations about anyone, but, based on what you just told me, there's at least an eighty-five percent chance you're human."

Anne cracked a smile she had not seen coming. It was likely the first real smile that day, and it felt good.

"What about you?" she asked Edwina. "Do you get scared?"

"In general, no. But then I've been doing this more than twenty years. In this case, yeah. A little bit. Well. If I'm being honest, I'm a medium bit scared."

"For him? Or for yourself?"

"For him," Edwina said. "But bear in mind I'm not the one taking him into my home."

Chapter Twelve

Scream

The boy arrived at her home as scheduled, but not in an ambulance. Not exactly. It was some sort of van that may or may not have belonged to the hospital.

When they lifted him out on a stretcher, Anne looked at his face and thought she might never be able to calm him down again. He looked as though he were being marched to the electric chair by aliens or evil spirits.

Then, as they were carrying him up her walkway, his eyes landed on her. And everything about him changed.

It was a strange experience for Anne, because his simple act of setting eyes on her face seemed to quell the most immense panic she could ever imagine seeing. She didn't want to read too much into his reaction, but she wondered if the boy might have thought they were taking him somewhere else. Someplace horrifying.

She fell into step beside the two men along her walkway.

"Did you tell him you were taking him to his foster mom?"

She directed her comment to the one in back, because she figured the guy at the front of the stretcher had enough to think about, like walking backward without tripping.

The man looked at Anne as though she had addressed him in a foreign language.

"I didn't tell him anything," he said.

"Would that have been so hard?"

"It's not my job to tell him stories, ma'am. Just to bring him here."

"You're telling me you take on a job to transport an injured child, but you don't think it's appropriate to put him at ease?"

"Now how was I even supposed to know where he was going?"

"I knew," the other man said. "But I didn't think he understood anybody."

They had reached her front porch by then, and were waiting for her to open the door.

"I have to go put the dogs away," she said.

The men expressed their frustration, one with a sigh, the other with a slight eye roll.

"I wasn't expecting you this soon," she added.

"Go do that, ma'am, please," one of them said. The one who assumed it was no use talking to the child. "He's getting heavy."

She ran into the house and closed the dogs into the laundry room, because she thought the boy might be afraid of them.

Then she opened the front door and they carried him inside. Anne watched his eyes. He was on his back, facing straight up. He scanned the ceiling with a look of absolute wonder. By the look in his eyes, she felt as though he might have been viewing the Sistine Chapel, and not a modest home in Boise.

"Where are we taking him?" one of the men asked.

"I cleared a bedroom for him upstairs."

She had, in fact, very emotionally and regretfully repurposed Louisa's room, but she didn't tell them all that.

"That's a mistake," the other man said.

"Why? You can't carry him up there?"

"We can. If we have to. But then what happens when you have to bring him down?"

"I have a large husband and a teenage son. We'll manage."

They looked at each other, shared an almost imperceptible shrug, and hauled the boy up the stairs.

—

"Are you hungry?" she asked him.

He stared into her eyes and said nothing. Now and then he turned his head to the left to look through the filmy curtain at the blue sky outside.

"I'm going to get you something to drink," she said.

She left him alone briefly—which, she realized, she was terrified to do. At the hospital he had been strapped to his bed. She certainly was not going to do that to him. But what if he tried to move in some way, or even get down off the bed? He could take a tumble. Reinjure his freshly set broken bones and undo the healing.

She toyed with the idea of a baby monitor or a nanny cam in that room with him. She couldn't spend the next few months never taking her eyes off him.

She poured him a glass of water. Then she thought better of that choice, dumped the water out in the sink, and got him an orange soda from the fridge. She opened a kitchen drawer and pulled out a bendable paper straw.

Her heart pounding, she carried them back upstairs.

She knocked lightly and then swung the bedroom door wide.

The boy hadn't moved.

She sat on the edge of the bed and popped the top of the soda can. It made him jump.

"Sorry," she said.

She pulled the straw out of its wrapper and plunked it into the soda. Then she held it out for him to drink.

For a moment, he just looked at what she was offering. He was focusing on the end of the straw, which made him go slightly cross-eyed. Which made him look cute. And it was the first time Anne had seen him that way. As a cute young boy.

Then he opened his lips slightly, closed them on the straw, and took a tiny sip. His eyes lit up. Just illuminated, like a kid on Christmas morning. As though he had never in his life tasted anything so delightful.

He drained the can in a few long pulls, and when the straw made a sucking sound with the last of the drink, he jumped again.

Anne set the can on the bedside table and began talking to him.

"We don't know your name," she said, "and it'll be hard not knowing what to call you. Do you have a name that you want to tell me?"

The boy stared into her eyes and said nothing.

"Okay. Well. If you don't have one, or you don't want to tell me what it is, I thought maybe we could give you a name. I was thinking *Thomas*. If that's okay with you. Thomas was my husband's father's name. Is it okay?"

Nothing.

"I'm sorry the men who brought you here didn't tell you they were taking you to my house, like I promised you. I can see how that must have been scary for you."

She did see a wash of fear come into his eyes and pass away again as she reminded him of his medical transport. But he offered no words or other communication.

She stopped talking. She wasn't afraid to say more. She was simply no longer sure that more needed saying, and she noticed that his silence had a peacefulness to it. She sat on the edge of his bed for quite some time, and they looked out the window together, watching puffy white clouds scud across the blue sky.

In time she heard the front door open and close downstairs.

"My other children are home from school," she said.

She watched his eyes lose that sense of silent peace.

"I had another one of the mothers pick them up because I knew I'd want to be home with you. And my husband has to work today."

She said it not because he needed to know any of that. Really, just to keep talking.

His eyes grew wider as footsteps came up the stairs.

"My children are good children," she said. "They would never hurt you."

She looked up to see Janie standing in the open bedroom doorway, her eyes almost as wide as the new boy's. She stood silent and still and stared at Thomas, and he lay silent and still and stared back at her.

"It might help," Anne said quietly to her daughter, "if you just treated him the way you would treat anybody else."

Janie looked at her. Then back at the boy.

"Hi," she said. It came out hushed, but audible.

She raised her right hand and offered him a little wave.

For a moment he only watched her. Then he wiggled the fingers of his left hand in a sort of mini-wave. Anne assumed he was right-handed, but his right hand was completely engulfed in a sling that was clearly intended for a larger patient.

Janie's face softened and lit up. And something corresponding lit up in Anne, though she could not have defined it. Pride? That seemed wrong, as nothing he did was related to her parenting. Relief? Maybe relief.

"He understands me!" Janie shouted, too loudly.

It made the boy jump again.

Janie noticed, and lowered her voice.

"Mom, I'm not afraid of him!" she said.

Anne opened her mouth to speak. But in that moment, Peter's voice came bellowing up the stairs.

"Why're the dogs locked up?"

"No, don't let them out!" Anne shouted back.

But it was too late.

They came bounding up the stairs and burst wildly into the bedroom, where they leapt onto the bed to get a better look at the newcomer. Jasmine planted herself with one paw on either side of his torso and began licking his face.

The boy opened his mouth as if to scream. But, for a strange second or two, nothing came out. Anne grabbed Jasmine and pulled her off, but then Plato stepped in and sniffed the boy's face, bumping Thomas with his cold nose.

Then came the sound.

It wasn't exactly like the metallic shriek she had heard from him at the hospital. This was a full-on horror movie scream. It was the scream of a person who's just met a murderous ghost in a house they had already known was haunted. It was the scream of a person being murdered.

Peter came dashing into the room, and the scream only got louder.

"Take the dogs!" Anne said. "Get them out of here! He's afraid of dogs."

The kids each took one dog by the collar and dragged them out of the room.

"Close the door! Close it before they can get back in!"

The bedroom door closed with a loud thump.

For a few beats, the terrifying sound continued. Anne thought she could hear the strain it was putting on his throat. It flitted through her head that she would have to talk to the neighbors. Try to convince them not to call the police every time they heard a murder taking place at her house.

The sound grew quieter, then disappeared.

"Okay, sorry," she said, attempting to breathe again. "I get that you're afraid of dogs. I thought you might be, since that store owner kept siccing his dogs on you, and since that's probably how you got that bite on your ankle. I'm really sorry. They're nice dogs. They would never hurt you. But they can be a little too enthusiastic. I didn't mean for you to meet them like that."

His eyes were still wide, and they gave his face a rattled appearance, as though he was still in shock. Which he probably was.

"Oh," she said. "I just remembered. They prescribed all kinds of medications for you, including one that's just for sedation. So you won't be too upset until you get used to it here."

She reached over to the bedside table for the pharmacy bag.

The boy shook his head. Rather vehemently, it seemed to her. It was a more distinct gesture than she had ever seen from him.

"You don't want something to calm you down?"

He shook his head again.

"Some of the medication you'll *have* to take. Painkillers and antibiotics."

She waited. He did not shake his head at those.

"Okay. I guess that last one is up to you. I'll just stay with you until you settle down."

To Anne's surprise, he allowed his eyes to close almost immediately. She sat with him for maybe two minutes. Then—owing to his exhausting morning, or because he'd left the hospital on a lot of drugs, or more likely both—he fell asleep.

———

Janie was at the kitchen table when Anne got downstairs.

The girl did not look at her as she sat down.

"Not all of our growth will happen in a straight line," Anne said.

"I have no idea what that means," Janie said, still staring at the tabletop.

"It means that sometimes we'll make progress, but then we might lose some of that progress again."

"Oh."

"He's afraid of dogs."

"Yeah, I noticed that."

"He's afraid of dogs because he was living in the woods all alone, and the only way he could get something to eat was to steal from this little store. And every time he did, the owner sicced his two dogs on the poor little guy, and one of them bit him and it started an infection so bad he almost lost his leg."

"Oh," Janie said. "Ow. Now I feel bad for him again."

Then they only sat for a moment without talking.

"But now I'm afraid of him again," Janie said, her voice mildly whiny.

"I know."

"Is he ever going to be . . ." But then she didn't finish the thought.

"What? Is he ever going to be what?"

"Like . . . normal. Like a normal kid?"

Anne sighed.

"Honestly? I don't know, Janie. I don't have the whole story of what he's been through, and there's a lot we don't know about him. I think I can be safe by saying he'll never be the boy he would have been if he hadn't gone through such an ordeal. But I'm sure he'll be more relaxed than he is now. He's already fairly trusting with me. And he was doing pretty well with you before Peter let the dogs out."

"That's true."

"I told you this was going to be hard."

"I know," Janie said. "But I wasn't ready for *that*."

Peter stuck his head into the kitchen.

"Sorry," he said. "Didn't know."

"I understand that."

He walked across the kitchen and sat at the table with them.

"Kid sure can scream," he said.

"I can't find the lie in that," Anne said.

"He'll stop doing that after a while, though. Right?"

"This is definitely what we're hoping," Anne said.

———

She checked on him again, but he was still asleep. Or drugged into unconsciousness. It was hard to keep the two sorted out.

She pulled the window curtain all the way closed, because so much sunlight was shining onto his face. It didn't seem to bother him, but it bothered Anne on his behalf.

Then she sat down in a chair between the window and the bed and indulged herself by watching him sleep for several minutes. He was so young and small and innocent in his sleep, and she already loved him. Which might have been setting herself up for the world's biggest fall. She was sure Chris would have said so. Then again, these attachments didn't have an on/off switch, or, if they did, Anne's was missing.

She sighed, and decided she'd best pay some attention to her two conscious children.

When she got back downstairs, the living room was cluttered with a hospital bed, a folded wheelchair, and a masked middle-aged woman Anne had never met.

"Hi . . . ?" Anne ventured, almost turning the word into a question.

"And the patient is where?" the woman asked.

She wore white orthopedic shoes and a very practical short haircut. She was wearing an old-fashioned windbreaker type of jacket, and held a clipboard squeezed under her armpit.

"Can we start with you telling me who you are?"

"Oh. I told your daughter. I thought she'd tell you when she went and got you."

"She didn't come and get me. I just happened to wander down."

The woman narrowed her eyes at Anne, and Anne didn't like it, because she took it as a veiled comment about how she raised her children. Then again, Anne was very tired, physically and emotionally, and she might have been taking it too personally.

While she was thinking this, she missed the woman's name. She came back into the moment just in time to hear that she was a nurse.

"Not that I don't appreciate your coming," Anne said, "but I have to question the timing of your first visit. He was an inpatient only a few hours ago."

The nurse pulled the clipboard out from under her arm and stared at it.

"Says here he was released to you day before yesterday."

Anne sighed, and plunked down onto the sofa, because the sudden flurry of complications felt exhausting to her.

"I have no idea why it would say that," she told the nurse, "but it's not correct. He just showed up here a handful of hours ago. And he's sleeping, and I don't want to disturb him. But thank you for bringing the hospital bed and the wheelchair."

"I didn't bring those," the nurse said.

She plunked herself down on the couch next to Anne, who had purposely been trying not to invite her to make herself comfortable.

"Who brought those?"

"No idea. They were on the porch. I had your son bring them in. So, should we go take a look at the patient?"

The comment represented something of a breaking point for Anne, who was already feeling as though she'd jumped into water over her head.

"No," she said. "No, we should not. As I told you only seconds ago, he was in the hospital just this morning, and now he's resting peacefully, and I don't want him disturbed."

Driving Anne's vehemence was fear. She could feel it. She couldn't handle another storm in that moment. She was afraid of the boy waking up with a stranger in the room and having another screaming fit, throwing the whole household full of raw nerves into another state of panic.

"Maybe tomorrow," she added.

The nurse seemed to ignore her tone and volume.

"It'll have to be day after tomorrow, if I don't see him today. Where do you have him? Just so I know."

"He's in one of the upstairs bedrooms."

"That's a mistake," the nurse said.

"Why is it a mistake?" Anne asked. Even though it was the second time she'd heard this assessment.

"It'll be hard to get him down the stairs in his wheelchair."

"Well, maybe he doesn't need to come down for a while."

"He'll have medical appointments."

"Oh."

"Show me your downstairs," the nurse said, pulling to her feet.

Then the woman pretty much began poking around on her own, without relying on a tour guide. Anne found herself mostly just following the nurse around her house.

"There's no place for him downstairs," Anne said as she followed the woman into her dining room. "Unless I put him in the dining room."

"So put him in the dining room. He'll be able to join family meals that way."

"I'm not sure he's ready for family meals. And besides, this wouldn't work, because it doesn't have a door that closes. I need someplace that I can keep the dogs out of. Until he gets used to them."

"Keep the dogs outside."

Anne felt another little twig snap inside her nervous system.

"I will *not* keep my dogs outside," she practically shouted. "This is their house, too. And it's not your place to give me advice on things like that."

Again she waited for the woman to react to her angry tone. Again, the nurse ignored it, or did not notice.

"His social worker would be the one to advise about such things."

"His social worker has been placing children in this family for a very long time, and she knows there are two friendly dogs who live here. *Inside.*"

"But now you have a child who's afraid of them."

"It's only his first day meeting them."

The nurse turned and walked out of the dining room. Anne helplessly followed her into Chris's office.

"This room would work well," the nurse said.

"Except it's my husband's office."

"So? Move his office into the upstairs bedroom. Move the bedroom stuff down here. Put the boy in his wheelchair and wheel him to the table for family meals. It's important. He shouldn't get too isolated."

Anne opened her mouth to blast the woman again for overstepping. But she remembered that the nurse would be back in two days to do important medical checks on the boy, and it would be best not to alienate her.

"I'll discuss it with my husband. Now if you don't mind."

And with that she took a piece of the woman's jacket between her fingers and walked her to the door.

The woman presented Anne with her card as she stepped out onto the porch.

"In case you have questions."

"Thank you," Anne said.

And she closed the door.

When she turned around, Peter was standing in the living room, staring at her.

"Who was that?"

"An interior decorator, apparently."

"Why did we call one of those?"

"We didn't. It was just a joke."

"I don't get it."

"Don't worry about it," Anne said. "It was just a joke in my own head."

———

She was sitting on the boy's bed, feeding him some bits of turkey breast and mashed potatoes, when Chris rapped on the bedroom door.

"Can I come in?" he called through the door.

The boy's eyes flew wide and he briefly choked on his dinner.

"It's okay," Anne told him. "It's my husband. He's a safe person. You trust me, right?"

The boy nodded slightly, his eyes still wide.

"Then can you trust me if I say someone else is safe?"

At first, nothing. Then a much smaller nod. Much less sure.

"Come on in, Chris," she called. "But don't let the dogs in, whatever you do."

Chris opened the door and stepped in, quickly closing it behind him.

"Hey, honey," he said. "Introduce me to your friend."

"Chris, this is Thomas. Thomas, Chris."

"Hey, Thomas. Can I come over and sit on the end of the bed with you?"

The boy nodded his smallest nod yet, his eyes still wide.

Chris sat at the very end of the boy's bed.

"I don't bite," he said.

"Bad choice of words," Anne said. "Tell you later."

"Did he come with the name Thomas?"

"He didn't come with any name. So I gave him that."

"Well, that's nice," Chris said.

His father, the elder Thomas, had died the previous year, and they were coming up on an anniversary of his death that she knew would be hard for Chris.

"But let's not get in the habit of talking about him like he's not here, okay?"

Chris turned his attention to the boy again.

"You've had a rough go of it," he said to Thomas. "Life hasn't been good to you lately, has it?"

A silence fell. After a few seconds of it, the boy opened his mouth, and Anne was sure he was going to say his first words. Instead what came out was a huge, almost convulsive sob. Thomas dissolved into tears at a level Anne hadn't seen for many years, despite having been around a lot of troubled kids.

"Me and my big mouth," Chris said, and he could barely be heard over the sobs.

"No, it's okay. He needs to get this out. Let me just stay with him so he doesn't choke or something. And to help him blow his nose. Then I'll be in."

———

It was almost half an hour later when she found Chris in their bedroom. He was propped up on pillows on the bed, working on his laptop.

"Really sorry about that," he said. "He okay?"

"Yeah. He's asleep again. It's okay. Honestly. It is. Now we know that expressing empathy for what he's been through makes him cry. That doesn't mean we should pretend not to notice. He needs someone to acknowledge that he's had it rough."

"Well, that's charitable. Thanks. I'll stop kicking myself now."

Anne walked off toward the bathroom to change into a nightgown, brush her teeth, and wash off her makeup.

Then she stopped.

"He really needs to be downstairs," she said.

"I'm about to lose my office, aren't I?"

"Not lose it. Just . . . what if it was upstairs? In the room he's in now?"

She avoided saying "Louisa's old room," because it still hurt. For both of them.

Chris sighed deeply.

"Yeah. Okay. I guess it would be okay. On one condition. We have to hire someone to do the moving. I've finally got my back halfway rehabbed to a state I can live with."

"Done," she said, and walked into the bathroom.

But a moment later she stuck her head back out into the bedroom and looked at her husband, who sensed her gaze immediately and returned it.

"I'm not giving him back," she said.

"Hell, I could've told you that yesterday."

"He only got here today."

"I know."

Chapter Thirteen

Deprogramming

It was three days later, at breakfast.

Thomas had been moved downstairs. Chris and Peter had gotten into the habit of lifting him into his wheelchair in the morning, with Anne guiding his legs to avoid bumps.

They had begun to wheel him into the dining room for family meals.

Her two older children were chattering at each other about something school related. Chris was leaning over a cup of coffee with his forehead resting in his palm. Thomas was looking out the window and eating a piece of peanut butter toast.

For the moment, the dogs were outside.

She had replaced his oversize sling with one that fit him properly, and, now that it was uncovered, he could use his right hand reasonably well, provided he didn't have to lift it too high. She was simply careful not to hand him food that had much weight to it. He kept his forearm braced on the table, and held light food in his hand, and leaned forward to take bites. He only just barely made it work. Still he seemed to like that better than being fed.

The older kids had fallen into bickering at a fairly high volume. Anne looked over to see if Thomas was scared by it, but he seemed okay. He had finished his toast, and was staring out the window, as though his mind were millions of miles away.

"That was not Mrs. Patina," Peter said. "That was Mr. Morris."

"No, it was Mrs. Patina," Janie said.

"I was there," Peter said. "I have eyes in my head."

"I have eyes, too!" Janie shouted. "What do you think I am, some kind of underground troll person?"

"You sure you want me to answer that?"

"Kids," Anne said. "Volume."

They both stopped talking and looked at Thomas, who only stared out the window. It had actually been Anne who'd been troubled by the level of their voices.

"Thomas," she said in the brief silence. "More toast?"

The boy didn't seem to hear.

Janie and Peter took up bickering again, but with a decibel or two less volume.

"Thomas," she said again, raising her voice to be heard. "More bacon?"

Still she could not get his attention.

"Thomas!" she said a third time.

He looked away from the window and straight into her eyes. Then he opened his mouth. His voice sounded scratchy and faint from lack of use, but his grasp of the language was clear. "My name is Remy," he said.

The room fell silent.

All eyes turned to the boy. But nobody seemed to know what to say.

It was Anne who spoke first.

"Well . . . okay," she said. "Thank you. That's good to know. Thank you for telling us that. We didn't know."

That seemed to satisfy the boy, and he looked out the window again.

"Can I just ask you one other question?"

He looked back at her. Into her eyes again. He had a way of drilling his gaze into hers as though he had lost something important there.

"Do you have a *last* name that you want to share with us, too?"

The boy seemed to think very hard about that. He tilted his head, as if that would help to clear his mind. He scrunched up his forehead. Then he looked back at Anne and shrugged slightly.

"Okay," she said. "That's okay. That's good for now. Will you all excuse me for a minute? I have to make a quick phone call."

She ducked out of the dining room, retrieved her phone from the kitchen counter, and dialed Edwina's cell. She knew Edwina would not be in the office yet.

"Everything okay?" Edwina asked in place of *hello*.

"Yes. Fine. He just told me his name is Remy. Does that help at all?"

"He talks."

"When he's ready. Yes. Perfectly."

"No last name?"

"Not that he can remember. Or is willing to share, I'm not sure which."

For a moment there was only silence on the line.

Then Edwina said, "It *might* help. If he'd said his name is John, that wouldn't help much. But Remy is a pretty distinctive name. Let me talk to the police and see if there's anybody missing by that name. I'll call you back as soon as I know more. If I'm not calling, I don't know more."

And she quickly ended the call.

Anne walked back to the breakfast table, trying to seem casual. As if something momentous had not just occurred.

"So what do we call him?" Peter asked. "Thomas? Or Remy?"

"His name is Remy," Anne said. "So we call him Remy."

—

167

It was two hours and twenty minutes later when Edwina showed up on her doorstep.

"Surprise inspection," she said when Anne opened the door.

"Is that a joke?"

She stepped out of the way and Edwina came in.

"Of course it's a joke. You know I don't spot-check you after all these years. I have info. But I still want to look in on him while I'm here."

"Sure. He's with the nurse right now. She's cleaning out that infection site in his ankle and I couldn't bear to watch. Tea?"

"Please. But first I have to stick my head in and ask him a question. It can't wait."

Anne guided her friend down the hall and rapped lightly on Remy's door.

"You may come in," the nurse said.

Anne purposely did not look in on the procedure, but she heard Edwina say, "Darn. Doesn't that hurt him?"

"I used a local anesthetic," Anne heard the nurse say.

"Remy," Edwina said. "You remember me, right? I need to ask you a question. It's very important. We were so happy to know that you're Remy. It helps us to know who you are. So tell me. Are you Remy Blake? Is that your last name? Blake?"

Anne glanced over Edwina's shoulder to watch the boy's reaction. He nodded rather vigorously. Enthusiastically, even. It seemed to delight him to hear his name spoken. He even smiled a little. Or . . . almost. Which wasn't all that surprising, Anne realized. We all want to be recognized. Known.

"Great news!" Edwina said cheerfully. "Thank you." Then, to the nurse, "Thanks, Hannah. I'll let you get back to work."

Anne and Edwina walked together to the kitchen, and Edwina sat down at the table.

"Details," Anne said, and began filling mugs with water to heat in the microwave. "I want details."

"Okay. So, as you gathered, his name is Remy Blake. Three years ago the police got a report about his welfare, and so did DCFS in Pocatello. But nobody knew where he was, so all anybody could really do was be aware of the situation. In case he popped up somewhere."

"Well, he popped up," Anne said.

She set the time on the microwave and started it heating, then sat down at the table to better hear the details.

"His father's name is Roy Blake. His mother was Marian. She died about a year and a half before we got this report. Hepatitis C. They're from Pocatello, as you probably gathered. The neighbors were concerned about the boy. The father sold the house, scooped up the kid, and disappeared for parts unknown. These neighbors, their names are Art and Jeannie Gaffney, and they have a boy the same age. Les. Lester is his name. Apparently the two boys were fast friends. Really close. So the family knew Remy pretty well. I guess it goes without saying that if a father has sole custody after the mother's death, there's no law against him taking the boy and moving away. But the Gaffneys were concerned about Remy because they felt like Roy's mental state had been deteriorating since his wife's death, and that he was falling under the spell of some pretty wild ideas. He'd been bragging about buying a piece of property so remote that no one would ever find them. And Remy was only five. They were concerned enough to report it to the police before it happened, to see if they could get some kind of mental health evaluation on the father. But by the time the police came to take a report, the house was empty and they were gone."

Edwina fell silent. Anne simply held still and absorbed all she'd been told.

The microwave beeped, and Anne jumped as if someone had fired off a gun.

"Jeez," Edwina said. "I hope his mental state isn't rubbing off on you."

Anne tried to laugh, but it didn't quite work. It didn't come out right. She got up to make the tea as she spoke.

"Nobody can say the Gaffneys worry too much."

"You can say that twice."

"That's a lot to find out."

"Let's hear it for distinctive given names," Edwina said. "So far there's just one important thing I haven't found out."

"And that would be . . . ?"

"What happened to the father."

"Right," Anne said. "That's a pretty key question, all right. If they find him, they wouldn't give the boy back, would they?"

"Oh, heavens no. He'd be in prison for child endangerment, unless his mind is so far gone that he'd be institutionalized instead."

Anne felt herself sigh inwardly at the reassurance. She already couldn't bear the idea of losing him. And it had only been a few days.

"So, do we just ask him straight-out what happened to his father?"

"I guess it couldn't hurt," Edwina said. "But let's sit here and drink our tea first and wait till the nurse is gone. He shouldn't have to answer questions about his dad and get an infection site cleaned out at the same time. It's too overwhelming."

Anne sat down with the two cups of tea. She blew into hers, feeling the steam rise into her face.

"So, the Gaffneys," Edwina said. "I had a phone conversation with the mother this morning. She gave me a real earful about Roy Blake. It's a lot, so I'll let you hear it straight from them. They desperately want to bring their son and come for a visit, if you'll allow it. The son has been worried sick, and really broken up about losing his best friend. Even after all these years he still talks about Remy. I'll give you their phone number and then it's up to you."

Anne heard a sound, and looked up to see the nurse standing in the kitchen doorway.

"I'll be leaving now," Hannah said. "I'll be back day after tomorrow."

"How's that infection?" Anne asked.

"It's responding to the antibiotics. Slowly. But it is."

Then she walked out without any more formalities spoken.

"Come on," Edwina said. "Bring your tea."

They walked down the hall together. Anne rapped lightly on the door and then stuck her head into his room.

"Can we come in?"

He offered no opinion one way or the other, so they stepped inside. Anne sat down in a chair a fair distance from his bed, and Edwina sat on the padded window seat, farther away.

"What would you think about a visit from your friend Lester?" Anne said.

Remy's face and eyes sprang to attention.

"Lester?" he said. As though he couldn't believe his good fortune. As though he needed confirmation that anything so exciting could actually be true.

It was only the fifth word she had ever heard him say.

"I'll tell his family you want to see him," Anne said. "But meanwhile I have another question. And this is a harder one. But I need to ask it. It might upset you, and if it does, I'm sorry. But we just need to know. Remy . . . do you know what happened to your father?"

Remy's eyebrows dropped lower. His face scrunched up into an odd expression. He seemed more confused than upset, as if Anne had posed a very complicated math problem and now he had to try to work it out in his head.

He glanced out the window for a moment, as though the answer were hiding in the bushes outside.

Then he looked back at Anne. Straight into her eyes, as was his way.

"I don't remember," he said. His voice was small, like a shy little mouse. "I'm sorry."

The sincerity of his apology broke Anne's heart a little bit. Or a little bit further, it might be more accurate to say.

"You don't have to be sorry," she said. "I just needed to ask."

———

"'I don't remember' is an interesting answer," Edwina said as Anne walked her out to her car. "I was expecting him to say, 'I don't know.' Like his father just disappeared one day and he didn't know what happened to him. But 'I don't remember' suggests that he knew at one time. And it's not the kind of thing that slips your mind, like where you left your car keys."

"I'm not sure what that adds up to," Anne said.

"I'm wondering if it was traumatic and he's repressed it."

"I'm sure just about everything in the last few years has been traumatic for him."

"I'm just thinking . . . I don't know. Maybe I shouldn't even say this. Maybe I'm wrong and it won't even happen. But . . . just be prepared for the fact that all this stuff might wake up in him at some point. He's being a sweetheart right now, which nobody saw coming. But when he starts to really feel safe in your home, that's when he might start expressing the trauma."

"I refuse to think about that today," Anne said.

"You're right. Sorry I brought it up."

And with that, Edwina climbed into her car and drove away. Anne watched her go for a moment.

Then she went back inside and called the number she'd been given for the Gaffneys. She spoke to the mom, Jeannie, who was so excited to hear from her that she didn't stay on the phone long. She wanted to get herself in the car, pick up her son at school, and start driving.

—

Anne was pretty sure it was a three-and-a-half-hour drive from Pocatello. So she was surprised when Lester and Jeannie showed up less than three hours later. Maybe Anne was wrong about the distance, or maybe Jeannie had broken a few traffic laws to get there.

It was nearing midafternoon when they knocked on her door.

"I could put on a mask if you want," the mother said, "but we're vaccinated."

She welcomed them into her living room.

"Before we go in there," she told them, "I just want to make sure Edwina warned you about his physical condition. His injuries. Otherwise it's going to be quite a shock."

Jeannie was an unusually tall woman, well over six feet, with hair down past her waist and a brow knitted into what looked like a permanent state of concern. Her son was a couple of heads shorter, with a pleasant face and a stylized haircut—shaved on the sides and long on top.

"She said he had two broken arms and two broken legs," Jeannie said, her voice a hush. "Is that really true?"

"Pretty much. Two broken legs. One is an old injury that healed badly and had to be reset. A shattered elbow from when he was hit by the car. And a rotator cuff injury. Also old."

She wanted to ask this woman if she thought Remy's father was a man who would break his son's bones. But she didn't want to ask in front of her eight-year-old boy.

Jeannie made a strange, disgusted sound in her throat that did not seem to resemble a word.

"It's just awful. Did you hear all that, Les? Are you prepared for all that?"

"I just want to see him," Lester said. "I don't care what he looks like."

She led them down the hall, where she knocked lightly on Remy's door. "Somebody here to see you," she said, opening the door a crack.

Then she swung it wide, so he could see.

His face changed entirely. It lit. It softened. It morphed into the face of an eight-year-old boy pretty much like any other. In that moment there was nothing the slightest bit wild about him.

"Lester!" he said. His voice was stronger than she had ever heard it.

Lester walked past her and sat on the edge of his bed.

"Hey, Remy. Hi. Oh. Just so you know. I go by Les now."

"Why?"

"I dunno. Just sounds cooler."

The women stood in the open bedroom doorway and watched as a silence fell between them. Then Remy started to cry. It wasn't a desperate sobbing as it had been a couple of days earlier. His eyes just filled up and spilled over. He blinked viciously, as though he could hide the tears or get them to go away. Like any eight-year-old boy, he likely wouldn't be caught dead crying in front of a friend if he could help it.

The cruelty of his condition was such that he could not raise either hand quite high enough to hide the tears, or wipe them away.

"How 'bout if we leave these two alone to catch up?" Jeannie said. "I have so much to tell you. You know. Privately."

"Sure. I'll make us some iced tea. Or lemonade. Whatever sounds better. And we'll sit out in the yard. It's such a nice day." It *was* a nice day. But Anne had chosen the yard because she knew she could keep an eye on the boys through the window. "Just one thing, though. Les? Remy can't blow his own nose, because neither of his arms are very bendy. So if he needs to, you'll help him, right?"

"Yes, ma'am," Les said.

She glanced at Remy to make sure he was okay alone with his friend. But he was staring up at Les as though Les were some kind of benevolent, angelic spirit, sent to save him.

Anne quietly let herself out.

—

They sat at the outdoor table together, sipping iced tea. Staring off toward the mountains. Now and then Anne looked through the downstairs window at the boys, but each time they were only talking quietly.

"I feel guilty," Jeannie said. "Like it was my fault. Because the first time Roy left him with us for the weekend, I didn't call the police. It wasn't until he asked us to watch him a second weekend in a row that I realized he was up to something, that he was making some kind of preparations. But by the time the police came out and took a report, it was too late."

"You can't blame yourself. You did more for Remy than anyone."

"There's so much I need to tell you about Roy Blake," Jeannie said, letting Anne's comment slide away. "You have no idea how long I've been waiting to say all this to somebody. But . . . in all fairness, I just want you to know that not everything I have to say about the man is bad. We used to be friends. Good friends."

"Did that end when he moved? Or before that?"

"We tried to stay friends with him after Marian died, but he took a real dark turn. Oh, he was always a little . . . let's just say I always avoided talking about politics. And anything involving the state of society or the world. Art would get into it with Roy, but not me. But they lived three houses down, and the boys were besties, and we played bridge. And we had movie nights. But after Marian died, a lot of things changed with Roy. He adored her, and he didn't do well with the grief. At all. He loved his son, but I don't think he was the least bit prepared to raise him on his own."

She allowed a pause, so Anne slipped in the question she had been wanting to ask.

"Do you think he would beat Remy? I mean, enough to break a leg, or some ribs, or tear a rotator cuff?"

"The Roy I knew, no. I don't think that's the kind of man he was. But I have to allow for the fact that he was changing, and the Roy Blake out in the wilderness with Remy might not've been the Roy Blake I knew. You know he was a survivalist, right?"

"I'm . . . not sure I did know that."

Anne took a sip of her drink because she felt restless and uneasy, and needed something to do with her hands.

"You know what that is, though. Right?"

"I think I do," Anne said. "I'm picturing a person who stockpiles weapons and food for the apocalypse. Someone who thinks the world as we know it is about to end, and the government is tyrannical and coming to take their guns and their freedoms, and they're determined to be one of the few who survive it."

"Bingo," Jeannie said. "Exactly that. And you know why I'm telling you this, right?"

"I'm not sure. Maybe."

"His social worker . . . I forget her name, but she told me how scared he was. Remy. How he didn't want anyone to touch him in the hospital, and how he screams. And you probably all think it's because he was surviving on his own, and yeah, I'm sure that's part of it. But you need to know that his father taught him to be terrified of the world. Roy took him into the middle of nowhere and got him to see the world like a survivalist. I know I wasn't there. But he was already doing it before he left, so it's a pretty good bet. Think about it. At the end Remy was living in the woods up above that little town, and coming down and stealing food from the store. All he had to do was walk up to those people and say, 'Please call the Gaffneys in Pocatello for me.' So why didn't he? Because his father taught him to be afraid of the world and everyone in it. That's why. He was five years old when his dad took him away. How's he supposed to know anything different from what he was taught? You need to know this, Anne. It's important that you know this. Because you're going to have to unteach him all of that. He's going to need some deprogramming. Or at least that's my opinion. My husband, Art, would tell you I'm too quick to offer my opinion. But, anyway, that's what I think."

Anne opened her mouth to answer, but her head felt swimmy. For maybe the dozenth time, it was hitting her hard that she'd stepped into a deeper pit than she might have imagined.

"I'm not even sure how to do that," she said.

"Who *is*? It's not one of those things you're born knowing. He'll probably need some professional help."

"We can get him that."

"Good. That's really good. Thank you. Thank goodness. I'm so relieved that he landed with somebody nice like you. It was really good of you to take him. I know it's a lot, the way things are now for him."

Anne looked in through the window again. The boys had not moved. Les was still sitting on the edge of the bed, looking down on Remy. Remy was still gazing up into Les's face like he was some kind of magical cure for everything that could possibly hurt in life.

She turned her attention back to the mother.

"So, another question. Do you think his father would abandon him?"

"Same answer as before, I guess. Not the Roy I knew. I have no idea what happened to his mind after they left, but it was sliding something awful before that, so nothing is off the table. Nothing is impossible. But he did have a heart condition."

"Roy?"

"Yes. Roy. I tried to tell this to the police. I tried to tell this to Child and Family Services. He had heart disease in his family. He had angina. He'd already had two minor cardiac incidents. And then what did he do? Did he take care of himself because his family needed him? No he did not. He smoked like a chimney. Drank too much. Ate almost nothing but red meat. When Marian was alive, she got after him about it, and he kept it halfway under control for her sake, but then she died and he just fell right off that cliff. It was like he wanted to make it worse. Art and I said that to each other. All the time. 'It's like he wants to go where Marian went.' And then he goes off into the woods with a five-year-old. Who would do that? No one in his right mind, that's what I think. Because what's the kid supposed to do if you drop dead? I wasn't there, so I can't say for a fact that I know what happened to Roy. But the odds are pretty high that he dropped dead. If I was a betting woman, I'd bet money that he dropped dead and left that poor kid alone."

"I wonder if we'll ever know," Anne said.

"What does Remy know? Will he say?"

"He says he can't remember. Which is not exactly the same as saying he doesn't know. We're thinking he might have repressed the memory because it was traumatic."

"Ya think? His last parent drops dead and leaves him out in the middle of absolute effing nowhere? Yeah. That's pretty much the textbook definition of trauma. Listen. Anne. Here's the most important thing I can tell you. Here's the thing I really need you to know. I'm the only person you know who knew Remy before. My family may be the only people you'll *ever* know who knew him before this disaster. And I've got to tell you, he was the sweetest boy you would ever want to meet. Heart the size of a truck. Helpful. Kind. So it's been really hard on me, hearing people talk about him like he's some kind of wild animal. I'm sure this experience hardened him, and it probably changed him a lot. But mark my words, Anne. That heart is still in there. That sweet little boy is still in there somewhere, and if you give him a chance, you're going to find that heart again. I know you are. I can feel it in my bones."

They both fell into silence.

Anne wanted to thank her for saying all that, but somehow her mouth wasn't working. Her words weren't accessible. She just felt overcome.

"You okay?" Jeannie asked.

"Actually," Anne said, "yeah. Better than I was before you told me all that. Thanks."

Chapter Fourteen

Regular

Anne sat in Dr. Klausner's office, chewing her fingernail when she was not talking, and picking at it when she was. She was aware that she was doing it. It bothered her that she was doing it. But she was caught up in the cycle of it, and didn't seem able to stop.

"So . . . ," she began. And stalled.

She had told him only the basic facts she'd learned about Remy's past. So far. She had not yet editorialized about it in any way.

She wanted him to say something to help her bring her thoughts into a straighter line. At the moment they were all over the map. But he only waited, unafraid of the silence. Because therapists were like that, apparently.

"So . . . ," she ventured again. "I'm not sure how to go about teaching him that the world is good."

"You can't," Dr. Klausner said.

"Okay. That's not quite what I was expecting. But okay. When he's well enough, I can bring him here to you."

"I can't either."

"Why not?"

"Because it's not the truth."

Anne shifted her eyes out the window, hoping to absorb this sudden turn in her experience with him. She was afraid if she looked right into his eyes, he would see her feelings about him. The doubts that had just fallen into place.

He wasn't speaking. He did not seem inclined to parse or explain or expand on what he had just said. She would have to draw it out of him, as always.

"You think his father was right?"

"Of course not."

"I'm confused. Hopefully you're getting at something that can make sense to me, but I'd be lying if I claimed to have any idea what it is."

"His father taught him that the world is bad. It's not. You want me to teach him that the world is good. It's not. The problem with the kind of survivalist mentality you describe in his father is not that it's completely wrong. The government remaining a free democracy is not assured. There are many very intelligent and experienced analysts of politics and society who feel a civil war is a real possibility. And whether it actually comes to a hot war or not, most feel we've never been more divided as a society. So Roy Blake wasn't seeing things that weren't there. He was just putting too much weight on his fear. And he was fearing the wrong things in the wrong order of priority. From what you've told me, he was terribly afraid of the government but not the least bit afraid of fatty foods and cigarettes on top of heart disease. A purely analytical mind would see that it should have been weighted the other way around."

Anne only sat still. His words felt like a lot to digest. Or even to chew up and swallow.

In a rare Dr. Klausner move, he went on to further explain himself without her having to push.

"You're probably too young to remember the Cold War," he said. "I was young but quite aware during the Bay of Pigs incident. We honestly thought a nuclear bomb could drop on us at any time. Kids were taught 'duck and cover' in schools, which served as air raid shelters for the rest of the community. A lot of people dug bomb shelters in their yards. If the big one came, they wanted themselves and their families to be among the survivors. So, in a sense, they were survivalists. But for the most part they weren't being pathologically paranoid. There really was a chance it could happen.

"Then again, your average person didn't sell their house and move to a property in the middle of nowhere, upending their lives and the lives of their children, because they also knew there was a chance it might *not* happen. They put the correct amount of weight on the possibility of disaster. We have to do this every day. We just don't think about it. We're used to it. We get in a car with our children and take it out on the highway. People die in horrible flaming car wrecks on the highway. Thousands of people every year, and we all know it. Some people are absolutely paralyzed by that portent of disaster. It causes them to seize up, and they're unable to drive. Some people are so afraid of the world that it takes everything they've got just to leave their home, if they even do. I work with these people all the time. But most of us can know all about grisly, flaming car crashes on the highway and still drive. We fasten our seat belts, drive defensively, and manage to live with the reality that we're now safer, but not safe. We learn to deal with that uncertainty. But there are those who have trouble dealing with it, and, as I say, I work with them all the time. But not by telling them that there's no such thing as a grisly, flaming car crash. Because that's not the truth. Now do you see where I'm going with this?"

"I'm afraid so," Anne said.

"What you told me about his going into town and asking for help . . . how his friend's mother said he could have asked anybody in town to make a phone call for him . . . that's true, to a great degree. In as dire a situation as he was in, that would have been a much better choice than the one he made. But now you have a line to walk. How much should you teach an eight-year-old child to talk to strangers, and trust them?"

For what might have been two minutes or more, neither spoke. Anne was adjusting to the enormity of what she was being asked to do. It felt like a garment she was trying on that didn't fit, yet somehow it was her job to make it fit. Except that was impossible, apparently.

"What if it goes the other way?" she asked. "What if he ends up convincing me that the world is too horrifying a place to ever consider leaving the house?"

She tried to throw it out there as an attempt at humor. But it wasn't. It felt like a real possibility. Still, she expected him to hear it as a light, humorous remark.

"Hopefully if that happens, it won't be permanent," he said. "What was your husband's reaction to all of this?"

Anne felt her face flush. It felt tingly and mildly hot.

"I didn't talk to him about it."

"You didn't tell him anything about your conversation with his friend's mother?"

"I told him Remy's father was a survivalist, and that Jeannie thinks his heart might have given out. But not much more."

Another long silence fell, during which Anne judged herself harshly. The truth felt well defined in her head: Confiding in her husband was good. Withholding from him was bad.

She waited for Dr. Klausner to call her on her shortcomings. Or at the very least require her to justify them.

He never did.

"I just feel . . . ," she began. "I don't know. In a way Chris has been really nice about all of this. Much more so than I expected. But in another way, it feels like he's disconnected from the whole situation. Like he did a really unexplained about-face and said yes to my taking on this very difficult, damaged child. But I'm not sure he's taking it on with me. I feel like he's just sort of . . . standing back and letting me succeed or fail on my own. Like he's not even all that deeply invested in which outcome we end up with."

A briefer silence, also filled with self-judgment. Chris had been a prince about her decision. He was home with the boy right at that moment, to enable her to keep her therapy appointment. And here she was accusing him of something. What must Dr. Klausner think of *that*? What must he think of *her*?

"Tell me again how long you've been married?"

"Nineteen years."

"Then I'd say there's a more than decent chance that if you feel he's disconnected, it's because he's disconnected."

It was possibly the first time it had ever dawned on Anne that her judgments of herself might be harsher than what others were thinking. It felt strange to be paying a near stranger hundreds of dollars an hour to tell her she could occasionally be right.

"I know this is a lot to ask," she said, "but is there any chance at all we might be able to get you to come to *us* at any point? Because I don't think we're anywhere near ready to get Remy to you."

"He needs three months or so before he's healed enough to be mobile?"

"Give or take."

"Theoretically, yes. I mean, under normal circumstances, no. Normally I would not. But in such an extreme case I'd consider making an exception. But I have to remind you that it's not only his body trying to heal. I really think it's best if we leave explorations of his trauma alone until he finds some kind of equilibrium. Not challenge him more than necessary, sooner than necessary. My advice for the moment is to gain his trust and help him settle in, but not too much more."

———

When she arrived home, Chris was sitting in the living room watching TV. One of those fishing shows that everybody in the house except Chris seemed to think were terribly boring.

Remy was not with him.

"How'd it go?"

"It was easy," he said. "He slept the whole time. Well. He woke up once. Just long enough to call you 'mom.'"

"Wait. He called me *mom?*"

"Well, sort of. He called you '*the* mom.' Which was weird. But interesting."

"But I wasn't here."

"I know. He was asking after you. He said, 'Where's the mom?' I said, 'You mean the mom as in my wife? The one who lives here?' He nodded. I told him you'd be back in an hour, and he closed his eyes and fell asleep again."

"Huh. Do you have to go back to work?"

"I don't think so. I think Mo's got the day covered."

"I'm going to go look in on him."

She walked down the hall to his room, with too many thoughts all swirling in her head at once. It felt like a dust devil in there. And those are always a little scary.

She opened the door to find him awake in bed, on top of the covers, staring out the window. He turned his head and looked at her. Smiled just the tiniest bit. Or maybe it was her imagination.

"Hi," she said.

He waved the fingers of his right hand slightly.

"You want to come out and watch TV with us?"

He nodded, looking surprisingly pleased.

"I'll get Chris and we'll move you into your chair."

She walked back to the living room, where Chris was absorbed in his program again. He looked up when she stood over the couch, looking down on him.

The dogs were sleeping on the rug in a spill of sunlight from the window. Chris turned his head to visually locate them.

"What if we don't lock them out next time?" he said. "What if we just tell them firmly not to go up to the kid?"

"We can try it."

"Hey, what are we gonna do for school for that little guy?" he asked, half watching the screen again.

"Well, we can't send him there. He's not physically well enough. And he'd be too overwhelmed. And besides, he apparently hasn't had any schooling."

"None?"

"His dad took him away when he was five. Now he's eight. That's a lot of catching up to do. I guess he'll need homeschooling."

"So *that's* what you'll be doing with all your copious free time." She ignored the dig.

"I'm going to ask Edwina about a tutor," she said. "Help me get him in his chair, okay? I want him out here watching TV with us."

"He's awake?"

"He is."

"I swear he was asleep."

"I believe you. But now he's not."

Chris tore his eyes away from the TV and pulled to his feet. He followed her down the hall.

"Want to know what's weird?" he said as they walked.

"Sure."

"I *like* the little guy."

"That's weird?"

But at a deeper level she understood what he meant.

"Kind of. I didn't exactly expect to. Did you?"

"I guess I didn't expect to so soon."

She opened his door, and he looked at them, his face bright. He looked genuinely pleased to see them.

Anne brought his wheelchair close to the bed and locked the brakes.

"Let me lift him by myself," Chris said. "Just take care of his legs."

They set him gently in his chair. Anne didn't watch his face, because it was so hard to see him wince.

"The dogs are in the living room," Anne said to the boy. "But they're sleeping. We'll make sure they don't come too close. Can you deal with that?"

No response.

"You let us know. Okay?"

Still no response. Or maybe a slight nod. It was hard to tell.

Anne nodded to Chris, who wheeled the boy down the hall to the living room.

They set up his wheelchair in front of the TV. Remy scanned the room for the dogs, who were still fast asleep in the patch of sunlight on the carpet. Then his eyes locked onto the screen and did not let go.

"Well, look at that," Anne said, settling on the couch with her husband. "Somebody else who thinks this fishing show is interesting."

"I haven't watched TV for a really long time," Remy said.

They both looked at the boy, surprised. It was not like him to volunteer words in less-than-urgent situations.

"You're welcome to watch ours anytime," Chris said. "We could even put one in your room if you want."

"I fished," Remy said.

"Did you?" Chris asked.

"Yeah. I did. I was good. But not in big, deep water like that. What is that?"

"That's a lake," Chris said.

"Not like that, I didn't," Remy said. "Not a lake."

Anne exchanged a glance with her husband. She was sure they both believed him. People do fish when they're living out in the wilderness. Their disbelief was centered on his willingness to discuss his life with them so easily.

Then he fell back into rapt attention with the program, and the ones after it, and said nothing more for well over an hour.

Her other two kids came home, said hi. Trotted upstairs. The dogs never moved, and Remy never took his eyes off the TV.

———

When the local news came on, that's when things really got interesting.

They were showing a construction project downtown. There were lots of people lining the streets in the footage. Anne wasn't sure why it was newsworthy, because she wasn't listening. She was watching Remy watch. His eyes had gone wide, but not so much with terror as with intense fascination.

He pointed toward the screen with just the fingers of his right hand. He didn't lift his arm to do it, which was understandable.

"What is that?" he asked them, glancing halfway to where they sat.

"It's the news," Anne said.

"No. Not that. *Where* is that? What city?"

"It's Boise."

"And what city is *this?*" he asked, pointing down at the floor of their home.

"This is also Boise," Anne said.

"That's a big city, right?"

"Yeah. Pretty big. Big by Idaho standards."

"Bigger than Pocatello?"

"Yes."

"It looks regular."

Again, Anne exchanged a glance with Chris.

"We're not sure what you mean by 'regular,'" she said.

"You know. Regular. I'm not sure how to say it. Like . . . how it all was when I was five. Lester said Pocatello was still regular. He said everything he saw driving over here with his mom was regular. I wasn't sure if I believed him. Sort of, I did, because he never used to lie to me.

But I thought maybe you *have* to lie about the . . . I don't remember what my dad called it."

A long silence. Neither adult tried to fill it. Anne thought it might be best to let him sort it out in his head.

"So he was wrong," Remy said at last.

"Mostly wrong," Anne said. "There are problems in the world, and he saw that. And they do exist, but they didn't explode all at once like he thought they would."

"A couple of times I thought he might be wrong," Remy said, "but then after a while I got confused and I couldn't tell."

"I understand," Anne said.

The boy still had his eyes trained to the screen. He fell silent for a time, watching footage of a city council meeting.

"If everything is regular . . . ," he said suddenly. His voice was surprisingly strong, and it startled Anne slightly. ". . . then what was that place?"

"What place is that, Remy?"

"That place. That awful place. Where I was before I was here. They tied me up and did terrible things to me and gave me something to make me sleepy so I couldn't fight back."

Again, Anne exchanged a glance with Chris. It seemed as though the dams around the boy's experiences and communication had burst all at once. And no one had been expecting it. Dr. Klausner had advised her not to challenge him any more than necessary. He had not told her to refuse to answer his questions, and she couldn't imagine he ever would.

"That was a hospital," Anne said.

"That was a hospital?"

"Yes. They gave you drugs so you wouldn't be in so much pain. They had to fix your injuries. You have broken bones. They had to set your broken bones so they would heal right. You had broken bones from before, too, and they didn't heal right. They need to be set. Something needs to hold broken bones in place so they heal well, so you can use them normally again. And then you have to hold them fairly still. I'm sorry they strapped you down. I didn't like that, either, but you were so scared, and you were thrashing around, and they wanted your bones to heal. You were badly hurt and they were trying to help you."

Anne stopped talking and just waited. And watched him. And let him think about what she'd said. Let it settle in.

"Why wouldn't they let me see their faces?" Remy asked.

"Oh," Chris said, close to her ear. "He doesn't know about Covid."

The boy had good ears, though.

"What is that?"

"Covid?" Chris said.

"Yeah. That. I never heard of that."

"It's a virus."

"I don't know what that is."

"It's a . . . ," Chris began. He seemed unequipped for the moment. But he was taking it on. Anne stayed out of his way and let him try. ". . . a sickness. That people can get pretty easily now. It didn't exist when you were five, but it's a pretty big deal now. People wear masks so they don't pass it around as easily. So they're not so likely to get it."

"How many people get it?"

"Millions," Chris said. "Tens of millions just in the US."

"Millions?"

"Yeah."

"Can you die?"

"Yeah. People can die of it."

"How many people die?"

Chris glanced over at her again, as if asking for her permission to tell the truth. She nodded faintly.

"More than a million so far."

"In the whole world?"

"No, just in this country."

Remy did not reply. At least, not for a very long time. Not until maybe five or ten minutes later. Anne had gotten to her feet and announced that she was going to start making dinner.

Remy turned his eyes up to hers. Completely open and unguarded. Then he opened his mouth and spoke.

"How is that regular?"

Anne sighed, and sat again. Plunked down as though someone had opened a valve and let all her air out at once.

"Well. Like I said before . . . there are always problems in the world. But we keep living in the world, because . . . well, I guess we think it makes sense, to keep living in the world. We think it's safe *enough*."

"A *million people* died," Remy said.

Then he turned his eyes back to the TV. A cartoon show had come on, and it seemed to enthrall him.

"I'm going to start dinner," she said again.

She rose and walked into the kitchen.

She opened the fridge, but then just stood there, staring in, seeming to have forgotten what it was she was going to get and what she planned to make with it.

The kitchen door pushed open, and Chris stepped in. She swung the fridge door closed, and leaned her forehead on it.

"You're doing fine so far," he said.

"Am I?"

"I think so. It's hard."

"Are we supposed to be telling him all this stuff?"

"I don't know. But I can't imagine lying is the answer."

"And the news. Should he be watching that? Even grown-ups have trouble with the news."

"Ask the therapist."

"Right. Good. That's a good idea. You know it's going to get harder, right? You realize all that trauma is just sort of lying dormant in there.

You know this is probably the easiest phase of the whole thing with him, right?"

"I do know that," Chris said.

He was still behind her, so they did not look at each other as they spoke. He wrapped his arms around her waist. She wrapped her arms around his, wondering when last they had been spontaneously affectionate.

Not recently.

"So what do we do?" she asked.

"We make dinner," Chris said. "Come on. I'll help you."

He had barely gotten out the last sentence when a scream from the living room split the air. At first it was vocal but not verbal, but it was followed by a panicky stream of words. "He's licking me! Get him off me! Make him stop licking me!"

"Ah, jeez. We forgot about the dogs. You want to help me?" Anne said. "I'll get dinner, you take care of *that*."

Chapter Fifteen

Seven Dead at Midland

In the morning, Anne packed sack lunches for the kids while Janie dawdled over breakfast. Peter was out in the backyard playing with the dogs. Jasmine especially. They seemed to be building up to an epic mock fight, causing Anne to worry he'd get his school clothes dirty. Remy was sitting in his wheelchair, watching through the sliding glass door. He seemed to be worried about more weighty topics.

"Nooooo!" Remy shouted suddenly.

Anne and Janie both jumped.

"What, honey? It's fine. They're playing."

"They're not playing. He's biting Peter! That dog is biting Peter!"

Anne sighed, and joined Remy at the glass door.

"Look at his face," she said.

"He's showing his teeth! It's terrible!"

"No, not the dog, honey. Peter. Look at Peter's face."

"Oh," Remy said. He sat very still for several beats. "He's laughing."

"Because they're playing."

"That can't be playing. That dog is biting him. How can you laugh when the dog is biting you?"

"It's not real biting, hon. It's play biting. She's not really biting down hard."

Still Remy's face was a mask of concern.

The doorbell rang.

"That would be your tutor," Anne said. "Janie. I have to get that. Talk to Remy. Please."

She excused herself from the kitchen to go let her in.

"Rachel," she said when she opened the door. "Good morning."

She was a young woman—very young—with shoulder-length dark hair. A full head shorter than Anne, and so thin she seemed to disappear from any given scene. Anne thought she had only very recently graduated from college, but she didn't ask, because it didn't matter. She was more than up to the task of first-grade curriculum.

"You look absolutely frazzled," Rachel said.

"I have three children," Anne said. "What else can I tell you?"

She stepped back to let Rachel in, and as they walked to the kitchen together, they heard a few more strangled expressions of panic from Remy.

"What's he upset about?" Rachel asked.

"He's watching Peter play with one of the dogs through the window, and he doesn't understand play biting. He thinks his new brother is being mauled. So, listen. Chris had to go in to work earlier than expected. There was some kind of disaster on the job site. I'm desperately hoping you won't mind if I leave you alone with Remy for fifteen minutes during his lessons so I can drive the kids to school. Of course, I'll wait long enough to be sure he's comfortable with you."

"So long as the dogs are out in the yard," Rachel said, "that would be fine."

They arrived in the kitchen just in time to see Peter coming in through the sliding door.

"Do *not* let them in with you!" Anne barked.

"I know, I know."

"Show Remy your hands."

"What?"

"Simple request. Show your brother your hands."

Peter frowned, furrowed his forehead, rolled his eyes. A sort of medley of teenagerhood. But he held his hands out for Remy's inspection, turning them over to show front and back.

"Why am I doing this?"

"He thinks Jasmine was actually biting you."

"Oh, no, buddy," he said directly to Remy. "No. Jasmine would never hurt me. We were just playing."

"I saw you laughing," Remy said, "but I couldn't figure out why. I would never laugh when a dog was biting me."

"She doesn't really bite down."

"Okay," Anne said. "Thank you, Peter. Now you guys grab your lunches, and I'll make sure Remy feels okay being with Rachel while we're gone."

———

They drove the first few minutes in absolute silence. Janie was in the passenger seat, her attention buried in her phone. Peter was in the back, his attention buried in his phone.

It was Janie who first caught wind of the news, and reacted.

"Oh no," she said, her voice a breathy whisper. "Oh no."

It sounded so dire that Anne pulled over to the curb and shifted into park to give Janie her full attention. The blood seemed to be draining out of her daughter's face, and fast.

"What?"

"Another school shooting."

Anne felt it like a kick in the chest. The way she always did. For a moment it seemed to make it harder to breathe.

"Where?"

"Close."

"How close?"

"Very close."

"Janie . . ."

"Midland," Janie said.

That just hung in the car by itself for a few beats. It seemed to echo, but it was an emotional, rather than audible, echo.

"That's less than fifty miles from here," Anne said.

"We played them three weeks ago," Peter said from the back seat.

"Was anybody killed?"

"No idea," Janie said. "It's still an active-shooter situation."

They sat in silence for a time. Possibly a long time. Anne was thinking that school hadn't even started yet, as if that proved this was all a big misunderstanding. But it was a foolish thought, because school would start in a matter of minutes, and ninety-nine percent of the students would have been in the building. What difference did it make whether the first bell had rung yet?

"Please don't make us go to school," Janie said.

It was unlike her to be so openly vulnerable, and it broke Anne's heart. Especially since she thought they should go. The student body would be following the news together. Mourning and working through their shock together. It would be healthier for the kids to be part of that, rather than hiding from the world at home.

"I think it would be better for you to go," Anne said. "But . . . I'll tell you what. I'll be home all day. If you seriously feel like you can't do it, call me and I'll pick you up. But these things happen a lot, and I think working through it with your classmates is the best plan."

"They don't happen a lot at *Midland*," Peter said.

Janie only sighed.

Anne shifted into drive and headed for their school again, but she felt as though she had to keep swallowing down her heart. As though it were trying to escape through her throat.

"I know you won't believe this," she said, more or less to both of them at once, "but it might actually be harder for me to take you to school today than it is for you to go."

"You're right," Janie said. "I don't believe it."

"Actually," Peter said, "we just have to go to school. You have to go home and decide whether to tell Remy. I wouldn't trade places with you for all the money in the world."

"I'm not going to tell him," she said automatically. Without thinking.

"He's going to hear it anyway," Janie said. "He watches TV."

"Well, maybe he shouldn't. We're going to talk to the therapist about that."

Anne pulled up in front of their school. It was less than a minute till first bell, but what looked like the entire student body was out on the front lawn, staring at their phones. Half of them still seemed to have a parent attached.

Anne put the car in park and stepped out.

The principal was running around trying to herd everyone back inside. Anne caught a piece of her sleeve as she hurried by, and she paused.

"Should I stay with them?" Anne asked her.

"Actually, we're trying to get the parents to go home. We'll have an assembly and then deal with this in the individual classrooms. If one of your children can't handle being here, we'll call you. In the meantime, we're trying to get things under control."

Anne turned around, kissed her children as though she might never have the chance again, and drove home.

——

She was trying not to hyperventilate as she walked in her front door.

Rachel met her halfway, in the hall.

196

"Did you hear? Oh my God, Anne, did you hear? Seven dead! Seven! Six students and a teacher. At *Midland!* That's not even fifty miles from here!"

Anne put a finger to her lips, but it was too late.

"How did seven people get dead fifty miles from here?" Remy called from the kitchen. "Did someone kill them?"

Rachel turned her eyes back to Anne's face.

"Oh, I'm so sorry," she breathed in a low whisper. "I had no idea he could hear me."

"Kid's got ears like you wouldn't believe," Anne said.

"I'm so sorry."

"It's okay. I needed to tell him. He would have found out anyway. He watches TV."

———

They sat together at the dining room table. Remy, Anne, and Remy's tutor—the very young woman with the big mouth.

Remy kept his gaze glued to the polished wood of the tabletop.

"What's Midland?" he asked after a time.

"It's a school," Anne said. "A high school. In Wayfield."

"And how did people get dead there?"

"Some kind of shooting," Anne said. "But I don't really have all the details yet."

"Fifteen-year-old student with his dad's AR15," Rachel said. She was staring at her phone. She had been staring at her phone the whole time. "He's in custody."

"Rachel!" Anne barked.

Everybody jumped.

"I'm sorry," Rachel said. "I wasn't thinking. I shouldn't have said that out loud."

"No. You shouldn't have."

"So," Remy began, "somebody just walked in there with a . . . whatever that is and started killing people?"

"I'm afraid so," Anne said.

The boy fell silent for a time. Then he raised his eyes and drilled his gaze straight into hers, the way he so often did. The way she told herself she'd get used to, but really, she was anything but sure.

"Tell me the truth," he said. "Is it starting?"

Anne opened her mouth to answer, but Rachel cut her off.

"Is what starting?"

Remy seemed disinclined to answer, so Anne took it on. Though, frankly, she wished Rachel would go away, or keep quiet, or both.

"Remy's father felt that something big was brewing in society, and that all manner of violence was about to break loose any minute."

"Oh, no," Rachel said to Remy. "Oh, honey, no. This is nothing new. This has been going on for a long time. This happens all the time."

As Rachel spoke, Anne tried to catch her eye, but did not succeed. Remy's eyes widened, and only then did the young woman seem to realize her mistake. She glanced at Anne, who shot daggers from her eyes.

"I think *I* should talk to Remy about this," Anne said.

Rachel opened her mouth, but no words came out. For a welcome change.

"It started a long time ago?" Remy asked, clearly addressing Anne.

"I think," she began, "that what started a long time ago is not really the same kind of thing your dad was worried about."

"How did you know all that about him?"

"Jeannie Gaffney told me."

"Oh."

"Maybe I should go," Rachel said.

"No, I'd like for Remy to have his lessons today. So let's talk this out a little bit more and then go back to his tutoring day being in session. Is that okay with you, Remy?"

Remy was not wasting a second before talking it out more.

"How long has it been going on?"

"School shootings specifically?"

"Yeah."

"Decades."

"I don't know what that is."

"A decade is ten years."

"So, longer than I've been me. How come I didn't know?"

"It's not really the kind of thing you want to discuss with a young child if you can help it," Anne said.

"How many times does it happen?"

"I honestly don't know, Remy. Far more often than it should."

They stared at the table together for a minute. Then Rachel handed Anne her phone. Its web browser was open to a search result. The article was fairly old. From 2019. The headline read "10 Years. 180 School Shootings."

She looked up at Rachel, who returned a questioning expression.

"I'm teaching him to read," Rachel said. "Sooner or later he's going to google it himself."

Anne handed her phone back.

"I think what we're going to do," Anne said to both of them, "is see if Dr. Klausner is willing to come to our house and do a session with the family and help me answer all of Remy's questions the right way."

"Are you saying I should be there?" Rachel asked.

"No!"

It came out too strong, almost angry, and caused a shocked silence to radiate through the room. And, in that silence, Anne's phone rang.

She slipped it out of her sweater pocket and saw it was Janie calling.

"Uh-oh," she said, and touched the screen to pick up the call. "Honey, what's up? Are you all right?"

"No. You have to come pick us up." Janie was clearly crying. "The school got this anonymous call that somebody here has a gun. It might not be true, but we all had to get out while they search the school, but if it's true then the kid with the gun might be out on the front lawn with us, and there are police everywhere, and Mom, I just really want to come home."

"Okay. I'll be right there. Tell you what. Is Peter with you?"

"Yeah. He's right here. We stayed together."

"Good girl. The two of you start walking toward home, and I'll come get you."

"Thanks, Mom."

Her daughter clicked off the call.

"What's wrong with Janie?" Remy asked.

"She's just scared and wants to come home. Rachel, I'm so sorry to do this to you again, but I have to go get them. I'm sorry if I've been a little short with you this morning, but I appreciate your being here, because I can't leave Remy alone. Just . . . no more talking to him about this, okay? We need to talk about it in therapy."

"No problem. Everybody's upset. Just go."

"You can leave me alone," Remy said.

It was a quiet sentence, and Anne was already up and headed away from the table when he said it. But it stopped her.

"No, I really can't," she said. "You're only eight. That wouldn't be right at all."

"I've been alone a lot."

It was the kind of sentence that could have echoed around in her, resonating for days, if she'd had the luxury of enough time to be stunned.

"Well, you shouldn't have been," Anne said. "That never should have happened to you, and if I have anything to say about it, it's not going to happen again."

—

Anne sat on the end of the living room couch with Janie and Peter on her left, Remy in his wheelchair on her right. Dr. Klausner sat in the recliner across from them.

"It was good of you to do this," Anne said, "especially on such short notice."

"As luck would have it," he said, "I got two last-minute cancellations. Two people who didn't want their sessions today for the same reason you *did*. Parents of high school students."

"Well, it helps us a lot. It's been a very upsetting morning. By the time I got the older kids home we'd heard from the school, and the phone call was just a hoax. Somebody's idea of a cruel prank. But it shook us all up, and I don't want to pretend to Remy that we're not upset. He knows better, anyway. He knows what he feels from us. Understandably, he has a lot of questions, and I don't know if the way I would answer them would be the right way, and I'm sure Janie and Peter could use some tools to put all this in perspective, too."

"Do you mind if we start with Remy?" he asked her older two.

Anne liked the way he talked to them. He seemed to seek their opinions the way he might an adult's. Also he really did wait to be sure they didn't mind.

"What are some of your questions, Remy?"

"How many times does somebody go into a school and just start shooting people?"

"Too often, I'm afraid."

Anne watched the boy's eyes widen.

"Why would somebody do that?"

"The short version," Dr. Klausner said, "is that the shooter is deeply disturbed. Sometimes people snap. It's a hard thing to understand, because we know *we* would never do such a thing, so it's hard to imagine that mindset. I wish I could give you a better answer, but it's not an easily answered question."

"It's okay," Remy said. "It's okay if you don't know that, because the other question is more important anyway. How do you go to school, then? If you know somebody could walk in and start killing people, how do you go?"

Dr. Klausner looked up at Janie and Peter. "You want to take that one on?" he asked.

Peter only laughed bitterly.

Janie actually tried to answer the question. It made Anne's heart swell with love for her daughter.

"I honestly don't know anymore," she said. "I don't know what I would've said if you'd asked me yesterday, because I don't remember yesterday. I don't remember anymore how I used to do it. I guess because it seemed kind of far away, like a thing that could only happen to somebody else. But now . . . today . . . I'm sort of on Remy's team. I mean, how do you do that? It seems impossible. I remember I did it before, but I don't remember how."

Anne reached over and squeezed her daughter's hand.

"I'm going to ask Remy some questions now," Dr. Klausner said. "And I'm hoping his answers will be helpful for all of you. Remy. How was your life before your father sold the house and moved away with you?"

"You mean when I was five and we lived in Pocatello?"

"Yes, if that's where you lived."

"Good," Remy said. "It was good."

"And how was your life living in the wilderness with him?"

"Really, really bad. So bad. I hated it. I hated it the very first day and I hated every single day after that. It was terrible. The worst thing ever."

"And how is your life now with your new foster family?"

"It's . . . good. I mean . . . everything hurts and I'm scared all the time, but I was hurt and scared before I met them, too. But the people are nice. It's good here."

"And, knowing that there've been school shootings all that time . . . when you lived in Pocatello, in the woods with your dad, and where you live now . . . given that the world was the same place, with the same problems, as long as you've been alive . . . doesn't it seem reasonable to say that you just proved that life is better when you live in the world, with other people, in spite of your fear?"

To his credit, Remy seemed to take time to think that over.

"Do you understand the point I'm asking you to see, Remy? It's okay if you don't, or if you need it explained more, or in a different way."

"No, I understand," Remy said. "I mean, I think I do. I think the answer is probably yeah. But the thing is, I don't know how to do that, though."

"The fact that you don't know how to do it right now doesn't mean you can't learn to do it over time."

Again, Remy seemed to think things through. Anne felt as though she could watch him mentally absorb ideas.

"I guess if I can learn to read," Remy said, "I can learn anything. Because that stuff is hard."

———

When her two older children had left the room, Anne addressed the therapist directly.

"I'm wondering if you and Remy could have a talk. With me or without me. Whatever you think is best. He seems dead set on watching the news. And it seems really important to him. And even *I* get upset sometimes watching the news. So I'm not sure if I'm handling that the best way by letting him."

"Okay," Dr. Klausner said. "Why not go ahead and leave us for a few minutes, and we'll discuss that."

Anne rose, feeling the jangling of nerves in her belly, and walked into the kitchen to make a cup of tea. Through the window she saw Janie and Peter shooting hoops together in the driveway. And she was not sure when she had seen such a thing before. If she had ever seen it.

Chris's voice startled her from behind.

"I'll be damned," he said.

"Oh. You scared me."

"Sorry. I'm just not used to seeing them doing stuff together like that."

"I know, right? I was just thinking that. Maybe their horrible day made them feel closer."

"Anything is possible. Where's Remy?"

"He's in the living room talking to Dr. Klausner about watching the news."

Just as she finished the sentence, the doctor stuck his head into the kitchen.

"We're done," he said. "And Remy says to tell you he needs to go to the bathroom."

"I've got that," Chris said.

And he hurried out of the room.

Dr. Klausner sat at her kitchen table. "You know why watching the news is so important to him, right?"

"I think I do," Anne said. "He's trying to figure out if the world is 'regular,' or if it's the way his father thought it was."

"Yes. Just that. He told me that for everything he'd been through—the physical injuries, and the fear and isolation, the grief over losing his parents—he said the very worst part of the whole thing was not knowing about the world. If it was the same world he'd known, or if it had exploded. He said it made him feel crazy. Actually made him doubt what was real. So it's terribly important to him to know. It's a real driving force in his life."

"So we should let him? I worry about what he'll see."

"Remy and I made two deals. One, he'll never watch more than half an hour a day. Two, that if he sees something disturbing, he'll immediately turn off the TV and tell you he needs to talk about it. Always answer his questions. Never censor and never lie. Don't tell him what he sees with his own eyes isn't true. Does that give you a clearer sense of how to move forward?"

"It does," Anne said. "It pretty much underscores my own thinking."

"Don't volunteer more detail than is needed. But never keep anything from him if he asks. Because that's his worst fear—that the world is falling apart but everyone is keeping it from him."

———

When she climbed into bed that night, Chris was already under the covers, reading. A political thriller. It struck her—and oddly, it was the first time it *had* struck her—that he was always already in bed and fully occupied when she got there. If he was looking to foreclose on intimacy of just about any variety, it was working well.

For a few moments she only watched him read. He didn't seem to notice. She needed to talk about the day, so she just started talking.

"You know what she said to me?"

For a few beats he did not reply. Then he set his book open on his stomach and sighed.

"Who?"

"Janie. Should go without saying. She's the only female in the household besides me."

"There's Jasmine."

"Right, and if Jasmine ever says anything to me, you'll be the first to know."

"I give up. What did she say?"

"A couple of hours after therapy she pulled me aside and said, 'Maybe he's right.'"

He frowned, possibly in disapproval, possibly in confusion.

"That's good, though," he said. "Isn't it?"

"How is it good?"

"Well, you want her to value his opinion."

"Did you think she was talking about Dr. Klausner?"

"I did assume that, yes. Who was she talking about?"

"Remy."

"She said maybe Remy is right."

"Yes."

"About . . ."

"About thinking the world is such a scary place that he doesn't get how anybody even goes out of the house. And here's the really bad part, Chris. I'm starting to see his point, too. Hundreds and hundreds of school shootings and we send our kids to school. How do we do that? He wants to know how we can do that, and I want to give him a good answer, but now I'm starting to wonder myself."

"Because . . . what choice do we have?"

"We could homeschool."

"And then what about when they want to go to a mall or a movie theater? Because those places get shot up, too. So we all just hide in the house forever? Because I have some bad news for you about home invasion robberies."

"I know all that," she said. "I'm just having trouble with it today."

"Well, of course you are. *Today.* Six kids and a teacher got killed a few dozen miles down the road. Give it some time. Your attitude is supposed to be rubbing off on Remy. It's not supposed to go the other way around."

Silence.

He reached for his book again, but she had one more thing she wanted to say.

"At some point you'll get in on the therapy, too, right?"

"Absolutely," he said.

It felt encouraging. It buoyed her spirits some.

Until he added, "At some point."

But Dr. Klausner had said there was no need to rush him. That she could give him time to get used to the idea.

She turned off the light on her side of the bed, rolled over, and let it go. The whole day—she just let it go. As best she could, anyway.

7. REMY

Chapter Sixteen

Bang

Remy was at the physical therapy place when it happened.

It had been something like ten weeks, maybe eleven, since the awful thing at the school that scared everybody so much.

It was his sixth physical therapy session over about ten days, and the first five had gone fine, except that they hurt.

His new mom would wheel him from the house to the car, and then help him stand up, and carefully move him over to the car door, and then help him settle into the seat.

It was hard, because he needed to be supported around his torso when somebody tried to help him get somewhere. A person holding his hands or arms didn't work. His left elbow and his right shoulder weren't quite ready to support his whole weight. And then he had those cracked ribs that had just finished healing, and those old broken ones that hadn't healed well. So the supporting arm had to be high, like under his armpits, but not so high that it pressured his right shoulder up. So it was hard. But it was getting a little better. At least he had all that plaster and metal gone, and the infection in his ankle was healed and didn't need to have a drain in it anymore, and that much was good.

Then, when he was in the front seat, she'd put his wheelchair in the trunk and tie the lid down with a strap, because the lid didn't slam with the wheelchair in there. Or sometimes Peter would put the wheelchair in the trunk and strap the lid for her.

Then his mom would put the seat belt across him, because his right shoulder didn't really want to do that diagonal movement across his body to the left.

They would drive away with Janie and Peter in the back seat, and go first to their school to drop them off.

It was scary being out in the world with all the other cars, and the construction going on, and the noise, but this was still Remy's favorite part of the thing, the being outside thing, because if he turned his head and looked over his shoulder at either Janie or Peter or both at once, they would smile at him. So that was good, and something Remy liked.

Still, it was always harder to breathe when they got out at the school and walked up those front steps and inside, because people walked into schools with guns and just started shooting. His new mom seemed to know it scared him, too, because if he looked over at her, she'd be giving him that look like she wished she could fix it for him. But all the people he knew these days seemed to be on his side, so Remy figured if anybody could fix it for him, they probably would have already done it by now.

But back to that specific day. The one in question. The bang day, as he had come to call it in his head.

His mom had wheeled him into the physical therapy place, but then Paulette, his person who worked with him, had gotten him up out of the chair and onto the treadmill. It had bars on both sides to hold on to, but that didn't help Remy much, because if he felt like he was falling, he wouldn't want to try to catch himself with his arms. Paulette had to get on the treadmill with him, and walk right behind him, being careful to step exactly when he stepped, which was hard. The treadmill was only going very slowly.

It hurt to put his weight on his legs, but it more or less worked. They held him. He might have winced, or showed it in his eyes a little, even though he was trying not to. But he never said "ouch" if he could possibly help it, because he liked Paulette and he liked his mom, and he wanted to do a good job for them, even though it felt harder to breathe with his mask on.

And then, just like that, it happened.

It happened so fast that Remy didn't really know what had happened until afterward.

It was just a . . . there was just this big . . . bang!

Then Remy was down on his belly on the treadmill, and Paulette was half falling on top of him, and they were both moving, because the treadmill was still going.

And Remy was screaming. He could hear himself screaming, but he couldn't really feel it, so it was almost like listening to someone else scream, except that Remy knew the sound of his own screaming.

He had a flash of a clear memory in his head. Landing on his hands and knees in a freezing creek because his father had purposely startled him. And the cause of the thing was the same.

Bang!

He could feel Paulette get up from being half on top of him, and the treadmill stopped. Maybe she stopped it. He didn't really think about that. He didn't really think about anything, except in his head he had pictures—like somebody with a gun shooting everybody in the place—so he kept screaming and didn't want to look up.

But there were no more bangs.

After a few seconds of no bangs he took that chance. He fell silent and looked around.

Everybody was staring at him. He could only see their eyes because they were all masked, but those eyes were all on Remy. There were people working with their physical therapists, and some people working at the big machines by themselves. Bicycles and weight machines, and these machines that were like bicycles for your arms. They were mostly older people, and they were staring at him like they'd never seen anything like him before. Like he was some kind of space alien, and like *they* were afraid of *him*, which seemed like a very weird way to react when somebody fires off a gun. Except he looked around and didn't see anybody with a gun. Just an older man with a slightly red face who leaned down and picked up a heavy-looking thick iron disc.

He looked right at Remy and said, "Sorry. I dropped this weight onto that other weight."

Remy realized his heart was pounding. It broke through into his consciousness in that moment. There was no gun, and it was over, so he was able to feel that his heart was hammering so hard that he wasn't sure if he would survive it. Maybe it would just explode.

Slowly the people around him went back to what they had been doing, but a couple of them shot weird glances at him.

They all thought he was crazy.

Remy had never been so utterly humiliated. Not even that time he'd peed his bed at the cabin. Not one other time in his life that he could think of.

Next thing he knew, his mom was on one side of him, and Paulette on the other, and they were helping him roll over and sit up and readjust his mask.

"You okay?" Paulette asked.

He was not okay. He was mortified. And he had hurt his shoulder and his ribs. Somehow he had instinctively thrown his left arm out rather than landing on that bad elbow, but apparently he had landed on his ribs and his right elbow, and it had wrenched his bad shoulder some. How much, he didn't know.

"I'm fine," he said.

Paulette got him back up and onto the treadmill again.

He wanted to go home, but he wasn't willing to say so. Instead he just moved his achy legs, his face burning with shame, while Paulette partly supported him. He didn't once look at his mom's eyes, because if she was ashamed of him, he couldn't bear to see it.

He couldn't tell if he'd actually reinjured his shoulder, or if it would just hurt some for a while and then maybe stop hurting on its own. His mind skittered back and forth from one outcome to the other, trying to judge, trying to decide. He didn't want any more surgeries, so he decided that if he had torn that . . . whatever, that cuff thing, he would simply keep it to himself.

It was one of the worst days of Remy's life, and Remy's life had offered some pretty stiff competition in that regard.

———

They drove home in silence for about half the way.

Then Remy said, "Mom?"

She looked over at him for as long as you can look when you're driving. She had a funny expression on her face. Remy had never seen it before, so he didn't know how to categorize it in his head.

"Is it okay if I call you Mom?"

"Yes. It's nice. I like it."

"But I'm supposed to, right? I mean, it's okay if I'm not supposed to, because I know you're not my mom the same way you're Janie and Peter's mom."

Her forehead furrowed up when he said that. She was gripping her hands on the steering wheel, then letting them go loose again. Gripping, loose. Gripping, loose. Probably because he had humiliated her, which was a hard thing to have to know.

"I'm your mom exactly the way I'm Janie and Peter's mom. I fostered them, and then I adopted them."

"Oh," Remy said. "I didn't know that."

"I'm sorry. I thought you did."

"Not really. I thought they were really yours and I was only sort of yours."

"No, I'm your mom just as much. And I'm glad you feel you can call me that."

"That was why I liked you when I met you. Not the very first time, but the time when I was in that room that was so small and with no windows. That lady in the white clothes opened the door and she said you were my . . . *something* mom. I don't remember the word."

"Foster mom."

"Right. Right. Well, I knew that meant you were sort of my mom and sort of not. I knew you weren't *my* mom—not the one I had at the beginning, I mean, because I remember what she looked like. Actually . . . I used to be able to close my eyes and see her face, but now I can't anymore, but I remember some kind of general things about what she looked like, and if I saw her again, I would definitely know her. But I know I'm not going to see her again. I know that, and I know I'll never see my father again."

He was watching her face as he said all this, and she got a curious look in her eyes when he said that last thing about his father. A confused look, almost.

Remy just kept talking.

"But the thing is, I knew you weren't *my* mom, but you were *a* mom, and you said you *could* be mine, and I really, really, really needed one. So that's why I liked you. That and because you showed me your face. Nobody else at that place showed me their face."

He paused, in case she wanted to say something, but she seemed lost in thought.

"I'm sorry if I'm talking too much. I mean . . . I am. I know I am. I can hear myself doing it. But the thing is, for a really long time I didn't have anybody to talk to, and I missed it. But I'll stop if you want me to."

"You talk as much as you want," she said.

But then, for a full minute or so, he didn't, and neither did she.

Then his mom spoke up. That was nice for a change, because he felt bad about talking too much.

"What did you want to say to me, though?"

"Didn't I say it?"

"I'm not sure. You said 'Mom?' with a question mark at the end. Like you wanted to tell me something. And then we got off into the mom thing and I'm not sure if you ever told me what you wanted to say in the first place."

Remy remembered then, and it made his heart feel as though it were falling down into his stomach.

"Oh. Right. I wanted to *ask* you something. Actually."

"Go ahead."

But they were almost home, so he felt like he needed to talk fast.

"Do you think I'm stupid?"

She kind of . . . stepped on the brake when he said that. Almost as though she hadn't meant to. Like it was one of those things that just sort of did itself. They both rocked forward a little in their seats. Remy was still worried about his shoulder, and his mind kept going back to that, but he tried not to think about it.

"Of course I don't," she said.

Somebody behind them honked his horn, and it made Remy jump and gasp. It made his mom step on the gas again.

They turned the last corner, and he could see their house near the end of the block. They lived on one of those streets with a circle at the end, and it made Remy nervous, because it meant there was only one way out. You know. In case of wildfire. Or society burning itself down to the ground.

She pulled into the driveway, shifted into park, and turned her head to look at him. He wouldn't look back, so she gently took his chin in her fingers and turned his head for him. He tried to look at her nose instead of her eyes because he was so ashamed.

"You had no schooling," she said. "Nobody taught you. It's impossible to know what nobody taught you."

"But that wasn't even really what I meant," he said, still looking at her nose. "I meant do you think it's stupid of me to be so scared all the time? Nobody else is."

"I absolutely do not think that's stupid," she said, and he quickly braved a glance at her eyes. "I think other people just haven't been through what you have. Now come on. Let's get you inside and we'll have a snack."

———

It was after the snack, and Remy was in bed and was supposed to be taking a nap. He usually took a nap after physical therapy because it was so hard.

But Remy had very good ears, and he could hear his mom making a call on the regular phone—the one that was not a cell phone—in the kitchen.

He figured she was calling someone to tell them about Remy's terrible morning, and how hard it was to be his mom. Maybe she was talking to that doctor. The one for people's heads. And that would have been awful enough, but to make matters worse, he heard her say the name Jeannie, which meant she was talking to Lester's mom.

Remy eased himself out of bed and teetered over to the door. His shoulder still hurt, and he was a little tippy walking all on his own, but he had to hear.

He had to.

". . . that thing you said to me," he heard his mom say. He could tell he had missed the beginning of her sentence. "That thing about his heart. His big heart. You said I'd find it again someday. That it was in there somewhere. But I just had to tell you this, Jeannie. I couldn't wait another moment to tell you. I don't have to find it, because it was never lost in the first place. He wasn't wild. He never was. He just wasn't talking to people, so they judged him by what they saw on the outside."

She was quiet for a long time, like Lester's mom was doing the talking.

While he waited to find out if she would say more, Remy could feel his heart get bigger. Or that's how it felt, anyway. Like it was filling up with something. Warm air or water. Swelling up like a balloon, until it took up more room than it was supposed to in his chest. It made it harder to breathe, but Remy didn't care. It was worth it.

When she started talking again, it was just chatty stuff about how the Gaffneys should come for another visit, or maybe she and Remy could come to Pocatello to see them.

Remy carefully put himself back to bed before she could catch him up and walking around by himself.

He fell asleep and napped for a strangely long time.

———

It was night. Early night, but after lights-out for all three kids.

Remy was not asleep. Maybe because he had napped so long during the day. Maybe because he had so much on his mind.

The moon was shining through his window and right onto his face. Into his eyes. It wasn't full, but it was pretty big, and it was an unusually clear night that night, and the moon seemed extra bright to him.

It made him think about his mom again. His first one. He hadn't even realized it out loud in his head, but he had been worried that she wouldn't be with him anymore. That she wouldn't look after him now because he no longer desperately needed her to.

It felt sad to think about that.

He heard a little soft knock on the door. It made his heart beat a little faster because he didn't know who was there. But it was such a polite, quiet thing. It was hard to think too many bad thoughts about it, even for him. He thought about the dogs, who still scared him some, even though he believed in his head that they didn't bite. But he was pretty sure dogs don't knock on the door.

"You can come in," he said.

The door opened a crack, and it was his new mom. He could see the shape of her in the light from the hall. It lit her up from behind.

"Were you asleep?" she asked quietly.

"Not really," he said.

"I thought that might happen. You took such a long nap."

She came into his room, closing the door behind her. She came to his bed, and lay down on the edge of it. He started to move over to give her more room.

"I'm fine," she said.

She reached over and stroked his hair—which had grown out quite a lot—kind of half combing it through her fingers and half petting his head the way you'd pet a dog.

"I want to tell you a secret," she said.

"Okay."

"If you tell it to other people, they might say I'm wrong. But I swear I'm not. I can feel in my gut that I'm not wrong."

"If it's a secret," he said, "then I won't tell anybody."

"It's not that kind of secret. It's a thing that people will try to keep from you, but once you find it out, you don't have a responsibility to keep their secret anymore. It would be better if more people knew."

"Okay. What is it?"

"Everybody's scared."

"Everybody?"

"Yes. Everybody. And almost everybody will tell you they're not. Maybe they don't want you to know, or maybe they don't even know it themselves. But I've been paying attention since I met you. And I'm telling you it's true."

"Even grown-ups?"

"*Especially* grown-ups. Kids mostly sit back and let grown-ups run things because they figure we know what we're doing. But a lot of the time we don't, and that's pretty weird for us."

He lay still for a time, not talking. Just taking that in. It was a lot to take in, but at the same time it was good. And she was still stroking his hair, and that was nice, too. It felt almost like she loved him.

"How do they do such a good job not letting on?" he asked after a time.

"Every strange thing you see everybody do," she said, "that's it. That's the fear. Every time you look at a person and their behavior is a mystery to you, that's their fear. All the rage you see in the world. All the arguments and the wars and the guns. All the loud music and the big monster trucks and the expensive, fancy cars, and the political rallies. That's all the fear that people don't want to admit they have. Every time you see these loud people walking through the world, putting out how they want the world to see them . . . 'Look at me. I'm so beautiful. I'm so smart. I'm so successful. I'm so rich, I'm so powerful. I'm so *right*.' Those are all the things people say because it feels so much safer than telling the truth. And the truth is 'I'm just a human, among billions of other humans, and I'm alive, and it's really hard being alive, and I don't want to admit it, because nobody around me is admitting it, and most of the time I don't know what I'm doing, and I'm scared.' So we all feel that way, but I think most of us don't know it's normal. We walk around thinking we're different from everybody else. Thinking it's just us."

For another minute or two he lay still and digested what she had said. He mostly understood it. Here or there he'd heard words he didn't know, but it didn't seem to matter. A spot in his gut felt it, and that was a kind of understanding. The most important kind, really.

"How can they be scared and not know it? You said before that some people don't even know it themselves."

"Not sure what to tell you on that one, Remy, except that the human brain is complicated. I think if anybody had asked me a few months ago I would have said no, I'm not scared. Not exactly lying, but . . . let's just say if someone had come into my room in the night, when everything was quiet, like I'm doing now, and told me what I just told you, I'm pretty sure I would have said, 'Holy cow, I think you're right.'"

He wanted to thank her for telling him that secret that nobody else was telling anybody—that probably no one else *ever* would have told him if she hadn't. But his words wouldn't seem to come up and out.

"You get some sleep now," she said.

Then she kissed him lightly on the forehead, and she was gone.

The moon stayed with him.

8. ANNE

Chapter Seventeen

Tipping

She sat on the couch in Dr. Klausner's office with Chris. They sat close enough, but not affectionately close. They did not hold hands.

She knew Chris was nervous, even though his face and voice didn't show it, because he quietly and subtly drummed his fingers on the leg of his jeans. Oddly, though, only until he started talking about Remy. Then the nervous gestures fell away.

"You know what he said to me? I don't think I told you this, Anne. Maybe I did. We were watching TV. The news. Kid loves to watch the news. He turned to me, and he straight-out asked me a question. Well. Two questions. First he said, 'Dad?' Then he asked if that's okay—to call me Dad. I said, 'Yeah, of course.' So then he asked me if I'm scared."

It was Anne who spoke up and questioned Chris, though it might have been the doctor's job. But this one was important to her. This was personal.

"What did you tell him?"

"Well, first I asked him a couple of questions just to be sure I was right about what he wanted to know. Like, was I scared when? And did he mean in specific situations? But he meant more like just in general. I thought about it for a minute, and then I said, 'Yeah. I get scared.'"

"That's such a good answer, Chris. Thank you."

"I have no reason to lie to the boy. He's a good little guy, which, face it, nobody saw coming. I mean, his medical needs are a nightmare, but *he's* not. He's just . . ." She really wanted to hear the end of that sentence, but he never finished it. He spun back to his original direction. "So then he asked me what I was afraid of. I said losing the people who mean the most to me, like my family. And losing the *things* that are important to me, like my contracting business. He said, 'But families are more important than contracting businesses,' and I said, 'Yeah, I know that, but the business is how I take care of my family. It's how I support us.'"

She waited to see if he would say more.

When he didn't, she said, "Thank you."

"For what? Supporting us?"

"For giving him an honest answer like that."

Anne turned her eyes to Dr. Klausner, and he met her gaze steadily. She felt as though they were talking in a way that did not include him, and she wasn't sure if that's how he wanted the therapy session to go.

"Can I ask him a question?" she asked.

Dr. Klausner gestured with his hand. Gestured in the direction of her husband as if inviting her to step into a room.

"Talk to your husband," he said. "It's why we're here."

She turned to Chris, and he ever so slightly averted his eyes.

"Why did you agree to take Remy so easily?"

He laughed it off when it first hit. Just pushed a little breathy laughing sound out of his throat as if to throw the question back to her.

"Didn't you want me to?"

"Of course I did. And I'm not being ungrateful. But there was something that didn't quite track about it. We'd had so many conversations about how hard it was going to be on the marriage if I wanted to take in another child. Especially a really difficult one. And then I chose pretty much the most difficult one on the planet, at least as far as we knew then, and you said, 'Sure. Let's do it.' I'm just curious as to where all that other stuff went."

An awkward silence fell in the room. Apparently she had struck some kind of nerve in him, because he did not seem to want to answer the question. Anne knew nobody was going to change the subject, bail him out, or let it pass simply because they found silence uncomfortable. She knew Dr. Klausner, and the way things went in his office.

Maybe Chris didn't know.

He seemed to grow increasingly uneasy with the focus on his silence. After a minute or two, his discomfort grew to the point where he seemed almost to squirm.

"Here's the thing about that, though," he said when he apparently could bear no more. "I was thinking I wasn't going to talk about . . . *that* . . . on the very first session."

It made a little part of Anne's belly go cold. Especially the word "that." There was a "that" there. He had just identified it. And now he didn't seem willing to tell her what "that" was.

They both turned their eyes to Dr. Klausner. To solve the impasse. To act as their referee.

Dr. Klausner cleared his throat and set down his pad and pen.

"I think," he said, "Chris, that once you hint to your spouse that an issue exists . . . that, as the expression goes, there's some '*there* there,' I'm not sure it's fair to say you want to address it at a later date. No one can force you to talk about an issue, of course, and we're not about to try. But please consider whether it's fair to your wife to drop that bomb and then just move along. I should think that would be very uncomfortable for her."

Anne watched her husband's eyes as the doctor essentially sided with her. She could see the moment sink in on his face. She watched him realize he was trapped. Not by her, or by Dr. Klausner, both of whom he was free to defy, but by his own decency and conscience.

She heard a great rush of breath come out of him.

"Okay," he said. "Okay. This is hard. This is weird. Remember a few months ago, before we had Remy, when you asked me if I was having an affair?"

An immediate sense of cold washed over Anne. All of her. As though someone had submerged her in icy water.

"And you were," she said.

"No! No, I was *not*! Absolutely not."

"But . . ."

She knew the "but" was there. She could feel it coming.

"But . . . there was . . . someone. There were . . . you know. Feelings. But they were not acted on."

A long, ringing silence.

She wanted to ask him about his use of the past tense. There *was* someone. There *were* feelings. She wanted some confirmation that he was not simply using the past tense to make the news go down more easily. But if she asked, he might tell her. And, depending on the answer, that might be more than she could stand to know.

"Here's what I don't get," she said, her voice sounding vaguely foreign to her. Maybe because her ears were ringing. "What does this have to do with fostering Remy?"

"Well. Like you said. We'd discussed more than once that it would be a strong test for the marriage. At the very least. That it might just blow everything apart."

Anne felt her jaw drop.

"You said yes because you wanted to blow up the marriage?"

"No! That's not how it was at all. You didn't let me finish."

She glanced at Dr. Klausner, who offered her a miniature shake of his head.

"Let him talk, Anne."

She sat back, feeling her spine thump against the couch. Also feeling more than a little stunned.

"I was not wanting to blow up the marriage," Chris said. "Not at all. I was worried that the marriage wasn't all that strong. I know you felt that, too. Right, Anne? You can't tell me that wasn't a thing we both knew."

He waited. Probably for her to say something. She didn't. She had been told to let him talk.

"Okay. So . . . I kind of . . . wanted to know in that moment if the marriage was going to stand or fall. I didn't *want* it to fall. I wasn't trying to *make* it fall. Just . . . if it was about to fall anyway, I kind of wanted to know. You know. More or less . . . then."

He didn't say, ". . . so I could go be with this other woman while the window of her offer was still open." But it seemed like a reasonable thing for Anne to infer.

"What about you?" he said. "We talked over and over about how another difficult foster could blow up the marriage. And then you go and find a child more difficult than we even knew existed. You trying to tell me *you* weren't trying to tip things one way or the other?"

"No," Anne said. "I wasn't. I took him because he desperately needed taking."

A long and painful silence fell.

"But there was no cheating," Chris said suddenly. "In fact, there never has been. In nineteen years, never. I never once cheated."

She thought maybe she was supposed to thank him for that. It was *something* to be grateful for, in the great scheme of things. But, in that moment, gratitude lay beyond her reach.

"Is that really so wrong?" he asked. "I mean, I know it's not a fun thing to hear. But you *choose* an affair. You don't choose feelings. Things were rocky with us. All I can really do at that point is keep my marriage vows."

"And stress-test the marriage," she said.

"It wasn't a devious sort of thing."

Anne felt herself pull a few long breaths. In through her mouth, for some reason. Maybe she just needed a more spacious airway. Out through her mouth. She could hear the breaths. They sounded like sighs.

"It's a very, very difficult thing to hear," she said. "But I can admit that it was not devious on your part."

"Good answer, Anne," Dr. Klausner said.

"Why is it good?"

"Because you told Chris how you feel, rather than lashing out in anger."

"Oh."

Silence. Anne still had not quite warmed up from her ice water dip.

"So what do we do now?" she asked Chris.

"We go on and have a marriage. We celebrate the fact that Remy turned out to be a blessing instead of a disruption."

"And the family is just supposed to wait while you decide between us and some other life entirely?"

"Oh, no," Chris said. "No. I thought I'd made that clear. I decided a long time ago. I told her I was staying a long time ago. I haven't seen her in months."

"Oh," Anne said. "No, I wasn't sure of that."

"I figured Remy would tip us one way or the other, but . . . I don't know about you, but I think he's brought us closer together. He's made me kind of . . . how should I say this? . . . appreciate why you take on the tough ones. Like, I really see that in a new light now. I feel what that feels like, to really rescue someone. And somehow it seems like when you rescue someone, they always manage to rescue you back. But . . . can I ask you a question? What does it mean to *you* to take on the tough ones? Why do you do it? I'm not saying you shouldn't, I think I made that clear. But what's behind your taking the ones nobody else wants to take?"

"I'm trying to prove that no child is too much," Anne said.

"I'm . . . not entirely sure what that means."

"There's a background to the statement," she said. "And I'll tell you. When we're not on paid time."

———

They drove in silence for most of the way home.

They were in Chris's truck, and he was driving. He was lightly drumming his fingers on the steering wheel. She couldn't hear it. It was too soft. But she could see it in her peripheral vision. It was making her nervous, and she wished he would stop, but it seemed better not to bring it up.

That should be our worst problem, she thought.

He whipped his head unexpectedly in her direction.

"Penny for your thoughts," he said.

It was a quaint old expression, and one she'd never heard him use. She wondered if his mother or his grandmother had used to say it to him, but she didn't ask.

"I was thinking about how weird it is when you sort of know something, like instinctively know it, but then somebody convinces you you're wrong. Or you convince yourself you're wrong. Or both. But then you find out it was just how you thought it was, and you think, 'Yeah, I knew that all along.' But it's two different kinds of knowing. The two things feel different. Knowing instinctively and hearing it out loud feel so different."

"I should never underestimate your instincts," he said.

"It wasn't pure instinct. It was something you said. It wasn't even just that you felt disconnected from the family. I mean, yeah, that did make me wonder. And I did ask. But you said something that tipped your hand. People have a way of tipping their hands. You said something like . . . there's a difference between being distant and actually, physically having sex with someone else. When you said that, I pretty much knew there was someone else but you weren't actually, physically having sex with her. If you listen to people, they'll tell you a lot, even when they don't mean to. And Miri had exactly the same take on it."

"You tell Miri stuff like that?"

"I tell Miri everything. You don't have one single guy friend you talked to about . . . that . . . situation?"

He never answered, which Anne took to mean he did. He probably told Mo about his affair of the heart in detail so excruciating that Anne chose not to imagine it.

"Remy did that recently, too," she said. "Tipped his hand on something. He said something that I think he didn't know was very telling. He said he knew he would never see his mother again, and he knew he would never see his father again. Just like that, one thing right after the other. Like they were the same situation."

"And you take what from this? Just so I'm clear."

"He knows his father is dead. Think about it. If somebody important simply disappeared from your life, and you didn't know what had happened to them, would you say you know you'll never see them again? Wouldn't you always hold out some hope that you would? It's kind of an actual . . . thing. A psychological thing. Did you know that's how parents become suspects in their own kid's disappearance? They call the police to come and find their kid, even though they know they killed their kid. And they say something to the police like 'He was a good boy.' And bam. Just like that, the police start questioning them for murder. Because the parents of a missing child don't talk about them in the past tense. They refuse to. They continue to believe their child will come home. That they'll see them again. They don't talk about them like they're dead. It goes against human nature."

They rode for several miles in silence. In fact, they didn't speak again until he pulled the truck into their driveway.

"If he's genuinely an orphan," Chris said, "it'll certainly smooth the way to adoption. You want to adopt him, right?"

"I would like that very much."

"We'll get through this," he said. "Right?"

"I hope so," Anne said. "But right now I can't really think in those terms. I need to digest this. I need to feel what I feel about it. Just for the moment you need to leave me alone."

He opened his mouth to speak. She beat him to it.

"About this particular thing, I mean. I don't mean leave me alone in general. That's where we've been for months."

"I knew what you meant."

"I don't want you to think I didn't notice that you kept your marriage vows and didn't cheat. Don't think you're not getting credit for that. Of course that helps. It's the reason I said I hope we'll be okay instead of no, we won't. But it's still this whole big thing for me to work through."

"Understood."

They stepped out of the truck and into the house, where Anne paid the babysitter. Of course, they didn't talk again until she was gone.

Chris was standing by the door, but he didn't lock it behind the woman. Anne figured that meant he was on his way out again.

"I should get back to the job site," he said.

"Sure. Okay."

"Can I ask you a question?"

She sighed inwardly. She was exhausted from the questions, both the ones she had asked and the ones she had answered. But she wanted to hear what remained on his mind.

"I guess," she said, and her exhaustion came through in her voice.

"Are *you* scared?"

"Oh yeah."

"All the time?"

"Pretty much all the time."

"What are you scared of?"

"Sending the kids to school. Or anywhere, really. Days like this."

It seemed to land with a thump on the carpet, that last sentence.

"I'm sorry," he said.

"Marriages have days like this. Life has days like this. That's what makes it all so utterly unnerving."

"I should get back to work," he said.

"I should check on Remy."

He walked out the door. She walked down the hall and stuck her head into his room.

He was lying on his bed, playing with some plastic horses. Acting out little scenes, apparently. Having them interact like a miniature society on his bed.

He looked up when she opened the door, and his face fell.

"What's wrong?" he said.

"Just a tough day."

"You okay?"

"It doesn't really feel that way right now. But I know I *will* be okay."

"Thank you for not saying 'nothing.' Like when you ask somebody what's wrong, because you can see something is, but they say 'nothing.' I hate that."

"Yeah," Anne said. "I hate that, too."

———

She called Miri at work.

"What's up?" Miri asked. "You sound weird."

"I have to fill you in on something," Anne said. "Be prepared to feel like we pay really good attention to signals and clues."

9. REMY

Chapter Eighteen

Go Back

It was around four months later when everything got shaken up again.

It was too bad, Remy thought, because in the meantime he had been happy. Or, at least, he had been *his* version of happy. He knew it might not be quite as good as somebody else's happy, but it felt good to him, and he was more than willing to take it. Looking back, he figured it might have been more what somebody else would call relief.

Remy had no problem with that.

He'd even had a birthday, and turned nine, and his family had baked him a cake with icing and candles, and sung to him. It was so amazing it made him cry, not because he got to blow out candles and rip wrapping paper off presents—although that was nice, too—but because he knew how old he was again. If felt as though he hadn't existed during that other, terrible time, and now he was real again.

And then his new mom got that phone call.

Remy knew there was something bad about it, because she was on that call for a weirdly long time, and he could hear in her voice that it was a thing she found upsetting. But then, when she got off the phone, she didn't want to talk to him about it. And that was not like her. She didn't say she was fine and nothing was wrong, which they had more or less promised each other they would not do. She just said she was going to call Dr. Klausner and see if he could fit them in for a session, and that she would let Remy know what he said, and they could talk more then.

She had never done anything like that before, and it made Remy nervous. Unusually nervous—a sensation that pinged around in his muscles like mild electrical charges.

He looked out the window all morning, and everything seemed calm enough on their little cul-de-sac, as his mom called it. Still, though. Even while he could see that it hadn't reached their house yet, Remy figured it had started.

Somewhere, it had started.

—

At 2:00 in the afternoon they sat in Dr. Klausner's office. Remy could feel that his mom was scared, which made him even more scared than he'd been before, even though the scared he'd been before had felt like maxing out the system.

"There's something I need to talk to you about," his mom said.

The doctor just mostly sat there.

"I know," Remy said, "and I don't get why you didn't just talk. Usually you just talk. Right at home. Right where you are. Right then. I don't get why we had to come all the way over here just to talk about a thing. We never did before."

"I wanted Dr. Klausner's help telling you this," she said, "because I thought it would be something you'd find upsetting."

"It's starting," Remy said. "Isn't it?"

"It's nothing like that," his mom said.

"Somebody called," Remy said.

"Yes. It was a sheriff's deputy."

"I don't know what that is."

"Like a policeman, but not in the city."

The word ripped through Remy's gut like the steel casing of a bullet. And just that fast, too. What would the police want with him? He was afraid of the police.

He opened his mouth, but no words came out. He had been terrified back into the world of silence.

"So here's what I need to tell you," his mom said, "and I'm afraid it's not good news at all. There were some hunters poking around on the very northern end of the state. Just a few dozen miles south of the Canadian border. They were looking for elk. But they stumbled on something very different. They found some . . . human . . . remains."

She stopped. She just waited, watching him. Maybe to see how he was doing so far. Maybe to see if he had questions, or had something to say.

Remy wasn't sure about those last two words. He opened his mouth to ask more about that, but his words were still gone.

"Do you know what I mean by 'human remains,' Remy?"

Remy shook his head.

The jolts of electricity in his muscles had actually calmed some, because what she was saying didn't sound as bad as he had feared. It sounded . . . weird. And kind of icky. But she didn't seem to be saying that society was burning itself to the ground, and she'd given no indication that the police were coming for *him*.

It sounded, really, like something unrelated to their family.

"It's what's left behind after a person dies. If the person died recently, it's their body. You know. All of it. Whole and together. But if they died a very long time ago, it might be far less. Maybe just some bones."

She waited. But Remy had nothing to add.

"So the hunters reported it, and that brought the sheriff in. The sheriff pretty much knew who it must be, because the property was in your father's name. But they were able to use dental records to find out for sure who it was who died. And it turned out it was your father. Not your new father," she added quickly.

But Remy already knew who she meant.

The electric tingles and knives were completely gone now. In their place, Remy felt absolutely nothing. There was no sensation in his body. It felt as though it had been carved from stone. Heavy and solid like that. And his mind felt silky calm, but in a dark, unpleasant way, like something you couldn't see through even if you tried.

"Remy," his mom said, "did you know your father had died?"

Remy tried to please her by going into his mind, his memories. But there was nothing there. And it wasn't only that he could find nothing about his father. There was nothing there at all. His brain seemed to have fallen asleep and there was no real way to search it, and no apparent purpose for trying.

He shot his mom what might have been a desperate glance and shrugged slightly.

"Okay," she said. "Not important for now. Here's what's important. The police are concerned about *how* he died. You know. Of what. It's hard for them to know much, because it happened so long ago, but there are a couple parts of the scene they found that make them worry about foul play. Do you know what 'foul play' means, Remy?"

He shook his head slightly. He wouldn't have known the term on any day, but on that day he knew nothing. Nothing connected up with anything in his mind. Even if something was in there, it could not be successfully found.

"It means when somebody does something they shouldn't have done. Oh, but that's not a very good explanation, is it, Dr. Klausner?"

"I think," Dr. Klausner said, "that inexact or confusing terms won't help this go down more easily, even though I understand why they're a temptation. As gently as you reasonably can, just tell Remy what they think happened."

"The police are worried that someone might have . . . hurt him . . ." She paused. Glanced at the doctor again. "Killed him. Because they found what looked like a shallow grave that somebody had dug. It looked like somebody had tried to bury his body but then maybe got interrupted or scared away and left everything just the way it was."

Something fired in Remy's brain. But it was just a flash of a second. It was gone so fast that he literally didn't know what it had been. He found himself reaching for it, the way he might reach for a dream in the morning while it slipped out of his mental grasp—knowing it was something, and that it was interesting, and so close. So frustratingly beyond his reach. But it would not come back. There remained only a blank confusion in its wake.

"Here's the thing I really need to talk to you about," his mom said. "The police are hoping you might come out there, and look at the spot where they found him, and see if there's anything at all you can remember. I told them you don't remember, and they understand that. But they just think . . . and I don't entirely disagree with them . . . that if you actually were to go back to that place, it might jog some memories. But only if you feel like you can."

"Go back?" Remy said.

Then he felt surprised, because he hadn't known his words were there with him again. The request seemed to have scared a couple out of him.

"I'm not going to force you," she said. "If I have to, I'll tell the police we just refuse. That you're too emotionally fragile. Do you know what 'fragile' means?"

Remy shook his head.

"Easily broken."

Remy felt his forehead furrow up when she said that. It felt like his eyebrows were trying to get closer down to his eyes. It was the first sensation he had felt from his body since this conversation had drilled down to its core.

He was not easily broken. He was the least easily broken person he knew. He had starved in the wilderness by himself, and it hadn't broken him, at least not permanently. His body had been broken in every imaginable way, and still he came struggling back. How could anyone think he was fragile?

It made him a little mad. No, a lot mad. He was strong, and everybody should have known it. Everybody should have been giving him credit for being hard to break.

"I can go back," he said.

His new mom and the doctor just looked at each other for what felt like a long time. Then his mom asked if he wouldn't mind waiting in the outer office for a few minutes, until it was time to go.

Remy did what was asked of him, but he didn't sit down in one of the comfy leather chairs out there. He stood by the door, on the oddly soft carpet, so he could hear.

He wanted to know if they were giving him credit for being hard to break.

"I'm not sure what to do," he heard his mom say. "How do I know if this is a mistake?"

"This is one of those situations where you can't know the outcome going in. Actually, all of life is full of those situations where you can't know the outcome going in. But here's my opinion on the matter. If he had said he wasn't sure he could do it, I'd say take his word for it. But he says he can. So I'm not sure who we think we are to say, 'No, you're wrong. You can't.'"

Remy wasn't sure he understood all that, but it sounded like the doctor was giving Remy credit for at least knowing if he was strong or not.

But then the doctor added, "That sedative they gave you when you first took him home from the hospital? Have it in your purse. Just in case we're making a bad call."

———

They left in the morning, after driving Janie and Peter to school.

There had been some talk about them taking the day off school, and maybe his dad taking the day off work, and everybody going along for extra support. He'd been in his room when his new mom and dad had talked about this, but he'd heard them.

But Peter had football practice after school, with the most important game of the year that weekend, and if he was going to stay home, then Dad had to stay home, so there would be someone to look after him that night, and besides, he was busy at work. And by the time it was all said and done it was just Remy and his mom going, and that felt oddly okay. He liked them all, but so long as his mom was there, everything was pretty okay.

They drove for hours. *Hours.*

In fact, they drove for so many hours that Remy started wondering how they were going to get home on the same day. Maybe they weren't. Maybe they would have to sleep over a night and then go home. Remy hoped they didn't have to stay in the cabin. He never wanted to go inside that awful place again.

It was already coming on to winter, and although it hadn't snowed much, it was cold. A few fine flakes of dry powder seemed to drift onto the windshield of the car here and there as they drove.

Remy hadn't been outside Boise since coming home from the hospital. In a way, that made it scary. In another way, he liked it, because everywhere they drove, everything was regular. And, right up until that moment, Remy had not entirely believed it wasn't starting. Somewhere.

"So was he really wrong?" Remy asked his mom.

"Your dad?"

"Yeah."

"Well. Honey. I don't like to speak ill of the dead. But, like I said before, I think he was mostly wrong, yes. I've told you before that some of the things he was afraid of are real. But I think he put too much weight on them. I think he was afraid of the wrong things, and I think he was wrong to take a five-year-old child into such a harsh environment, especially if his health was any concern at all."

"I didn't understand all of that," Remy said. "But tell me what he should have been afraid of instead."

"Maybe the combination of cigarette smoking and heart disease, which are two bad things to put together. Maybe whether or not he could take care of you properly out in the middle of nowhere like that."

"Oh," Remy said. "What was he right about? You said *mostly* wrong."

"Well," she said, "that gets into some complicated territory."

"Not following," Remy said.

Still, he loved the way she talked to him. He loved *that* she talked to him. It was like birthday parties. It made him feel like he really, truly existed.

They had been driving through national forest land almost from the start, but on a real highway that still felt like society. Like a place where people really lived. Cars would pass them going the other way, or pass them from behind, and there were little towns all along the way with fast food places and gas stations. It didn't feel like where he used to live with his father yet. But he could feel it hanging over his head that it would, in time.

Probably that's why he was talking so much.

"I'll explain it to you the best way I can," she said. "But I have to be honest and say I don't really understand it fully myself. But I'll try. Your father thought the world was about to collapse. That everybody was about to start killing and enslaving everybody else. And you can see with your own eyes that it hasn't happened. But there is such a thing as war, and I can't absolutely promise you that we won't have one. I can just encourage you to live your life as though we won't, because we probably won't. But I can't make you any guarantees.

"I can give you an example. Dogs. That's a good example. When we met you, you were terrified of dogs, because your only experience with dogs was with the ones that chased you and bit you. Now you know Plato and Jasmine, and even if they still make you a little uneasy, you know they won't bite you. And I like that you're not as scared of dogs as you used to be, but I wouldn't want you walking right up to every dog you see and trying to pet them, because some dogs do bite. Here's another example. When you were living in the woods over that little town, you could have asked the people there for help. They wanted to help you."

"They did?"

"Yeah. They did. There was an older woman there who wanted to help you. She kept calling Child and Family Services to see if they could find you and get you a social worker. But they couldn't find you."

"That must have been the lady who left me the water."

"Yes, I think so, too."

"But the old guy in that store. He didn't want to help me. He hated me."

"He hated having somebody steal from his store. But he didn't want to hurt you. He wanted you to be with a social worker, too."

"Oh," Remy said. "I thought they would kill me. I mean, I thought maybe they would help me and maybe they would kill me, and I couldn't figure out which was true."

The drive was taking them into more and more remote areas of forest, and Remy was feeling increasingly uncomfortable. It made it hard to sit still.

"What was this supposed to have to do with whether my dad was right?" he asked his mom. Because talking was better at a time like that. The more talking, the better. "I sort of lost track of what we were talking about."

"I'm sure your father would have told you not to talk to strangers."

"He did. Especially if they were anybody official."

"See, now I would tell you just the opposite. I would tell you if you were in trouble to go to a police officer, but maybe not just a random stranger. But, anyway, here's the point I'm trying to make. He was right to tell you not to talk to strangers. Anybody in their right mind would teach their kid not to talk to strangers, because now and then a stranger can be terribly dangerous for a child. So I'm not going to tell you, 'No, that was wrong.' What I'm going to tell you is . . . that was *too much* fear of strangers. If you're in that much danger, the stranger would have been the better bet. There's such a thing as too much fear, but there's also not enough fear, and somehow we have to find the right spot in the middle."

"How?"

"Well, see . . . that's where it gets tricky."

"You're not going to tell me?"

"I'm not sure I know *how* to tell you. I'm not sure I even know how to do it myself. I don't know if the spot I find for my own self—you know, between too much fear and too little fear—is right. That's why I thought it would be good to have Dr. Klausner. I thought maybe he could help us with that. But, honestly, I don't even think *he* has any set answer for that. I think it's one of those things . . . you just walk the best line you can with it, all your life."

Remy wanted to think about that, but he couldn't think. His brain was doing that thing again—feeling dark and smooth, and very still, like the surface of a pond. But you can break the surface of a pond and go underneath it. This surface resisted breaking.

They drove quietly for a few minutes. It was snowing harder now, the kind of snow that settles on the ground and sticks. The snow on the road was slushy and dark from having been driven through by other cars, but on either side of the road it was a few inches deep.

Then Remy said, "Mom? This is scaring me. To go back."

"I know, honey. If it gets to be too much, tell me."

"How do I know what's too much?"

"I . . . don't know. Just keep me posted on how you're feeling, okay? And we'll see."

—

They pulled into a gas station in Coeur d'Alene. His mom stepped out and filled up the tank.

It was snowing so hard that Remy could barely see her. There was snow on the car windows and snow between the car and her, and she was just a shape in all that white.

When she stepped back inside, she had snow on her eyelashes and her hair, and she had to shake it off her coat.

He expected her to start up the car and drive again, but she didn't. She took her cell phone out of her pocket and made a call.

Remy jumped, because he could hear the ringing through the car's speakers.

"Johnson," he heard a big, deep man's voice say.

"Oh, good," his mom said. "You're there. This is Anne Sebastian. I'm with my son Remy. We made it as far as Coeur d'Alene, but I've got to tell you, I'm worried about going any farther. We've been driving for hours, so I don't want to just put the whole thing off to another day. I don't really know what to do. I'm kicking myself for not bringing my husband's four-wheel-drive truck. I'm kicking myself for not checking the weather reports farther north. No snow in Boise, and none in the forecast as far as I know. I have chains in the trunk, but my husband is much better at putting them on than I am. Maybe here in the city I could find someone to put them on for a fee. I have to be honest, though. It doesn't feel right to go farther. It doesn't feel safe."

Then Remy felt better, because they weren't going to go. And also, he noticed that it was quite a stream of words that had just come out of her. That was interesting, he thought, because maybe she preferred a lot of talking, too, when she was scared.

The officer's big, deep voice made him jump.

"No problem, Mrs. Sebastian. No trouble at all. The last thing we want to do is put you two in danger. You're doing us a huge favor, helping us get this one off our books. You just tell me where you are. Find a safe place to park your vehicle, and we'll come to you and your son. We have the proper equipment, and we'll get you up there safely."

She told him the name of the gas station, but said she couldn't tell him the name of the street it was on, because she couldn't see the sign through all that snow. He said that was okay, he knew where it was.

When she hung up the phone, Remy said, "Oh. We're still going, huh?"

And she said, "Yeah. I'm sorry about that."

———

They stepped out of the car when Johnson finally showed up for them, and stood there in all that swirling snow. To Remy he looked like a mountain of a man. More than a full head taller than his pretty-tall mom, with broad shoulders, and close-cropped blond hair. He didn't have a hat on, either. He just stood there, collecting snow on his head.

His mom shook the officer's hand, which Remy thought was encouraging, because *she* wasn't afraid of him. He started to reach a hand out to Remy to shake, but Remy took a step back and ducked halfway behind his mom.

"My son is afraid of law officers," she said. "I hope you won't take that personally."

"I won't," he said, "under one condition: that you tell me it wasn't you teaching him to feel that way."

"That was his father."

Then they all just stood there getting snowed on for a few seconds. As though life were something like snow—just too awkward and difficult to plow through.

"His father was a survivalist," his mom said.

"Oh," the officer said. But it sounded like a much longer word the way he said it. "Well, that really just explains so much. You two dressed warm enough? We're not going to be in an SUV with the heater running the whole time."

"I brought some heavy parkas for after dark. I didn't figure we'd make it back to Boise tonight. They're in the trunk."

"Best go get them," the officer said.

He waited until she had them, then walked Remy and his mom to his big sheriff's vehicle. It was one of those utility vehicles that people use for off-roading, and its loud, beefy engine was running. It had huge, knobby tires—almost like the tires you'd see on a tractor—and it was very high off the ground. He opened the back door for them, and his mom helped him up and inside.

"You want me to put a mask on while we're in the vehicle?" the officer asked, climbing into the front.

"Not if you're vaccinated."

"That I am. Seat belts," he added.

"On it," Remy's mom said.

She had already buckled his seat belt and was working on her own.

"We're going to go by the station first. We've got a plow that's going to go up that forest road with us, and my partner has a flatbed truck with two snowmobiles on the back. We have a snowcat, but I'm sorry. It's off looking for a couple of missing hikers. It'd be a lot more comfortable than flying down that dirt road with the wind in our hair, but we can only work with what we've got."

—

Remy knew the intersection of the forest road and the private dirt road that led up to the cabin. He would have recognized it anywhere. The road itself was covered with snow, but Remy had seen it that way many times. There were two trees with curved mirrors on them, so his father wouldn't get creamed taking his truck out onto the paved forest road, on the rare occasions he did. They'd been put there by the previous owner, so far as Remy knew. Then again, his dad had done a lot of work in secret, so it was hard to be sure.

They were spotted with snow, but still there.

All the officers knew it was the right road, too. The snowplow in front of them stopped. The SUV they were riding in stopped. The flat-bed truck with the snowmobiles pulled up behind them.

Remy squeezed his mom's hand, hard. She squeezed back.

They stepped out into the eye-searing afternoon sun.

The snow had stopped falling, but it was deep. They stood in the plowed road, waiting for the two officers behind them to unload the snowmobiles. It took a while. They had to set up ramps and carefully back the snowmobiles down to the plowed tarmac.

Johnson just stood there in the road with Remy and his mom. He leaned over so his face was just a little closer down toward Remy. Remy instinctively moved one step closer to his mom.

"You lived here with your dad, son?"

"Yes, sir," Remy said.

"How long?"

"I don't really know, sir. Felt like a long time. More than one winter. I know that."

"How old were you when he brought you up here?"

"Five."

"How old are you now?"

"Nine."

He looked over at Remy's mom and clucked his tongue.

Remy moved to the other side of the paved road, because it was farther from the cabin. Farther from his past.

The officer was talking to his mom, and he seemed to think Remy couldn't hear him. Remy had really good ears, and nobody seemed to get that.

"See, now *that* I don't get. Even knowing what you told me about the man back in Coeur d'Alene. I mean, he had a kid. You don't have kids, fine. Do what you want. But five is awful young for a place like this. Wild animals and bitter cold and no help if something comes up. No friends, no community for a kid, no way to communicate with anybody. No school. I got a seven-year-old and I wouldn't even bring him up here on a camping trip. I mean, not without this fine support team." He nodded toward the snowmobiles, which were being driven their way. "Freddy, you stay back here on the road, okay? Make sure if anybody's brave or crazy enough to come along, that they can get by all this. Mike and I'll drive the snowmobiles the rest of the way. The boy and his foster mom'll ride on the back with me."

The guy he figured was Freddy stepped off his vehicle.

The guy he figured was Mike said, "Wouldn't they be more comfortable one of each behind us? So they don't have to double up on that little seat?"

"I think the boy would be most comfortable with his mom," Officer Johnson said.

He turned and gave Remy a little knowing wink, and Remy decided it was possible that his father had been wrong about official people, in addition to everything else he'd been wrong about. Or, anyway, at least mostly wrong. And not just because the officer let him stay with his mom or because he winked at Remy. Mostly because he said out loud that Remy should never have been asked to live here.

———

"This is our first stop," the officer said, shouting to be heard over the wind and the engine roars.

He pulled the snowmobile off to the side of the road, and cut the engine.

The edges of the dirt road had been marked with long, flexible sticks with reflectors on top, which Remy thought was good. Because with all that snow, it would be easy to drive right off the edge of that road without meaning to. And running a vehicle off the road was no joke. The knowledge of that still lived in Remy's gut.

Remy and his mom stepped off into the snow and followed the officer to the edge of the road.

They stood together, looking down over the spot where Remy had crashed the truck. Remy could make out the huge lump of the truck under all that snow. It appeared to be just as he had left it—on its side, and utterly ruined. If he hadn't known the spot, though, he might not have known the lump was a truck. A stranger to the situation might not have known.

"We want to ask you what you know about this, son. But I think Mike and I'll need to go down and knock some snow off it, so you can see what it is we're asking about."

Remy felt cold all over, but somehow it didn't feel like the kind of cold that came from the weather outside. It felt like it had started inside his core and was radiating outward.

"I know what it is," Remy said.

He could hear himself talking, but he couldn't quite feel it, and in a strange way it felt like a surprise. Just the idea that he could look down on this wreckage of his past—literally and figuratively—and still talk. Of course, he didn't think it out in those words, or really any words. Instead it was all feeling. As though he were floating over his own right shoulder, looking down at this kid and wondering what anything so awful must feel like, and how he was functioning through it.

"You do?"

"Yes, sir. It's my father's truck."

"Yes. Correct. That's exactly what it is. When we first found it there was no snow, and we ran the plates, and it's registered to your father. And, I have to say, it's one of the things that got us thinking about the possibility of foul play. It gives us the impression that maybe somebody was trying to tear out of here real fast. So, if you know, son . . . do you have any idea how this truck got crashed?"

Once again Remy looked down on himself with curiosity, and with almost a sense of admiration. Because this little boy underneath him seemed so calm, and he was still talking.

"*I* crashed the truck," Remy said.

"*You* did."

"Yes, sir."

"When you were five?"

"No, sir. I was older than that, but I don't know how old I was."

"Why did you try to drive the truck?"

"I didn't know what else to do."

That just seemed to hang in the clear, diamond-crisp air for a moment. Remy thought he saw the officer exchange a glance with his mom.

"So your dad was already gone by this time."

"Yes, sir," he said. Or, at least, the boy underneath the spot where he hovered said that. "I wanted to drive to Pocatello. I knew I couldn't really drive that far, but I figured I could drive someplace, and anyplace was better than here alone, and anyway, sooner or later I'd run out of supplies. But I couldn't really see over the dashboard, and I couldn't really reach the pedals, and I was going around this curve, and it started to go off the road, and I tried to stomp on the brake but it turned out to be the gas. I'd never driven anything like a truck before."

The officer seemed to stall there, waiting to see if there was more. He pulled in a deep breath that Remy could hear. When he blew it out again, it was a frozen cloud.

"What'd you do then? Walk to the road?"

"No, sir. I couldn't, because I broke my leg in the accident. I had to just get myself back to the cabin and stay until it healed."

The officer exchanged a look with his mom again, who nodded.

"Yes," she said. "True. He had a badly broken femur that had never seen any medical attention. It had to be rebroken and set properly when he finally landed in the hospital."

"So you lived here all by yourself with a broken leg."

"Yes, sir."

"That's a lot for a boy that age to have to do."

"Yes, sir."

"Well. Okay. That solves that mystery. Let's move this show along."

———

When the cabin came into view, Remy started to yell. But mostly to be heard over the sound of the snowmobile engines and the wind.

"Don't stop there! I don't want to see that cabin again! I won't go in! It's the worst place in the world, so don't even stop! Don't make me go in! I won't! I'll do anything you want except that!"

The snowmobile kept going.

It swung to the left of the cabin and started up the hill, between trees. The drive was marked with sticks, the same way the road was. But this was not a road. It was more or less the path his father had taken to go hunting.

The trees had deep drifts of snow on their branches, and the sun was warming them. Now and then a drift would just sort of collapse, and it would be snowing, but only for a few seconds, and only right under that tree.

Then Remy was floating over the snowmobile, looking down at himself—at the part of himself that was still on the seat, which he'd used to think of as all of him.

They came over the crest, and he saw the creek, its running water sparkling in the bright afternoon sun. It had ice over parts of it, and drifts of snow on the branches of its downed trees, but the water flowed underneath it, because it refused to hold still long enough to freeze.

If you don't want to freeze, you have to keep moving. Some things you learn and never forget.

They pulled into the clearing, and the snowmobiles stopped. Their engines fell silent.

It was the clearing that Remy had memorized. He had memorized every tree, every slope of the ground, so he would know never to come back here again. And now, here he was.

He wanted to know how he felt about that, but he couldn't tell.

For a second or two, he was no longer over his own shoulder. He was inside himself, and his head filled with an image. He saw himself down on his knees, tugging and pulling at his father's huge, rigid body. But the big man never budged an inch.

Then he was above himself again, and the boy underneath him was crying, but not with any sound.

The snow had fallen evenly all over, about a foot deep. So there was snow in the shallow grave, but he could still see the shape of it.

"*I* dug the grave," the boy below him said.

No one said anything. They just waited. Maybe to see if there was more.

And there was. Much more.

"He went off hunting, and he didn't come back all day and all night, so in the morning I went out looking for him. I found him in this clearing. He had a deer with its feet tied, and he must've been trying to drag it home. They were both stiff. I tried to dig a grave for him because I didn't want the animals to get him. But I couldn't move him over into it. He was too heavy."

A perfect silence fell. It felt perfect to Remy because he was utterly detached from the scene. And there was something strangely pure about being nowhere. It felt safe.

"I'm sorry I didn't tell you this sooner," Remy heard himself say. "But I honestly couldn't remember."

He saw his mom reach over and put a hand on his shoulder, but he couldn't feel the hand. He was completely and utterly numb.

At the corner of his eye he saw the officer cross himself the way Lester's family did in church.

"Son," the man said, "on behalf of the world and all of humankind, I apologize for the hell you had to go through in your short life so far. I have no idea why so much gets dumped on any one person, especially just a little slip of a child, but, damn, boy. That's a tough row you had to hoe."

He breathed clouds of steam into the clearing for another few seconds. Then he seemed to rouse himself, as if waking from a nap. He glanced behind him at his partner, Mike.

"Welp," he said, "that closes this case, all right, and I can't thank you two enough for coming all this way."

They rode back through the freezing afternoon in silence.

10. ANNE

Chapter Nineteen

Breakdown

"I *did* tell you on the phone that Roy Blake had a heart condition," Anne said.

"You did indeed," the officer said. "And so did the Gaffneys. And I believed you both. But you can have a heart condition and still meet with foul play, so we had to be sure."

They were standing outside her car in Coeur d'Alene. Remy was belted into the passenger seat. She turned her head to check on him. He was leaning forward in a weird way, as if that would get him back to Boise faster.

Johnson's big SUV idled close behind him, making it slightly harder to be heard. Her car's engine was running, too, albeit more quietly, to keep everything warmed up in its engine, and inside.

"Couple other things before you go," he said. "He owns that land."

"Who does?"

"The boy, unless Roy Blake had other kin. We sure couldn't find any. Even if he has a greedy cousin somewhere, that's his son. That's a pretty direct relation."

"I doubt he wants it."

"I was thinking more like, get a lawyer. Clear the title. Sell it, and put the money in a trust for his future. That's a 175-acre parcel, so that might be a college education right there. And there's not a lot of private land up here. Mostly national forest and American Indian reservation."

"You sure *anybody* would want it?"

He cracked a crooked, ironic smile.

"Oh, I expect you could sell it to a survivalist," he said.

Anne shook her head, but might have smiled in spite of herself. She turned to open her driver's side door, but the man had more to say.

"One last thing. We searched the cabin up and down. Let me tell you, there was not much in there. There was a big tent, probably used for supplies, but that was picked clean except for some bear canisters and shelving. But we found this under one of the mattresses."

He reached over and opened the passenger door of his SUV. He popped the glove compartment open and handed Anne a dog-eared five-by-seven photo of a woman.

She was wearing a polka-dot dress. She looked to be in her thirties, with long red hair and fair skin, and a faint, tentative smile that struck Anne as simultaneously hopeful and afraid.

"His mother?" the officer asked.

"I don't know," she said. "But *he* will."

She opened the door of her car and leaned in, handing the photo to Remy. He took it in both hands and stared at it for what felt like a long time.

That was the moment when the child broke.

Anne wasn't surprised. In fact, she had been waiting for it. Expecting it far sooner. But in that moment it arrived, and it was a bigger storm than anything she had seen coming.

At first she thought he had simply begun to rock, which didn't seem especially alarming. There was surely nothing wrong with self-soothing at a moment like that. The first time his forehead hit the dashboard she thought it was a mistake. She thought he'd judge the distance better on the next rock.

The third time his head hit, she was in the driver's seat, trying to stop it.

He was surprisingly strong.

She wrapped him up in her arms and tried to keep him from rocking forward at all. It more or less worked. He froze for a second or two, and she thought it was over. Then he slammed his body sideways, which she had not known to prevent. She heard the sickening crack of his skull hitting the passenger window.

The only way to stop him seemed to be almost lying down on top of him. Pinning him with the weight of her body. His head was smashed against the inside of the car door, his neck at a weird angle. But she didn't dare loosen her grip. And he did not exactly hold still. He seemed unable to do so. He lurched in her arms, over and over again, every muscle in his body taut. It felt something like spasms. Maybe that's what it was.

She pinned him that way for what could have been several minutes. All the muscles in her upper body had begun to tremble with the strain. Even her legs ached from the way she was bracing herself.

Still Remy did not, or could not, give it up.

She heard a knock on the passenger window, and it startled her. And it startled Remy. She could feel it. She looked up to see Johnson just outside the window.

She carefully reached out with one finger and powered it down.

"I figured you'd left," she said. She could hear the breathlessness of the exertion in her own voice.

"I haven't," he said.

"You can go. We'll be okay."

"I'm sorry, but I really can't. Because I'm not at all sure that's the case."

Anne said nothing. Because she really had nothing to say. Nothing helpful seemed to lie within reach.

"I would open this door and try to help you restrain him," Johnson said. "But knowing what I know about him, I'm afraid it might make it worse."

"It would definitely make it worse."

Still the child bucked and strained in her arms, and she wasn't sure how much longer she could overpower him. And she had no idea what would happen after that.

"Here's the thing," the officer said. "A couple things, actually. Thing one, I feel responsible for this. You tried to tell me on the phone that it might be a lot for him, but I wanted you to do it. How am I going to feel if I walk away and he hurts himself?"

"Remy," she said quietly into his ear. "Remy, please. Please try to hold still."

A pause fell in his bucking and thrashing, but it was barely enough time to count to two. He could not seem to control his reactions.

"I talked it over with his therapist," she said. "Remy said he could do it, and we didn't want to forbid him from trying."

Silence, except for the little grunting escapes of breath as Remy fought her to resume bashing his head on something.

"What's the second thing?" she asked the officer, who appeared to be squatting on the passenger side of her car, his face in the open window.

"This is self-harm behavior, and I'm obliged to report self-harm behavior. You know. So nobody ends up getting harmed."

It spread through Anne's mind, with alarming speed, where he was going with this. If she couldn't restrain the child, and keep him from giving himself a concussion, he might have to take Remy away from her. For how long, she didn't know. But even a few hours would be a disaster. He would be strapped to a bed again, surrounded by people who would not show him their faces. He would think "it had started." And she would not be there to help him.

"If you're talking about a 5150," she said, "you have no idea how much damage that could do." She purposely used the number code for a three-day psychiatric evaluation, because she knew the child would not understand it.

"Give me another option," he said. "Make me happy."

"They gave me a liquid sedative when I brought him home from the hospital. Because he was just in a panic."

"Where is it now?"

"In my purse."

"Where's your purse?"

"In the back seat."

"All right," he said. "Let's try that."

His face disappeared from the window, and Anne heard one of her rear car doors open.

"Remy," she hissed. "Look at me."

At first, nothing. For several beats, he did not. Then his eyes found hers. He must have been nearing a state of exhaustion. Anne's muscles were on the verge of giving out, and she was nearly twice his size.

She saw a bright light out the open window and glanced up to see that Johnson had turned on the flashlight on his phone, and was using it to study the label on the medication.

She looked back into the boy's eyes.

"I know you didn't want this," she said. "I know it scared you to have the sedative. You said you thought people were drugging you so you couldn't fight back. But this is me, Remy. It's me. You know me. You trust me. If you want to stay with me tonight, I really need you to take this. It's so important to me, Remy. If you're ever going to listen to me and trust me, please do it now."

A hand came through the window holding the little plastic oral syringe. Anne took it from him and looked at it closely. He had filled it with the correct amount of liquid—the number of milliliters indicated on the label.

"Please trust me, Remy. If you take this, it'll quiet you down. And then nothing bad will happen to you. You'll just stay with me, and we'll drive, and then maybe sleep, and then drive some more, and then we'll be home, and it'll all be over."

She fell silent, wondering if she had just lied to the boy. Maybe it wouldn't calm him down enough, and the officer would take him away and commit him to an institution for a few days. And even if that didn't happen, they would get home, and it wouldn't all be over. His mother would still be dead. His body would still have been shattered. He still would have had to unsuccessfully attempt to bury his own father. His trauma would still be real.

They held each other's eyes steadily.

In Anne's head, though she desperately needed to stay positive, were the words *I failed.*

I tried to take on too much. I knew it might be too much. It is. I failed him.

"Please, Remy," she said.

It was a final, desperate try. She was allowing him to see her desperation. Sharing with him that she was helpless. That she couldn't do everything she needed to do.

That she could simply fail.

For a moment, Remy only stared into her eyes. Then he opened his mouth. Surprisingly wide. She squirted the medication onto his tongue. He winced and made a face, not liking the taste.

"Thank you," she breathed.

———

Time went by. The officer did not leave.

Anne had mixed feelings about that. He was there if she needed help. He was also there to call time on her attempts to keep the child with her.

In time she could feel the rigidity in Remy's body soften.

Her own muscles were trembling. Screaming.

What felt like hours later, but was probably fifteen or twenty minutes, she softened her hold on him, because she had to. Nothing happened.

He looked up at her, and his eyes looked filmy and soft as though half-asleep. Anne breathed deeply, and blew the breath out as a loud sigh.

They had survived that moment.

"I'm sorry," he said.

Then he closed his eyes.

———

The officer followed them to a motel. A place he knew. Not fancy, he said, but clean and safe.

It sounded like an easy thing to do. Just drive to this place with him behind her.

It ended up being another chapter in the disaster.

Remy was deeply sedated, and strapped into the passenger seat, but every time another car came toward them Remy reacted disastrously to its headlights. It would bring him thrashing up out of his stupor.

"No!" he screamed, and threw a hand across his eyes as if to save himself from the lights.

Then he would drift back down into his stupor. And the next set of headlights would have him up and shrieking again.

By the time they reached the motel, Anne's nerves felt positively sandpapered.

But as soon as they pulled into the parking lot, and there were no opposing headlights, Remy sank down into unconsciousness and stayed there.

Before she got out of the car, Anne noticed the picture of Remy's mother. It was lying under his dangling feet on the passenger-side floor. She retrieved it, and tucked it into her wallet, to save it for some future date when it might feel right to offer it back to Remy. Though the wisdom of when she should give it back to him lay well beyond her reach that night.

———

They masked up, and the officer hauled Remy in a fireman's carry into the lobby, because it didn't matter who carried him. The boy was entirely out. Exhaustion and sedation had overtaken him, and he hung like limp fabric over Johnson's shoulder.

She opened her purse at the desk, but he waved her away.

"This is on the department," he said to the young male desk clerk. "Because this is one of our star witnesses I have here over my shoulder."

He produced a credit card.

She filled out a form and passed it back to the clerk. He gave her a key card.

"I can take him," she said to the officer.

"No, it's okay. I've got him."

They walked toward the room together. It was on the second floor, and she found herself relieved that he was willing to carry the boy up the stairs. Anne could never remember having felt so exhausted. So utterly drained. Her legs trembled and barely held her, and she didn't know if they were suffering from overuse or fear. Probably both.

She opened the door with her card and stood outside while he gently spread the boy out on the bed. The motel had only had one room left, and it was a room with one king bed. But that was okay. He might wake in the night and she would need to be close.

Johnson joined her outside the open door, in the dark and the cold.

"You must be starving," he said.

"Oh. I forgot to even ask myself about that."

"I'll bring you a burrito from my favorite place, if that sounds good. I'll get him one, too, in case he wakes up hungry. Best burritos in the state, and believe me, I've tried them all."

"I . . . guess I'll take you up on that."

"You want something to drink?"

"Hot tea," she said. "Sometimes when I'm upset, a hot beverage is soothing."

"Oh," he said, and smiled. It seemed weird that anyone in the world could smile that night. "Like that obnoxious smart guy on that TV show."

"I don't . . ."

"Never mind. Not important. World's best burritos and one hot tea coming up."

———

They sat outside in the freezing night. He had hauled two chairs to just outside the room. She had opened the drapes so she could watch Remy through the window.

She hadn't asked why outside, especially in that weather. But she would not have been comfortable with a man in her motel room, and he was probably smart enough to know it.

He had brought a burrito for himself as well, and put one for Remy in the mini-fridge.

They ate together in the cold and the silence for a time.

"Are you staying to make sure he's okay?" she asked after a time.

"No, he's asleep. I'm staying to make sure *you're* okay."

They ate in silence for another few minutes. Anne's nose and fingers went from stinging to numb.

"I'm sure you know this," he said, "but most people wouldn't have taken on that level of trauma in a child."

"Maybe they were on to something," she said.

He smiled a bit ruefully.

"So why did you take him? If you don't mind my asking. I mean, it's a good thing. Speaks volumes about you, and all of it good. I just wondered if there was a 'why' to the thing."

"I took him because I didn't think anybody else would. And he deserved to be taken. He deserved some happiness."

"I believe all kids deserve that," he said. "But I agree this kid was long overdue. The world owes him a few." He wrapped the uneaten half of his burrito in its paper and foil again, and dropped it back into the bag. "Speaking of what kids deserve," he said, "I'd best get home and kiss mine good night."

He rose, and towered over her for a moment.

Then he reached into his wallet and produced a card.

"If you need me," he said. "I wrote my cell phone number on the back while I was waiting for the food to come up. I don't care if it's two in the morning. I'm more than an hour away, but I can get you somebody who can be here in minutes. You'll be okay driving home in the morning?"

"I think I might call my family. Ask them to drive up. My husband can follow us back to Boise, and my other two kids can sit with Remy in the back. Keep him calm."

"I'd call that using your head," he said. "He's lucky to have you, that boy. Don't give up on him. It's not his fault."

"I don't think I *could* give up on him now. He feels too much like my own . . ."

"Good. But I'm sensing there was a 'but' coming. And I talked over it."

And he was right. There had been a "but" coming.

Anne sighed, her breath billowing out visible. Frozen and so visible. Like an arrow pointing at her anxiety—a sigh everyone could see.

"I'm just not sure I'm . . . I might not be enough."

"Not a good enough parent, you mean?"

"Right."

"As opposed to what he had before?"

That just hung in the air for a moment like a frozen sigh.

"Thanks for the new way to look at it."

"Do me one more favor. I don't usually ask this, but maybe drop me a text when you get in. Let me know it all came out okay."

"I will."

He gave her a sort of combination nod and salute, and trotted down the stairs and into the night.

———

She called Chris while Remy slept.

"I have to ask you for a big favor," she said, in place of "hello."

"This is a big ask."

"You two in some kind of trouble up there?"

"Yeah, kind of. Remember how we said he was being really sweet and nice and easy to deal with, but we knew all that trauma was still in there, and it would come to the surface at some point?"

"And this is that point."

"Right."

"Where are you?"

"We're in a motel in Coeur d'Alene. Courtesy of the sheriff's department."

"Oh. That far. You haven't gotten much closer to home. What do you need me to do?"

"I was hoping you could drive up here tomorrow with the kids. I could put them in the back seat with Remy. When he got upset today, he tried to hurt himself. He cracked the passenger window of my new car with his head. I have some of that sedative the hospital gave us. But if he has to be sedated, I'd want someone to really keep an eye on him while I drive. You could follow us back so I'd have another set of adult hands in case of trouble. Like I say, I know it's a big ask. You'd have to take off work. The kids would miss a day of—"

"Honey," he interjected. "Anne."

"What?"

"Tomorrow's Saturday."

"It is?"

She stood holding the phone for a moment, absorbing the extent to which she had lost track of the world. She had known when she'd started driving that morning that it was Friday. But the whole world seemed to have evolved since then. Looking back, it did not seem possible that their trip had begun earlier that morning. She could almost believe it had begun in a previous lifetime, but not that it was still the same day.

"So you'll do it?" she asked him, her voice breathy in her throat.

"Of course we'll do it. Little guy needs help. We're his family. We help."

For a moment, Anne did not answer. She wanted to. She tried to. But she felt overcome.

"So it's true," she said after a time. "You really are all in."

"I really am all in."

"Thank God. Seriously. Thank God, Chris, because right in this moment I'm so aware of how much I bit off with this one. I don't know what I would do if I was in this alone."

"Well, you're not. We'll leave at five and try to get there by noon."

———

Remy woke screaming at 3:00 in the morning.

"Mom!" he bellowed. "Mom! Mom!"

"I'm here, Remy," she said.

It didn't stop him. He just kept screaming it.

"Mom! Mom! Mom!"

Anne turned on the light so he could see she was right there. Someone in the next room pounded on the wall, demanding silence.

"Remy," she said. "I'm here."

But he looked right past her, almost as though he was still asleep, but with his eyes open. They looked blank and unseeing.

"Mom," he said, a little more quietly. "Why did you have to die?"

Anne only lay still for a time, those words ricocheting around in her gut. How foolish she had been to think he would wake up screaming for his mom . . . and mean her.

In time his eyes squinted, reacting to the light. Then they seemed to focus.

"Oh," he said. "You're here."

"Yes, I'm here."

"Why did she have to die?"

"I'm sorry, Remy. I don't know. I wish I did."

"If she hadn't died, we would've stayed in Pocatello and been happy."

"I know," she said.

"I hate that she died."

"I know."

"Are you going to die?"

She opened her mouth to say no. She would not. But she had already told him a couple of things that might not be true. And she was not at all sure that their relationship could afford too many such breaches.

"Someday. Everybody will someday. But not anytime soon. I hope not, anyway. I doubt it. I'm healthy, and I'm careful. But you can never promise something like that."

"I wish you could promise."

"I know."

"Why did you take me?"

"Because you deserved to be taken."

"I didn't think anybody would. I heard the nurses say nobody would."

"They said that to you?"

I'll kill them, she was thinking. She didn't say so out loud.

"Not *to* me. But I heard them. But you took me."

"Yes."

"Are you going to give me back because of tonight?"

"No."

"You sure?"

"Positive."

"You promise?"

"Yes," she said. "*That* I promise."

She was about to try to talk him into another dose of medication. But before she could even broach the subject, he rolled over and apparently fell back asleep.

Chapter Twenty

Normal

Remy seemed to sleep very late. The sun poured through the filmy motel drapes and into his face, and still he did not stir. Anne figured he was exhausted from his ordeal of the previous day.

She glanced obsessively at her phone.

Chris had texted her a link that allowed her to watch her family's progress on the road. A little icon, moving along the highway in their direction. It struck her as a weirdly modern depiction of the old-fashioned cavalry, riding to the rescue.

It was about nine thirty, and her family was already on the section of twisty two-lane highway that touched the Washington border twice. In other words, they were making good time.

She got up to use the bathroom.

When she came back out, she saw that Remy was not asleep at all. He was just lying very still. The sun shone into his eyes, albeit through a thin curtain, but he did not squint or seem to blink. His face showed no expression. If she hadn't known better, she would think he was still heavily sedated. But that medication had to be administered every four hours to be effective. Whatever it was, it was not that.

She crossed to the bed, and settled close to him again, and put one hand on his side. He did not flinch or pull away. Neither did he react positively. He seemed not to be inside himself at all.

He was on his side, faced away from her at the edge of the bed, which is why she hadn't known he was awake.

"You want breakfast?" she asked.

He shook his head faintly.

"Want to get up and take a walk while we're waiting?"

Another soft head shake. Barely there at all.

"I should tell you what we're waiting for," she said.

Nothing.

"Your dad and your brother and sister are going to drive up here, and we're all going to go home together. Your dad will have to be following in the truck, but Janie and Peter will be in the back seat with you, and we can talk and play games all the way home. I thought that would be nice."

Nothing.

"Won't it be?"

Still nothing.

"Should we watch TV while we're waiting?"

That turned out to be the one thing that could get a reaction out of him. He rolled onto his back and nodded slightly.

Anne picked up the remote from the bedside table and found a kids' cartoon program.

Remy stared blankly at the screen for several minutes before speaking for the first time that morning.

"I want to watch the news," he said.

Anne sighed, but quietly. She wanted him to watch less news. But she had agreed to half an hour a day, at the therapist's direction.

She switched to a twenty-four-hour news channel, and they stared at it together.

It was several minutes later when she asked him a question. She wanted to know that he could and would talk to her about his situation. She wanted to press the issue of his willingness to communicate.

She briefly muted the news. He continued to drink in the visuals.

"Remy? Can you tell me anything at all about how you're feeling right now?"

He offered the world's tiniest shrug in reply.

"Please, will you try?"

A long, long silence, during which Anne saw no evidence that he was trying.

Then, in a very small voice, he said, "Ashamed."

She talked at him for the better part of five minutes about why he had no reason to feel ashamed. But he said nothing in reply. In fact, he did nothing to suggest that her words were getting through.

Then they stared at the muted TV together until the family arrived. He never asked her to turn it back up. He never said anything at all.

———

Chris knocked on their motel room door at about a minute to noon.

She crossed to the door and opened it, feeling the relief flow.

"Hey," he said, and leaned in and kissed her on the forehead.

Then he looked past her to Remy. Anne could see the fear on her husband's face. Which was interesting. She had never before known Chris was afraid just by looking at his face, and she didn't know if that meant he was more afraid than usual, or if she'd gotten better at seeing fear. Or both.

"Where are the kids?"

"Downstairs in the truck, running the heater and playing the radio." He walked to the edge of the bed and sat. "Hey, buddy. You doing okay?"

At first Remy showed no reaction at all. He didn't even pry his eyes away from the TV. Just as she was thinking he would literally ignore his new father, he wiggled the fingers of one hand in a tiny wave. It was exactly the way he'd used to acknowledge people when he was freshly arrived from the hospital.

Chris caught her eye.

Then he rose and met her by the door.

"Man," he said. "That sedative really knocks him for a loop."

"He's not *on* any of it," she said.

"Is that a joke?"

"I *so* would not joke about a thing like that. I gave him one dose late yesterday afternoon, after the head-banging incident. It's supposed to wear off in four hours. It's been . . . like . . . I'm not sure. Maybe thirteen hours?"

He looked over his shoulder at the boy again. They stood close together and watched him lie limply on his back, staring in the direction of the screen with eyes that seemed not to focus. Seemed not to see.

"So this is just how he feels right now?"

"Apparently so."

"Oh, well *that* can't be good," Chris said.

———

"We should play the license plate game," Peter said. "Mom. Remember when we went on that family trip to Washington, DC, and we played the license plate game almost all the way there?"

Anne met her son's eyes in the rearview mirror. There was a touch of desperation there. He and Janie were sitting on either side of Remy in the back seat, glancing too often at his face. Anne wanted to return a gaze that was steady and reassuring, but she probably failed. Peter probably saw desperation in her eyes as well. And maybe that was okay. Maybe that was just honest.

They were only a few minutes south of Coeur d'Alene. There was a lot of driving left to go.

"Or punch buggy," Janie said. "I like punch buggy better."

"That's because you really punch," Peter said.

"That's how you're supposed to play it."

"But you punch too hard. You're not supposed to be vicious about it. Remy doesn't need violence right now."

The car fell silent, Peter's reference to violence reverberating. Anne glanced in the mirror again, but Remy showed no reaction. If he was listening, he was doing nothing to let on. Either he was revealing nothing, or there was nothing there to reveal.

"Can't you just be normal?" Peter said to his sister. "Just be normal for this one ride home. Remy needs us to be normal."

And that was when something landed in Anne's head, though it felt like it landed in her gut at exactly the same moment. It might have been a knowing, or some kind of understanding. Or it might have been a false idea. But she had no better ideas—or any other ideas at all—and she had no reason to think they had anything to lose by trying a different approach.

"Or maybe he doesn't," she said, and the inside of the car vibrated in silence for a few beats more. "I asked Remy how he was feeling this morning, and he said he felt ashamed. And last night he wanted me to promise I wasn't going to send him back because he'd had that little . . . episode. I'm not sure, but maybe trying to act like the most normal family possible is not the right way to help him. Maybe he's feeling ashamed because he feels like everybody in the family is okay except him."

She watched his eyes in the rearview mirror as she spoke, flickering her gaze back and forth to the road as needed. For the first time, she saw a hint of reaction in his eyes. A hint of connection. Rather than appearing nearly catatonic, he seemed to be listening.

"Ha!" Peter said. "That's a laugh. That's a good one. Nobody in this family is normal."

"Maybe Dad," Janie said.

"Maybe. But not too much. Not so much that you'd be ashamed to have problems around him. Listen. Remy. You are *not* the only one. Jeez. When she first adopted me, I was a mess. And then when they took Janie . . . holy cow. That was bad."

"Bad how?" Remy asked.

A little spot in Anne's gut jumped hopefully. Because he had spoken. He had voluntarily engaged with the conversation.

"Every way you can imagine," Peter said.

"No, honey," Anne said. "Tell him for real. Tell him details. If you're willing. Whatever you're willing to tell him about your past. It might help him."

"You sure? It's not the happiest subject."

"I know. But it's not like he doesn't know there are bad things in the world. Maybe it would help him to know that you and Janie went through bad times, too. He can see with his own eyes that you're doing better now."

Silence. For a time.

Anne monitored Remy's face in the mirror. He was waiting.

"Details?" Peter asked. "You sure?"

"As much as you're willing."

"I'm not sure he's ready to know what my mom did to me. And also I'm not sure I'm ready to tell him. Yet."

"Okay. That's fair. Maybe just tell him what you were like when we first fostered you."

"Oh, I was a mess. I tried to burn down the garage."

In the mirror, Anne saw Remy's eyebrows lift slightly.

"*Why?*" Remy asked.

"I don't know," Peter said. "I sort of . . . can't remember. It seemed like it made sense at the time, but now I can't remember why I thought so. I just had all this rage. And then I threw a desk at a teacher and got arrested. And Mom and Dad had to come down to the police station and bail me out, and I was on probation for a year. I think they would have put me in juvenile detention, but Mom went in front of a judge and told him everything my mom put me through. You know. My other mom. My first mom. And I guess he felt bad for me and cut me some slack. That was the only time I was ever happy to hear those stories out loud, let me tell you."

"You know, you might be right, Mom," Janie said. "I didn't know Peter back then. I wasn't in the family yet, so I didn't see any of that. Just that Dad was still remodeling the garage, but I didn't know why. And I was a mess, but I thought Peter wasn't. I thought it was just me. So maybe Mom's right. Maybe Remy needs to know it's not just him. Remember I used to steal money from your sock drawer, Mom?"

"That was . . ." Anne paused. A light snow had begun to fall, little dry flakes ticking silently on the windshield. She said a tiny internal prayer that the road would stay open long enough to get home to Boise. "That was fairly minor, honey. You know. Compared to . . ."

"Oh," Janie said. "You mean the cutting." She turned her face to Remy and spoke directly to him. "I used to steal Dad's razor blades out of the bathroom cabinet and make cuts on the inside of my arms with them. And then one time I went too deep, and they had to rush me to the emergency room, and I had to have twenty-two stitches."

"Twenty-seven," Anne said.

She exchanged a glance with her daughter in the mirror. Anne made sure her glance conveyed gratitude. Because her daughter was helping. Even though it required the visibility she despised, and though it forced her to be vulnerable, Janie was helping.

"Okay, twenty-seven. Even worse. And what's really bad is that I told you and Dad it was accidental that I went so deep, but it wasn't really. I never told you that it wasn't really an accident."

"We kind of knew," Anne said.

"Oh. Okay. And then what was really even worse than that, Remy, was . . . even after that, I didn't stop. I just kept cutting myself."

At first Remy did not reply. Anne glanced at him in the mirror. He was looking down at Janie's arms, but they were covered with long sleeves. Janie's arms were always covered with long sleeves.

She tugged a sleeve back and showed him the scars. The network of fine white jagged lines that still cut Anne every time she saw them.

"Why?" Remy asked quietly.

Janie tugged the sleeve back down.

"It's kind of hard to explain," she said. "It's like you hurt so much inside, but nobody can see it and you sort of feel like you can't feel it. Like there's so much of it you don't know what to do with all of it, and like it's trying to get out, but you don't know how to let it out, but then you hurt yourself, and you can see it with your own eyes, and it hurts and you can feel it. I don't know how to explain it any better than that."

A silence fell in the car, and lasted for a mile or so.

"Don't go getting any ideas, though," Janie said to Remy. "I'm not saying it like it worked or anything."

"Don't worry," he said. "I'm so tired of things that have to heal. In a million years I'd never do that."

"Good. And then I wet my bed until I was twelve," Janie added for good measure.

"I wet my bed the first night I was at the cabin," Remy offered. He sounded . . . Anne couldn't quite put her finger on it. As if he was straining. Trying to reach for something.

"Yeah," Janie said. "Okay. But you weren't twelve."

Another silence fell, but this one lasted several miles. The snowflakes continued to tick silently onto her windshield, but they did not threaten to close the highway. At least, not so far. At the corner of her eye, Anne could see the small star-shaped crack Remy's skull had made in her passenger window. She knew these had been stories he could understand on some level, even if he didn't understand them with his conscious mind.

When she looked in the mirror again, Remy was crying. Not full-on breakdown crying. Just tears that welled up in his eyes and spilled down his cheeks, dripping onto his shirt. Peter had an arm around his shoulder from one side, and Janie had an arm around him from the other side. Just the support she had hoped they would be when she asked them to come. If anyone could understand the kind of trauma that bubbles up after you've been delivered to safety, it was these two.

Remy held her eyes in the mirror.

"You?" he asked.

"Me? What about me?"

"What happened to *you*?"

"Nothing as bad as what Janie and Peter just told you."

"What, though?"

So that took an interesting turn, Anne thought.

"Well," she said. "Let's see."

Somehow she had not expected the spotlight to fall on her in that moment. Somehow she had imagined the conversation remaining focused on abused foster children. On the children and not the parent.

"Okay. Well. My father left us when we were pretty young, and my mother told us it was our fault. Like we were just so hard to be around, and we were just too much for him, so he left us. Which was hurtful, and I think it still hurts me to this day, because I still foster and adopt kids that other people think are too much and keep them no matter what. So it's part of me, I guess, and part of why I'm not what you might call perfectly put together. But it's nothing like what you went through."

"I think it's worse," Remy said. "It was hard being with my dad, but at least I knew he wanted me. I feel bad for what you went through."

That just sat on the seats of her new car for a long time as they drove.

Anne made a mental note to call Dr. Klausner first thing Monday morning. For Remy, so they could all go in together, but also for herself. So she could see him alone and tell him that the remnants of her childhood were worse than she had given them credit for being. So she could try to describe for him how it felt to have that pain suddenly and unexpectedly seen. It was not nearly as unpleasant as she might have imagined.

"Punch buggy blue!" Janie shouted, followed by a muffled thump Anne assumed was her punching Peter on the arm.

"Ow!" Peter bellowed. "See? You punch too hard. Nobody wants to play that game with you, because you punch too hard."

And Remy. Remy giggled.

In that moment it was the most welcome, most amazing sound Anne could imagine. No, it was more welcome and amazing than she could have imagined.

It was a level of welcome she hadn't known existed until it arrived.

—

Dark came early, it being winter, and Anne had a lot of anxiety about the combination of Remy and driving in the dark. About other people's headlights.

Maybe it had been night when he was hit by the car. Maybe he had seen it coming. She wanted to ask more about it. But Dr. Klausner had suggested allowing his traumatic memories to come up naturally, in their own time, rather than dredging them up.

She glanced at him over and over in the rearview mirror. The first time she did, he met her eyes. Every time after that he had his forehead pressed against his knees, his eyes presumably closed.

He rode in that position for the rest of the drive.

—

With gas and food stops, it was well after eight when they got home.

Remy was clearly exhausted. He brushed his teeth, changed into his pajamas, and put himself straight to bed.

She tucked him in.

"Thank you for keeping me," he said.

She could see his face fairly well in the glow of the night-light. He still seemed vacant and lost. But at least he was talking.

"I promised you I would," she said.

"I didn't think you would, though. I thought you were lying to me. I thought when we didn't drive home in the morning that somebody was coming to take me. I thought you called somebody to come take me."

Anne made an effort to breathe. It had become unexpectedly more difficult, and she had to work at it. She reached in and stroked the stray hair off his forehead.

"I'm so sorry you thought that, honey. I can be trusted not to lie to you. I hope you know that now."

He nodded.

She kissed him on the forehead and let herself out. And immediately bumped into Peter just outside Remy's door.

"I want to go in and talk to him," Peter said. "Would that be okay?"

"I think it would be great."

She didn't ask him what he planned to say. She didn't hang around by the door to listen. Peter and Remy were brothers, and they would have many conversations that Anne was not privy to hearing. And that was okay. She trusted them.

She sat at the dining room table, digesting the day as best she could.

Then she remembered Officer Johnson. She found his card and texted him a simple message: "Home safe. He's a little better."

A few seconds later she heard an odd tone from her phone. A kind of *bloop* sound. She picked it up to see that he'd added a little heart emoji to her message.

It was about twenty minutes later when Peter came back out, smiling slightly as he passed her in the hall.

It was maybe another twenty minutes after that when she thought to go check Remy's bedroom door to be sure Peter had closed it. Peter sometimes forgot to close doors, to keep the dogs in or out.

She walked down the hall to Remy's door. It was standing open by more than a foot.

She started to pull it closed. But, before she did, she glanced in.

Jasmine and Plato were up on the bed with Remy, and they had him utterly sandwiched in. Jasmine was lying up against the front of the boy, her chin resting on his neck. She looked up at Anne with the saddest eyes, and without moving her head. Plato was curled up behind Remy, his face pressed into Remy's back.

For a moment Anne assumed that Remy was sleeping, and had no idea the dogs were on his bed. She wanted to call them away, but was afraid of waking him. Surely he would wake up in a panic to find them so close.

She tiptoed across the room and reached for Jasmine's collar, planning to guide her silently away.

Before she could, Remy spoke. His voice and his words made it clear that he was completely and perfectly awake.

"Did you know *they* had a really hard time, too?"

"The dogs?"

"Right."

Anne sat on the edge of the bed. Tucked herself into the only tiny, narrow space Jasmine had left her.

"I kind of did, yeah. I mean, they were three years old when we adopted them. And we got them at the pound. Somebody had abandoned them, so, yeah. I figured they'd been through some stuff, but I don't know exactly what. Why do *you* say they had a hard time?"

"You can just tell," Remy said. "*They* can tell *I* had a hard time. That's why they came in here. And *I* can tell *they* had a hard time by the way they want to make me feel better."

"So you want them to stay?"

"Yeah, I do. We're talking."

"Okay, then."

"Not with words."

"I didn't think you meant with words."

"I don't want you to think I'm crazy."

"I didn't think you were crazy."

She leaned over and kissed him on the forehead. Then she kissed Jasmine on the ear. Plato's face was still inaccessible, buried in Remy's back.

"Good dog," she whispered.

Then she let herself out.

———

She joined Chris in bed.

He was lying on top of the covers, still fully dressed except for his shoes, reading something on his tablet. He immediately set it down when he saw her come into the room. That was different. And the difference was not lost on her.

He raised his arm high in an unspoken invitation for her to duck under it and rest her head on his shoulder. She accepted.

"How's Remy?"

"Better," she said. "Depressed. But not at the very bottom of the pit like before. I have to tell you all about our drive home. It was fascinating."

"In a good way?"

"I think so, yeah. Intense, and not particularly easy. But yes. Good."

"I'd love to hear all about it, but before we get into that . . . do you know where the dogs are? They're usually sleeping on the rug at the foot of the bed by now."

"They're on the bed with Remy."

"Um . . . don't you think you should go get them? You know. Before he wakes up and starts screaming?"

"He was never asleep."

A moment of silence while he chewed that over.

"So he's made his peace with them?"

"Let's just say the three of them have discovered a commonality."

"As in, they're all rescues?"

"Something like that," Anne said. "Yeah."

———

It was the first session with Dr. Klausner after their return. It was about five days later.

Chris was there. Because she had asked for his support, and he had given it. She had just told Dr. Klausner about that, hoping the full subtext would come through. Then again, it's not as though she needed to hide from her husband that things were better between them. Maybe they would talk about it at a future session. This one seemed to be geared toward helping Remy.

"And your other two children are at school?"

"Yes."

"And will Remy ever attend school?"

Anne had one hand draped over Remy's shoulder, and she felt his muscles tense.

"Not in the foreseeable future, no."

She glanced down at the boy and saw him looking up into her face.

"What does the big word in there mean?"

"'Foreseeable'? It means as far as we can see now. We won't ask you to go to in-person school as far as we know now."

"Whew."

"You've been homeschooling him?" the doctor asked.

"Right now the state is providing a tutor. But I might end up home-schooling him, depending on how long they're willing to do that."

"Or we could pay for the tutor ourselves," Chris said.

She turned her eyes to her husband. She was feeling this intense gratitude and relief for having him back from all the subtle and miscellaneous ways he had been gone. He must have seen that in her eyes. He smiled at her, and the feeling intensified.

Meanwhile Dr. Klausner had turned his attention directly to Remy.

"No pressure here, Remy. It's okay if you don't have the words for it. But is there anything you can tell us about how it felt to go back to the place where you lived with your father?"

"It didn't feel like anything," Remy said. "I'm sorry. I know that's not what you want me to say, but I couldn't feel anything. It felt like I was made of mud instead of myself."

"That's fine," Dr. Klausner said. "That's perfectly normal."

Anne was watching Remy's face, and oh how it changed when the doctor said that last word. "Normal." His eyebrows lifted slightly in surprise. His eyes widened in wonder, as if viewing some sight that was almost too perfect to be true.

"It *is?*"

"Absolutely. That's how most people deal with trauma. We go numb. It's a reaction meant to protect us. We deal with the traumatic feelings in time, but in the moment it would all be too much for us, so we shield ourselves, and we take it on a little at a time. Some people even dissociate, which is a fancy way of saying they feel like they're outside themselves."

"Yes!" Remy shouted. Literally shouted. It made Anne jump. "Yes, I had that!" He was clearly excited now. "When we were looking at the wrecked truck and when we were on the snowmobile—and maybe a couple other times—I was up in the air looking down at myself. But I wasn't going to tell anybody that because I thought you'd all think I was crazy."

"Not at all," Dr. Klausner said. "It's a fairly common reaction."

Remy paused, as if building up to something. Anne thought she could feel him taking in a breath to say something big. He was leaning forward on the couch in a way that looked straining.

"So I'm *normal?*"

"Yes, I think you are," Dr. Klausner said. "I think you've been through an abnormal amount of stress and trauma, and that makes you seem different from the people around you. But your reactions to what you've been through seem completely normal, so I guess what I'm saying is that any child who had been through what you've been through would be having the troubles you're having."

Remy sat back, letting his shoulder blades thump into the soft couch cushions.

"That makes me feel so much better," he said.

"Good. That's what we're here for."

"When I was at the hospital, I didn't feel normal. I felt like everybody was looking at me like I was some kind of monster or something. The nurses whispered about me to each other and they called me a wild animal."

"They didn't know what was going on inside you," Dr. Klausner said. "They were afraid."

"Oh," Remy said.

He sat quietly for a moment. They all did.

"My mom never looked at me like that," Remy said. "That was what I liked about her right from the start."

"Your first mom?" Anne asked.

"Well, both. But I meant you."

Another silence.

"So, maybe," Dr. Klausner said, "you can tell us how you've been feeling . . . since. After going back there."

"I liked the car ride home. I was pretty happy then. Same reason I'm pretty happy now, because everybody was making me feel regular.

My mom was right. She thought I was ashamed because I wasn't regular enough for the family, and she was exactly right."

Dr. Klausner turned his eyes to Anne, seemingly for more explanation.

"On the way home," she told him, "I had the other kids tell him a little about what their lives were like when we first fostered them. The troubles they had, and some of the problems they caused the family. I thought it might help."

"It did," Remy said. "It really did help."

"You know, you said something on that drive that helped me, too, Remy."

He turned his face up to hers, fully open to the moment. Fully vulnerable and ready to receive.

"I *helped* you?"

"You absolutely did."

"How did I help you?"

"Remember you asked me about my life? What trauma *I'd* been through? And I told you about how my father left us, and how I was thinking it was my fault."

"You didn't just think it," Remy said. "Your mom *told* you it was your fault."

"Right. True. She did. Anyway. After I told you that, I said it wasn't as bad as what you went through, but you said it was worse, because at least you knew your father wanted you. You said you felt bad for me, having to go through that. I feel like a lot changed for me after you said that. I realized I'd been minimizing it. Which is just a complicated way of saying I treated it like it wasn't a big deal when it really was. And also . . . I've been thinking about it more since then, and I'm not sure it all happened the way my mom said it did. When you're a kid, you just take stuff like that in, and if it's a grown-up saying it, then you don't really question it. But now I look back and I think, well, maybe three kids *was* too much for him, but that's his fault, not mine. I mean, if you can't handle three kids, then don't have three kids, but don't have them and then blame it on them. And also, it's starting to occur to me that my mother might have told that story to cover over problems in the marriage that she didn't want to admit."

Anne stopped talking. Took a long breath. At the corner of her eye she could see Chris staring at her. Rather intently, it seemed. She turned and looked him straight on.

"What?" she asked.

"I didn't know all that."

"I told you."

"Yeah. You sort of did. But you told me about it like it wasn't that much of a thing."

"Right, I know. That's exactly what I'm saying. I didn't get what a big deal it was until Remy told me."

"I can't believe I helped you," Remy said.

Chapter Twenty-One

The Box

It was more than three months later, and Jeannie and Lester Gaffney were visiting from Pocatello.

It was a beautiful early spring day, and they sat outside watching the boys play. All three of the boys. Janie was at the mall with two of her friends, but Peter was playing a big-brother role, and playing it well. He was teaching the two younger boys to throw a spiral with a football. He had an old tire set up in the yard, and they took turns trying to sail a long pass across the yard and get it through that target.

"Les is gonna be so jealous," Jeannie said. "He's always wanted a brother. But me, I had to stop after one. I'm sorry, but that's a kind of pain I am *not* going through again. But why am I telling you? *You* must know. I have no idea how you did it. Or . . . wait. Are Janie and Peter your own?"

"Yes," Anne said. "They're my own. And they're both adopted."

"Oh, I'm so sorry. Stupid, stupid me. I said the wrong thing. I didn't mean that the way it came out."

"It's okay," Anne said.

That was true and it wasn't true, all at the same time. Each individual person who said things like that to Anne meant well enough, and each instance could be allowed to go by. But collectively, multiplied by everyone who interacted with her family, it was draining.

"You couldn't have kids of your own?" Jeannie asked.

So that was another one.

"We could have, so far as we know. But we chose to do this instead. It just seemed like there were an awful lot of kids already here, and everybody couldn't wait to step right over them to make more. This was just our choice."

"Well, it was a very noble thing to do," Jeannie said.

"Can I get your advice on something?"

"Sure. I'll help if I can."

"You'll need to come into the house with me."

They got up and walked inside, leaving the boys with Peter. Leaving them to learn to throw that perfect spiral pass.

Anne led Jeannie upstairs to her bedroom. Jeannie sat on the edge of the carefully made bed while Anne took the box down from the closet shelf. It was about eight inches by six inches, not very deep at all, and probably barely weighed a pound. It was made of a dark mahogany wood. She carried it over to the bed and stood in front of Jeannie, holding it about at her eye level.

"I give up," Jeannie said. "What is it?"

"It's Roy Blake."

Jeannie leaned in and looked at the box more closely, as if it might explain itself. Her face took on a puzzled expression.

"That little box? Is all his remains? No, there must be some mistake. I've seen people's remains after they're cremated. My father was cremated. Roy was a big man. That can't be all of him."

Anne sat down hard on the bed, bouncing Jeannie a little too much.

"See, this is my dilemma," she said. "This is what I wanted your advice about. I'm dreading showing it to Remy. Because if he asks questions about it . . . he might say the same things you just said. And then I'd have to tell him an ugly truth that he's bound to find upsetting.

This is all of Roy's remains . . . that they could find. There are animals up there. You know. Out in the wilderness there are coyotes and bears. They probably even have wolves up there, now that they're coming back. They found a skull, and I think maybe most of one femur bone. That's a hell of an image to put in the poor kid's head."

"Maybe he doesn't know how big a box you need for a whole cremated person."

"He very well might not. But I won't find out until I show this to him."

"And you have to show it to him?"

"I think I should. I keep being haunted by the mental picture of that shallow grave. That poor little kid out in the wilderness by himself, trying to dig a grave for his own father. And then he can't move him into it, because he's so small and his father's so big. So he has to leave him out where the animals can get him. It just seems so sad. I figure the least we can do is offer him the chance to do that moment over."

"Oh, I get it. You mean bury his father proper."

"Right."

"Well, that's a nice idea."

"I'm just not sure how much it might upset him to see how little of his father is left to bury."

"I think if I were you," Jeannie said, "I'd just tell him this is what a person comes down to when they're cremated. Maybe sometime in his life he'll see otherwise, but by then he'll be a grown-up and can handle things better."

"Maybe," Anne said.

But she was thinking she would not literally tell Remy that the whole of Roy Blake was inside the box. Because that was a lie. She had already lightly broached the subject of how much of his father had been found, back when he had first been found. Remy hadn't pressed for details. Maybe he wouldn't this time, either.

She got up and crossed to the window, still holding the box, and looked down over the boys playing football in the yard. They had changed up the game now. Peter was throwing passes, and the younger boys were going long and learning to be receivers.

She stood watching them with the box in her hands, visible in the window but far from their eyes, almost as though wanting to show it to Remy and not wanting him to see it at the same time.

"At least they put him in a good-looking wooden box," Jeannie said. "Pretty nice considering he had no kin, and nobody to pay for it."

"We had to pay extra for the box. He would have been sent back in a plastic bag inside cardboard otherwise."

A few seconds of silence, and then Jeannie joined her at the window. They stood shoulder to shoulder, looking down on the boys.

"He just looks so wonderful," Jeannie said. "He just looks so much better. Last time we saw him . . . Lordy, that was a shock. Every little bit of him broken, and hardly talking at all. It's like a transformation."

"He's still really scared. And grieving."

"Well, of course he is. But you need to take my word for this, honey. You see him every day, so you might not see it the same way I see it. That boy is coming *back*."

They watched the boys play for a moment in silence. Anne tried to see Remy more the way Jeannie did—more of a straight comparison with the way he'd been when she first met him.

"Can I pick your brain about something?" she asked Jeannie. "You said a few minutes ago that Roy had no kin. How sure are you about that?"

"Just as sure as I can be. His mom and I talked about family all the time. Both Roy and Marian were only children whose parents died young. Why?"

"Chris and I hired a private investigator to see if he has any living relatives at all. He's not finding anybody. But I wanted to ask you, too."

"You're not looking to give him back, are you?"

"No. Just the opposite. We've filed to adopt him. But we haven't told him yet, because first we want to be sure the way is clear. The one thing that could derail us is if a blood relative came in and wanted to take him."

"Well, you stop worrying right now, then," Jeannie said. "That boy has nobody. Which is why it's such a damn good thing he has you and Chris."

———

The company was gone, headed for home, and Chris was in the kitchen helping her get dinner on the table when she broached the subject.

"What if we talked to him about the box after dinner?" she said.

Chris's hands stopped moving.

"I thought we were going to get an appointment with Dr. Klausner for that."

"Yeah, we did say that. But he's so trusting with the family, and I'm just wondering if it isn't time to transition away from needing Dr Klausner so much. I mean, therapy is good for him. I'm not suggesting we stop therapy. But also I'm not sure we're at a place where we need the therapist every time we want to talk to him about something hard."

"Except the last time he got hit in the face with his past he melted down entirely."

"Yeah, but that wasn't just talking. He was standing in the place where he'd had all those horrible experiences. He'll be at home with his family."

"I'm willing to try it," Chris said, "if you think it's the right thing."

Anne trotted upstairs and got the box.

When she got back down, Chris had dinner on the table, and all three kids were seated. They turned and looked at her as she came into the room. It seemed ridiculous to try to hide the box after they'd already seen it, so she took a deep breath and set it in the center of the table.

And so, of course, the talk did not wait until after dinner.

"What is that?" Peter asked.

"It's something we need to talk to Remy about."

"Okay," Remy said. "Go ahead and talk to me."

"Remember when I got that phone call from the sheriff a few months ago? And I told you that some hunters had found your father's remains out in the woods? Well . . . I'm not sure there's any really gentle way to say this. So I'll just say it. Those are his ashes. We brought them back here for you in a nice box, because we figured your father deserved to be treated with respect. We know you wanted to bury your father properly, but you didn't get a chance to do that. So we thought you might want to do that now."

"Oh, that's a great idea!" Remy said.

Anne felt herself breathe, and only then did she realize the extent to which she had been holding her breath.

Please don't anybody comment on the size of the box, she thought.

"Why is it so small?" Janie said. She was holding her fork like a weapon and eyeing the box as though staring down a poisonous snake.

"Well . . . ," Anne said, ". . . because . . ."

But she wasn't sure the best direction to go with it.

Janie opened her mouth to say something else, but Anne caught her eye and stopped her with a small head shake. Janie's mouth snapped closed again.

"There are lots of wild animals up there," Remy said to his sister. "That's why I tried to bury him. So the animals wouldn't get him. But still, if we bury what we've got, that's better than not burying him at all."

Silence.

So he already knew.

The whole family just seemed to be staring at Remy. Waiting for him to break. He did not break. In fact, he did not seem deterred from eating. Homemade macaroni and cheese was his favorite, which is why Anne had chosen it.

He shoveled huge forkfuls of it into his mouth for a minute or so. Then he looked up and noticed that everybody was staring at him.

"What?" he asked.

"Nothing," Anne said. "We just all think you're taking this very well."

"Well, I knew he died," Remy said. "It's not like I didn't know that. We need to bury him up at the place."

"On that property with the cabin?"

"Right."

"You want to go back there?"

"Not really. I hate it there. But we have to bury him there. Because he wanted to be there. *I* didn't want to be there, but *he* wanted to. He liked it up there. I have no idea why."

They ate quietly for a time. It almost seemed as though Remy had moved on in his head. But after a minute or two he opened his mouth and showed that the subject was still on his mind.

"Are we *allowed* to go up there and bury him? Whose place is that now?"

"It's yours," Anne said.

"*Mine?*"

For the first time that evening, Remy seemed shocked. He even set down his fork and stopped shoveling.

"Your dad owned it. And you're his only living relative."

"*I* don't want it," Remy said, and picked up his fork again.

"We figured we could sell it and put the money in a trust for you. That's when money rightfully belongs to a child, but it's being saved. For college, or for when you're an adult."

"Okay," Remy said, his mouth rudely full again. "Just don't sell it until after we bury him up there." He looked around the table. "Will you all come this time? Because I really hate it there. And the more of you guys that are there with me, the less upset I'll get."

"Absolutely," Chris said. "We'll go as a family."

Dinner resumed, and the remains of Roy Blake were not mentioned again.

At one point in the meal Remy looked up at Anne and asked, "What happened to that picture of my first mom? Did we lose it?"

"No, we didn't lose it. It's in my purse. I figured I'd give it back to you when you wanted it back."

"I want it back now, please," he said.

———

Anne let herself into Remy's room at bedtime, and sat on the edge of his bed.

She handed him the old dog-eared photo and he slipped it under his pillow.

"Thanks," he said. "And thanks for tucking me in."

"Of course."

"Do you think I'm too old for that?"

"Not at all. Especially not tonight. I was worried you were upset by what we discussed tonight. But you seemed to handle it really well."

Amazingly well, she thought. But of course she didn't add that.

"A little upset," he said. "I mean, always, if I think about that, it's a little bit hard. But you guys were all there, and I was at home. And I was really happy that you got him back. I always felt really bad about leaving him out there in the woods. Any time I thought about that, it bothered me. Even though I didn't think about it a lot. But I had to *work* to not think about it. Now maybe I won't have to work at that so much."

She reached out and brushed the hair off his forehead. It had grown long, and he didn't particularly want it cut. And she hadn't pressed the issue.

"There's just one thing I want you to consider about the trip up there," she said. "It's a long drive. And probably part of it will have to be in the dark. We've never really talked about the way you feel about headlights coming at you. I figured it was because that was the last thing you saw before you got hit by a car."

"Yeah, partly that," Remy said. "But there was that other time."

"What other time was that?"

"There was this time when I tried to come down to town just as it was getting dark. I was going to try to get something from that store, because I was hungry. But somebody shone these big spotlights on me. They were so bright I couldn't even see. And they scared me so much because I thought that's how you know they caught you. So after that I went back up in the woods and didn't come down again until I was practically starved to death. I really just came down because starving was so slow, and I figured I'd just let them catch me and kill me, and . . . Why're you looking at me like that? Why do you have your hand over your mouth like that?"

Anne hadn't realized she'd brought her hand to her mouth until he pointed it out.

"Because . . . ," she began, dropping the hand, ". . . I think that was me."

"*You* shone big spotlights on me?"

"Not on purpose. I was just turning my car around in the road, and my headlights hit you. And I just stopped, and you stopped. And then you ran away."

"What were you doing up there?"

"I was looking for *you*."

"How did you even know about me?"

"Edwina told me they were looking for you near that little town. And I had you on my mind, so I drove up there to see if I could see you."

In the silence that followed, a thought settled in Anne's brain. No, of course she hadn't meant to scare him. But, if she hadn't, everything might have gone on the way it had been going. Who knows how long he might have evaded efforts to help him. Maybe by the time he was found, there would be no helping him. No real chance to bring him back.

"I can't believe you were thinking about me before you even knew me. That's so nice. When I was up there, I sure didn't think anybody was thinking about me."

"So here's a new way to think about headlights," she said. "You thought they were somebody wanting to catch you for terrible reasons. But really they were somebody who already knew they wanted you. For good reasons. Somebody who wanted to help."

"Yeah," Remy said. "I get it."

She kissed him on the forehead and moved to let herself out of his room.

Before she could get out the door, he spoke again.

"Maybe we could stop at that town on the way back," he said. "You know. At that store. I want to tell that man I'm sorry I stole from him. Except you have to go in first and make sure those dogs are locked up. Maybe we could even pay him back. I know it would really be you paying him back, because I don't have my own money. But you said I would, later, after we sell that terrible property. I could pay you back."

"I think that's a wonderful idea. And you don't need to pay us back."

"Okay, good night, then."

"Good night, Remy."

"When do we go?"

"Whenever you say."

"Okay," he said. "I'll think about it. You know, Lester is jealous of me. Because I have a brother."

"Yeah, I heard all about how he might be."

"I'm lucky to have a brother and a sister."

"And they're lucky to have you," Anne said.

11. REMY

Chapter Twenty-Two

The Decision

Everyone was weirdly quiet on the drive up there. Remy couldn't figure out why nobody could think of anything to talk about.

And it was more than an eight-hour drive.

Now and then his mom would say something about stopping for gas, or ask whether anyone was hungry or needed to use the restroom. Other family members would say whatever they had to say in response to that, and then silence would fall again.

Remy was worried that they felt terrible for him. Pitied him. Or maybe they were scared that he was going to lose it again. Both were deeply uncomfortable thoughts.

At one point he broke the silence himself, and it made everybody jump. That seemed like a bad sign.

"Am I supposed to say something about my dad when we do this?"

His mom turned around in her seat and looked into his face, and Remy figured by her eyes that she mostly felt sorry for him. That made him squirm, but it was better than the other option.

They were driving his new dad's four-wheel-drive truck, which was good, because his mom's car might not have made it up that long dirt road to the cabin. It had a big extra cab with a back seat. Janie and Peter were sitting one on each side of him, and Lester's family was meeting them there. So Remy felt mostly pretty calm. All things considered.

"It's completely up to you, honey," his mom said. "You can if you want, but you don't have to."

Then there was more of that awkward silence.

After a while Peter asked, "Do you *want* to say something about him?"

"I feel like I should," Remy said. "But I just can't decide what kind of thing it ought to be. I think you're only supposed to say nice things about people who die, but not everything I think about him is nice. And the biggest thing is . . . I still don't know if he was wrong. I keep asking, and I keep getting these answers that I don't really understand. Like 'He was right about what he saw, but he was wrong about the best way to deal with it.' Stuff like that. No offense, but that's kind of confusing when you're trying to figure out if he was right or wrong. I keep going back and forth, and I'm so tired of that. I've been doing it ever since he took me up there, and it makes my brain tired. Like, I'd think, he really loves me and he's trying to keep me safe. But then I'd think, this is the worst thing he could have done to me. And it's driving me crazy that I can't figure out which is right."

His mom turned around in her seat again.

"Honey," she said, "this is where life gets a little complicated. Life would be really simple if only one thing could be true at one time, but it never seems to go like that. The truth of this situation seems to be that he *meant* well, but he didn't *do* well. Maybe he loved you and wanted to keep you safe, but the decision he made was a bad one and put you in danger. It's called a paradox, and unfortunately the world is full of them. And it helps if you can just kind of . . . make your peace with those. As best you can, anyway."

Remy chewed that over in his head for a while. A few miles at least.

Then he said, "I'm going to say something about him when we bury him, because I think if I don't, I'll be sorry later. Just . . . until I open my mouth, I'm not really sure what it'll be."

———

The Gaffneys were waiting at the wrong spot on the forest road, but fortunately it was where his family would drive right by them. If it had been farther up the road, that would have been a problem, because it's not like there was any cell phone reception way up there.

Remy leaned over his brother and waved out the window to Lester, and Lester waved back. His dad was driving a big red truck that Lester's family hadn't had back when Remy lived in Pocatello. It reminded him that a lot of time had gone by. That he'd missed a lot.

Then Lester's family followed them to that awful little spot in the road with the two filthy curved mirrors. And they turned and headed up.

Remy's stomach felt crampy and sore, but he talked to the place in his own head. He said, *You can't hurt me anymore, because I have a real family, and they'll drive me away from here anytime I ask.* And it really did make him feel a little better to think that.

Then they came to a tree that had fallen down across the road.

Everybody piled out, including Lester's family, and they all just stood, looking at the big trunk of this tree. Like it would move if they just kept staring.

It was a gorgeous spring day, maybe 60 degrees, with a cloudless sky that was so blue it looked almost navy. The contrast of the green trees against that sky was a beautiful thing to see. It struck Remy that this place really was beautiful if you knew you could turn around and drive right out again anytime you wanted.

"What did your father use to do when this happened?" Remy's new dad asked.

"He'd take the gasoline chain saw and cut it up and then split the rounds into stovewood, and we'd burn it to stay warm."

His dad turned to Lester's dad, and he was wearing a sort of crooked smile.

"Happen to have a gas-powered chain saw on you, Art?"

And Lester's dad said, "Darn it, I knew there was something I forgot."

Remy's dad turned his attention back to Remy.

"How far a walk up to the cabin from here?"

"It'd take us maybe twenty minutes. Or maybe half an hour, depending on how everybody walks. But I never had a watch when I was out here. So that's a guess."

His dad looked around at all the faces.

"Ready, guys?"

"Bring the box," Remy said.

"I have the box," his mom said.

"And the stone."

"I'll get the stone," his dad said, and walked back to the truck to retrieve it.

His new parents had ordered a stone specially for the occasion. It didn't look like a gravestone, exactly. It was more like a smooth river stone, but it was engraved. It said Remy's father's name, and the year he was born, and the year he died.

Some of them walked down into the gully on the side of the road to chart a path around the tree. Lester and Remy climbed over its trunk, even though they got a little scratched up doing it.

Then they all walked along the road in silence. Remy had to wonder about Lester's family, just like he'd had to wonder about his own. Were they feeling sorry for him? Or were they afraid he was going to lose it? Or both?

After a while they passed the wrecked truck, and everybody noticed it. Remy could see them turn their heads to look. It had started to rust, and the forest floor was growing up to cover it, but it was still hard to miss. But nobody asked him anything about it, or talked about it out loud, and that felt like a relief.

And then, just like that, the cabin came into view. Which seemed impossible to Remy, because they hadn't been walking long enough. He must have been wrong about where they started walking. But no, he knew how far it was from the cabin to the truck's crash site. He had made the walk many times.

"How long were we walking?" Remy asked his dad.

His dad looked at his watch and said, "Twenty-eight minutes."

Then Remy knew time had played a trick on him.

He looked around at the faces. Everybody was standing still. Nobody was talking. Everybody was just staring at the cabin. And the looks on their faces . . . well, Remy would have found them hard to describe. But they weren't looking at it as though they liked it. That much was sure.

Remy's dad walked closer to the cabin, and then everyone followed him. Except Remy. Remy was already closer than he wanted to go.

Remy's new dad pulled the cabin door open. The door wasn't locked. Remy hadn't bothered to lock it, or even make sure it was pulled closed. His dad looked inside. And then he stepped back, and everybody else stepped up and looked inside. Even Janie and Peter and Lester. They all looked in.

Remy's mom looked back and saw him standing there by himself, and she walked to him, and stood close beside him with one arm around his shoulder, and that was nice.

"It's bad," Remy said quietly, "isn't it?"

"You mean the cabin?"

"Right."

"As a place to live?"

"Right."

"Well, it's not much. I mean, most people have a lot more to make them comfortable."

"They look shocked," Remy said.

"I . . . suppose they are."

"There's no bathroom," Lester called to him. "What did you do when you had to go to the bathroom?"

"You had to go out here," Remy said, indicating a swath of forest with a sweep of his arm.

"What if it was ten below?"

"Then you had to go out here in ten below."

They all stared inside a little longer. All except Remy and his mom.

"I feel a little bit ashamed," Remy said. "Because they're all looking at it. But also it makes me feel better, because it helps me decide something. He was always telling me the place was great, and I thought it was terrible. And I was right. It's terrible."

"Yes," his mom said. "You were right. It's terrible."

"See, now *that's* an answer I can understand."

The two families came walking back to him, and Lester's mom looked particularly disturbed.

"Honey, there's no kitchen," she said to Remy. "How did you cook?"

"On the woodstove. Or we'd make a fire in the fire ring outside."

"But no refrigerator. How did you even keep things fresh?"

"If it was ten below," Lester said, "it wouldn't matter."

"But it wasn't always, honey."

"Most of our supplies were in cans or dried, but if my dad shot a deer, we had to salt it and dry it. Can we walk up and do this now? This is making me nervous. There's a shovel in that little tiny shed against the back of the cabin. Unless those hunters or somebody else stole it. I sure hope nobody stole it. Maybe we should have brought one from home."

Remy's dad disappeared behind the cabin and came back out with the shovel, and Remy breathed again.

"I had one in the truck just in case," he said.

"I'm sorry if I made you uncomfortable, Remy," Lester's mom said.

"It's okay," Remy said. "It's not your fault. I just hate this place, and I just want to do this and get out of here."

He started walking up the hill.

"Wait," his mom said. "Where are we going?"

"We have to bury him up where he died."

"Oh. Okay."

Remy thought he heard a sigh or two, but they all trudged up the hill after him.

"You know what I never asked you?" Remy's mom said. She was walking right beside him. "I always wonder about this and then forget to ask. I know you broke your leg in that truck accident. And I'm guessing that's how you injured your shoulder. But I know your ribs were broken at some point. And I still don't know how you broke your ribs."

"I fell out of a tree," Remy said.

"Oh. Well, I'm sorry you had to go through that, but it's not as bad as what I was thinking. It's nice to picture you being a kid and having some joy."

Remy stopped walking suddenly.

"What joy? I don't know what you're talking about."

"You know. Climbing trees. That's something I think all kids enjoy."

"My fish hook got stuck in a branch. My dad wouldn't go out for supplies and it was my last hook, and if I didn't bring home any fish, then we didn't get to eat."

"Oh," his mom said. "Then I guess I'm sorry I asked."

They walked a bit more without talking.

Remy could have found the spot in his sleep. He had memorized everything about it. But none of that mattered, because the reflector sticks the sheriff had put up to guide them to the scene were still in place.

As they walked on, Remy could hear Lester's dad talking to his dad.

"I had no idea Roy was so far gone," Art said, "and now I feel bad, because I should've known. For Remy's sake I should've known. It's just weird, you know? Because I *knew* the guy. Well. We spent hours arguing about the state of the world. About politics. I never changed his mind and he never changed mine. But then it got to a point where we both knew it was best to leave all that alone. I could see the situation was sliding, but I sure never thought it would slide all the way down to here."

Just as he finished saying that, the spot came into view. The spot Remy had vowed never to revisit. And this was the second time he had been there since making that vow.

The snow was gone for the season, and the grave Remy had tried to dig stood out very clearly. Then he was looking down on himself from a spot directly over his own head, but it was okay, because Dr. Klausner had said that was normal.

"Right in the middle of this?" Remy's dad asked.

He had the shovel in one hand, and was pointing it into the shallow grave.

"No, right on the other side," Remy said, "because that's where I found him."

Remy stood silently for a time and watched his new dad dig. Everybody did. It didn't take long at all. Just a couple of minutes, because the box was so small.

Remy took it from his mom and set it down carefully inside the nice deep hole, and his new dad filled it in.

"I'm going to say something about my dad," Remy said. He was talking loudly so everybody would hear. "My first dad. Because I know that's what you do when you bury somebody. And I was really nervous all the way up here because I still didn't know what to say. Because I hadn't decided about a lot of things. But now I've decided. He was wrong."

That hung in the air a moment. Remy felt as though he could hear it echo, but that was just an imaginary thing. Behind that, he could hear a chorus of birds that were very real. They were maybe the only thing about the place he'd liked, though he had never once focused on them before.

"I know he figured people can hurt you, and probably that's true, but usually they don't, and anyway, nothing is worse than being all alone. So if you make yourself all alone, then you're hurting yourself as bad as anybody else could ever hurt you. So he was just wrong. And I'm sorry. I know you're supposed to say all nice things about people after they die, but I've spent all this time trying to figure out if he was right or not, and I just had to say out loud what I decided. He was wrong."

He stood quietly for a moment, aware of the roaring sound of wind blowing by his ears. And those lovely birds.

"But now I have a question," he said. Before he could even say what the question was, the tears started leaking out. No matter how hard he tried to clamp down on his emotion to stop them, they just kept leaking. "If I know he was wrong, and I know what he did was a bad thing for me, does that mean I'm not supposed to love him and be sad he died? Because he was still my dad."

Remy purposely looked away from all the faces because he could see he had made them sad, too.

"Of course you loved him," his new mom said. "Of course it's sad that you lost him."

"One of those things where life won't let only one thing be true at a time?"

"Exactly," his mom said.

"Can I have the stone, please?"

By now he was crying openly and not trying to hide it. Not because it didn't embarrass him, but because there was nothing he could do to stop it.

His dad picked it up off the ground and handed it to Remy. It was heavy. It was about the size of a football, but much flatter. It was almost more than he could carry. But he strained to set it in place. With the engraved side down.

"Honey?" his mom said. "I think the side with the writing goes *up*."

"No," Remy said. And he shook his head hard. "He would *not* want anybody to know he was here. Trust me. I know my dad. He always wanted it to be secret, where he was. This way *I* know, but next time some hunters are walking around up here looking for elk, they'll never know he's here."

"Okay, honey," she said. "If that's the way you want it."

"That's the way *he* wants it. Now come on. It's a long walk back, and I can't wait to get out of this place."

—

He said goodbye to Lester on the other side of the downed tree. The civilization side.

In a way it was different, being with Lester. Because Remy was different. He could never go back to being the boy he'd been when they were best friends. But Lester *was* his friend. He still was. It was just different.

Lester grabbed him in a bear hug, which he had never done before. Not once. Up until that moment they had been boys just the way they figured people expected them to be. But now they were hugging each other tight.

"I'm sorry it was so bad," Lester said near his ear.

"Not your fault."

"I know. I'm not sorry like I did it to you, I'm just sorry. I thought about you every day, and I tried to think what it was like for you, but I never thought of anything this bad."

Remy opened his mouth to speak. But, honestly, he had no idea what he should say, or if it would make him cry again to say it.

Then Lester clapped him on the back, turned sharply away, and followed his family back to their red truck.

"We'll visit," he called over his shoulder.

So that was too bad, because Lester was gone. But now they got to drive out of that place for the last time, and that was better than anything.

———

When they stopped in front of that little store, Remy felt his stomach flip over. It was a sickening feeling. He had known they were coming here. He had asked for this stop. He had been listening to his new parents discuss how to find it. But still he had not been prepared for the way it would feel to see it again.

It was worse than seeing the cabin, because at least the cabin didn't remind him of anything *he'd* done wrong.

His dad parked the truck by the gas pumps. It was near dusk, and there was no one else in the lot.

"Whoa," his dad said. "Good thing we filled up in Coeur d'Alene on the drive up. Look at those prices."

"It's always like that in the middle of nowhere," his mom said.

His mom stepped out of the truck and stood on the tarmac. Peter climbed out to let Remy through.

Remy tugged on his mom's hand.

"You have to go in and make sure his dogs are locked up."

"Okay, I know. I said I would."

"Don't close the door," Remy said to Peter, his voice breathy and desperate to his own ears. "I might need to get back in fast."

He watched his mom walk to the open doors of the store. He could see the old man behind the counter, and it filled his gut with dread.

"Where are your dogs?" his mom asked the old man.

"Well, that's an odd question if I ever heard one. Why? You planning on robbing me?"

"No, nothing like that. I just want to bring a young boy in who's afraid of dogs."

I used *to be afraid of dogs,* Remy thought. *Now I'm just a little bit afraid of dogs when I don't know them, and a whole lot afraid of* those *dogs.*

"They're upstairs in my apartment," the man said.

Remy's mom motioned for Remy to come.

At first, Remy gave his legs a signal to walk, but they never seemed to receive it.

His mom motioned again for him to come in.

This time he could see he was walking. The open doors of the store were getting closer. But he couldn't really feel his legs working. He couldn't feel his feet touch the ground. It felt more like having a dream about walking. Not so much like really doing it.

He reached his mom, and she placed a hand on his shoulder, and he felt it. She gently guided him up to the man's counter.

"This is Remy," she said. "And he wants to apologize to you."

"Happens all the time," the man said. "What'd he do, take a candy bar? Just give me the money for it and we're all square. It's wrong to steal," he added, shaking a finger at Remy. "But you fessed up to it, and that's the main thing."

Remy looked up into his mom's face for direction. He had no idea what to say.

"I'm afraid it was a little more complicated than that," she said. "He stole from you on multiple occasions. Once he even broke out the back doors of your store in the night and took everything he could carry."

The man's eyes narrowed. Remy felt as though he could watch the old guy think. Then he turned his burning gaze onto Remy and looked him up and down. It made Remy feel squirmy, but he held still and took it.

"That was not this boy," the man said.

There was a definite tone to his voice, like that closed the subject for good.

"It actually *was* this boy," his mom said.

"No. Absolutely not. I got a good look at that little monster on more than one occasion. That boy was barely human. He was like a wolf boy. He was a wild animal. This is just a regular kid. You got this wrong somehow."

Remy winced as each of the judgments hit him. *Monster. Wolf. Wild animal. Barely human.* Then, when he was sure the man was done hurting him, he leaned down and tugged up the leg of his chinos. Pulled the back of his sock down with the other hand.

"It *was* me," he said. "See? This is where your dog bit me."

For a weirdly long time, the man said nothing at all. He just kept running his eyes all up and down Remy.

"I'll be damned," he said. "I wouldn't've known you in a million years. I didn't think they'd bite you. I figured they'd just run you off."

"They were getting tired of me," Remy said. "Just like you."

His mom took her checkbook out of her purse.

"We want to pay you for what he took. If you can give us some idea of what that would cost."

The old man turned his eyes onto Remy's mom, and in much the same way. Looking her up and down as though he assumed he could find some visual key to understanding her, but hadn't found it yet.

"You fostered him?" the man asked.

"Yes."

"That was brave."

"It's working out fine."

"I hope you plan on keeping him. Because not everybody would."

"We've filed to adopt him," she said.

It was the first Remy had heard about it, and it made him feel good. Like something warm in his belly. He had not expected to feel good in that store, in that moment. It was a weird feeling. Like thinking the headlights wanted to catch you and kill you, when really they were somebody trying to help.

He opened his mouth to say something about it, but the conversation took a different turn.

"I guess it's good that you had the guts to come back here," the man said to Remy. "But maybe your foster mom forced you to. I don't know."

"No," Remy's mom said. "It was his idea."

"Okay, well, very nice, very noble, but here's what I don't get. Why didn't you just walk up to me or anybody else in this town and say you were hungry and had nobody looking after you? We would've gotten you some help and something to eat while help was driving up here. But instead you just took. And there's no excuse for that."

He fixed Remy with his withering gaze as he spoke. And Remy withered under it.

"I thought you would kill me if you caught me."

"Well, that's just crazy talk."

Remy's mom stepped in to rescue him.

"Remy's father was a survivalist," she said. "He thought society was pretty much on the brink of collapse."

"Isn't it?" the man said, with a twisted half smile.

"Okay. Point taken. But his views were a bit more . . . extreme. He taught Remy that the only way to stay alive was not to let anybody see him or catch him."

"Oh," the man said. He looked Remy over again. Up and down. This time it felt less withering. "Well, that's a hell of a thing to do to a kid."

"I know," his mom said. "Right?"

Remy got a feeling that he couldn't describe, but that he'd felt before. He'd felt it when his mom said the cabin was terrible, and when he'd overheard that officer saying he'd never bring his kid to a place like that. It was a feeling like being right when you hadn't expected to be. He

316

wondered why people hadn't said more things like that all along, and fewer things like "Well, there are two sides to everything." Maybe they were trying to be fair to his father. But this was much more fair to *him*.

"Okay, I take back what I said, then," the old man said to Remy. "I guess that's an excuse I can understand. Tell you what. Insurance paid for the door and a little bit for robbery. Gimme two hundred dollars and we're even."

Remy's mom set her checkbook down on the man's counter and wrote him a check.

She tore it off the pad and held it out to him, but he didn't notice. He was scanning Remy with his eyes again.

"So listen," he said, directly to Remy. Remy turned his eyes up to the man, ready to receive whatever he dished out. Even if it was bad. "I'm sorry for what I said before. Calling you a wolf boy and hardly human. You're obviously just a regular boy like everybody else, and if that's what you are now, then that's what you were all along and I just couldn't see it. And I apologize for that. You'd just got yourself in a bad spot and I shouldn't have judged you for it."

"Thank you," Remy said.

The man took the check from Remy's mom, and they walked back to the truck.

"You okay?" she asked him.

"Yeah. Good."

When they got to the truck, Peter didn't get out and make him sit in the middle. He just moved over to let Remy in.

"I get a window?" Remy asked.

"You shouldn't always have to be in the middle," Peter said. "Everybody hates the middle."

They headed out of the parking lot and onto the road, and Remy's dad turned for home. It was eight hours away, if not more, but they were headed for it, and that was something. Remy was exhausted, especially in his mind. He leaned his head on the window, let his eyes go into soft focus, and thought about nothing at all. At least, as far as he knew.

The closer they got to the highway, the more cars they saw. It was a relief to Remy, because he hated to be where there were no people.

It was almost dark now, and their headlights shone in his eyes, but he didn't squeeze his eyes closed, or even wince. He just let the light in, because he was happy to be where there were lots of people again.

And, anyway, he was half-asleep.

"Penny for your thoughts, Remy," his mom said.

"I don't know what that means."

"It's just an old-fashioned way of asking what you're thinking."

"About the headlights?"

"About anything. But, well . . . yeah. Mostly that."

"I wasn't really thinking anything about them. Or I thought I wasn't. But now that you ask, I guess I sort of am. I'm thinking if I'd been walking down this road all dirty and starving, maybe every one of these people in every one of these cars would have stopped and tried to help me, but I just didn't know it."

"That's a really nice thought," his mom said.

Then they all fell quiet, but in a nice, comfortable way, and Remy fell asleep with his head against the window.

When he woke up again he was home.

His dad carried him to bed, and he fell back asleep in his clothes and slept for a really long time.

When he woke up, that awful place and time were behind him. The worst of all he had been through was over.

And, even better than that, he knew it.

12. ANNE

Chapter Twenty-Three

Doing Life

She jogged beside Miri through a busy part of the city, and they hit every green light. It felt like the universe offering some sort of positive comment on something, but Anne didn't say that out loud, because it was silly. It was just one of those things you think, and it matches with how you feel, but you don't mistake it for objective reality.

As they crossed a street together and reached the curb, Anne was able to tell that Miri was struggling. She could hear it in her friend's breathing.

"Break?"

Miri stopped, leaned on a light post, and panted. She did not try to speak.

"Still the Covid after all these months?"

Miri panted for another full minute or more before answering.

"More than I like to admit," she said.

"That coffee place I like is just on the next block."

"*Now* you're talking."

They walked together side by side for half a block or so. Anne could hear that Miri was still working to get her breath fully back.

"So now that we're talking alone for the first time," Miri said, her voice still breathy, "the difference with you and Chris is like night to day. I felt it the first time I walked into a room you were both in."

"Feels completely different to me, too. In some ways I think it feels better than the early years, before the kids. Obviously, that was . . . you know. All the passion. The high highs. All that stuff people crave. But this is . . . I don't know. I mean, I do know, I'm just not sure how to say it. Wider and deeper? More real?"

They stopped just outside the patio of the coffee place.

"You sit," Anne said. "I'll go. I've got a mask. What do you want?"

"Triple espresso."

"That'll get you back on your feet."

———

She rejoined Miri at the table with the drinks. Her friend was watching people go by.

"Here's what really struck me most," Miri said. "About Chris. He loves Remy so much."

"He really does."

"Then again, who wouldn't? That kid is amazing. Know what he said to me? He said Janie and Peter are his heroes, because they go to school. He said that's his goal. To be as brave as they are and go to school. He just totally opened up to me, which kind of blew me away, because of everything he's been through."

"He loves being around people because he was without them for so long."

"I get why Chris would fall for him, but he was always the cautious type. You know. About making that kind of connection with a foster."

"But Remy's adoption is going to be final anytime now. It's a done deal. There's nothing to get in the way."

"Good. Who's taking care of him while we're gone?"

"He's with his tutor all day."

"Oh. Okay. That's helpful."

Their coffees arrived at the table, and they thanked the barista, and then stared off into the distance and blew on the hot drinks, and sipped carefully.

"Here's the thing about Remy, though," Miri said. "And it's not anything against him. But he makes you look at the world. Really look at it. Which is a bizarre experience. Like, we're all so casual about it. We wake up and walk out into the world like, 'What could possibly go wrong?' And meanwhile we're in the middle of a global pandemic, and there are mass shootings every time we turn around, and we're at each other's throats politically and every other way I can think of, and we just live our lives anyway. And I never even thought about how we do that until I met that kid. How do we do that, Anne?"

"Miri," she said. "I'll be damned if I know."

"But you went through the same thing, right? He made you look at everything differently?"

"Oh yeah. All of us. Janie and Peter, too. But now I think it's better that we did go through it, because before . . . it was almost like this state of denial. Like, 'Sure, bad stuff happens, but it won't happen to us.' But this is different. This is something you do with your eyes open. You look at the world, see it for exactly what it is, and then make this conscious choice to be part of it. It's a better deal, really. I like it. In a shaky, ambiguous sort of way."

"Here's hoping it rubs off on me," Miri said, and raised her cup in a modified toast.

They drank their coffee in silence. Because, just in that moment, nothing more needed saying.

Then they finished their run. They took it slow, for Miri's sake. But they finished the day they had planned.

Because, Anne thought, *that's what you do. You do it for your kids, or your spouse, or you do it for yourself. But one way or the other, you do it. You just do.*

BOOK CLUB QUESTIONS

1. Remy's father justifies taking his five-year-old son to live in the wilderness by saying that in their new home they'll have the most important thing: freedom. Do you believe freedom is truly the most important thing?

2. What evidence do you think Remy's father based "the conflagration"—when civilization burns itself to the ground—on? To what extent do you think he had his son's best interests at heart?

3. Anne's father left her when she was a young girl, and her mother blamed her and her siblings for being "too many and too much." In what ways did Anne internalize this rejection and allow it to affect her adult life?

4. After Remy moves in with Anne and her family, he is very interested in watching the news to learn if the world is "regular," or if it's the way his father thought it was. Based on what he sees, how do you think a child would interpret today's world after being isolated for so long?

5. Remy's worst fear is that the world is falling apart but that everyone is keeping it from him. Anne and her family have to constantly weigh how much to tell Remy, while still staying honest so he'll trust them. How would you navigate a precarious situation like this in your own life?

6. The theme of fear-driven behavior runs throughout the book. At one point Anne says, ". . . the truth is 'I'm just a human, among billions of other humans, and I'm alive, and it's really hard being alive, and I don't want to admit it, because nobody around me is admitting it, and most of the time I don't know what I'm doing, and I'm scared.'" Does this statement resonate with you?

7. At first, Remy is deathly afraid of Anne's dogs, but as time moves on Anne finds the dogs happily sleeping on his bed with him. What is the commonality between the abandoned children and the abandoned dogs that make up this family?

8. Anne, Chris, and the other siblings go with Remy to bring his father's ashes back to the homestead. Remy is conflicted over his feelings about his father and says, "If I know he was wrong, and I know what he did was a bad thing for me, does that mean I'm not supposed to love him and be sad he died?" Have you ever lost someone in your life and struggled with what to feel? How did you reconcile it?

9. At the end of the book, Anne and Miri discuss how to keep going when facing the overwhelming challenges in today's world. Anne suggests, "This is something you do with your eyes open. You look at the world, see it for exactly what it is, and then make this conscious choice to be part of it." Do you agree with her philosophy?

ABOUT THE AUTHOR

Catherine Ryan Hyde is the *New York Times*, *Wall Street Journal*, and #1 Amazon Charts bestselling author of more than forty books and counting. An avid traveler, equestrian, and amateur photographer, she shares her astrophotography with readers on her website.

Her novel *Pay It Forward* was adapted into a major motion picture, chosen by the American Library Association (ALA) for its Best Books for Young Adults list, and translated into more than twenty-three languages for distribution in over thirty countries. Both *Becoming Chloe* and *Jumpstart the World* were included on the ALA's Rainbow Book List, and *Jumpstart the World* was a finalist for two Lambda Literary Awards. *Where We Belong* won two Rainbow Awards in 2013, and *The Language of Hoofbeats* won a Rainbow Award in 2015.

More than fifty of her short stories have been published in the *Antioch Review*, *Michigan Quarterly Review*, *Virginia Quarterly Review*, *Ploughshares*, *Glimmer Train*, and many other journals; in the anthologies *Santa Barbara Stories* and *California Shorts*; and in the bestselling anthology *Dog Is My Copilot*. Her stories have been honored by the Raymond Carver Short Story Contest and the Tobias Wolff Award and have been nominated for *The Best American Short Stories*, the O. Henry

Award, and the Pushcart Prize. Three have been cited in the annual *The Best American Short Stories* anthology.

She is the founder and former president (2000–2009) of the Pay It Forward Foundation. As a professional public speaker, she has addressed the National Conference on Education, twice spoken at Cornell University, met with AmeriCorps members at the White House, and shared a dais with Bill Clinton.

For more information, please visit the author at www.catherineryanhyde.com.